Birds of a Feather

Mysteries of Sparrow Island®

BIRDS OF A FEATHER

Carolyn Greene

Guideposts Books

CARMEL, NEW YORK

www.guideposts.org
(800) 431-2344
Guideposts Books & Inspirational Media Division

Cover and interior design by Cindy LaBreacht
Cover art by Gail Guth
Map by Jim Haynes, represented by Creative Freelancers, Inc.
Typeset by Nancy Tardi
Printed in the United States of America

This book is dedicated with love and gratitude to Priscilla Drobes. Thanks for offering me the opportunity to participate in this fun new series.

And to my "family" at Old Powhatan Church for all your encouragement and support.

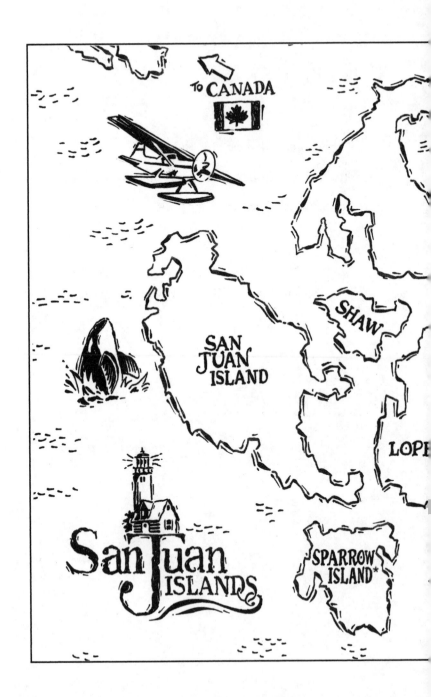

TO
U.S.A.

ORCAS

LUMMI

N
W E
S

CYPRESS

GUEMES

TO
ANACORTES

FIDALGO
ISLAND

*SPARROW ISLAND IS FICTITIOUS

CHAPTER ❦ ONE

LIFE WOULD BE SO MUCH simpler if people just had all the answers up front, Abby Stanton thought. Water the hole *before* chucking the blue huckleberry bush into it or douse it after? Since she was in a hurry to finish the project today, Abby decided to investigate the matter later and pray the plants would thrive despite her uncharacteristic decision to proceed without knowing all the answers.

Abby plopped the leggy shrub into the freshly turned dirt and covered the roots. A little mulch, a spritz from the hose and then she moved down the perimeter of the yard to the next hole. An early spring breeze blew in from the bay, bringing with it the scent of brine and the sea and a crisp snap that crept through her sweater.

"*Gayluss—*" Bobby stopped, then tried again to pronounce the word on the plant tag he was reading. "*Gayluss—*" He turned to Abby. "How do you say this?"

She leaned over and looked through the glasses on her nose. The afternoon sun cast a shadow over the paper, so she moved to one side to see the printed words more clearly.

"*Gaylussacia frondosa.* It's a Latin term for huckleberry."

The ten-year-old parroted the words, repeating them as if to embed the information into his already overstuffed brain.

He continued reading. "Also called whortleberry, bilberry or dangleberry. It's from the *Eri*—"

Abby peeked over his shoulder. "*Ericacae* family."

"Right," he said, as if she were the one having difficulty with it. "Or 'heath family' if you have trouble saying Latin."

Abby pulled a shrub off the nearly empty wheelbarrow. "Would you help me put this bush in so it can join the rest of the heath family?"

"Why aren't we mixing 'em up? Huckleberry, rugosa rose, huckleberry, rose. Like that."

Abby held the plant while her young friend patted the mulch around the roots. When he was done, she rubbed at the new brown spot that had recently graced the back of her right hand. If her image-conscious older sister saw it, Mary would certainly lecture her on the dangers of the sun's rays. It was still only early April, but Abby made a mental note to use sunscreen the next time she came outside.

"So why don't you mix 'em up?" Bobby pointed at the tiny bushes they'd already planted. "Then when they're growing berries and flowers, they'd be blue and red, blue and red."

With a finger to her chin, Abby paused and considered his belated suggestion. "That's a nice idea, but I think we'll just keep them with their own kind so it doesn't confuse the eye."

"So the *Gaylussacia frondosas* are like sparrows, huh?"

Abby lifted an eyebrow at his unusual comparison.

He shrugged. "You know. Birds of a feather flock together."

"Yes, I suppose it's something like that."

Bobby attempted to blow a bubble, but the pink wad shot out of his mouth. "Oops."

He toed loose soil over the blob.

She and Bobby had often discussed ecology. She knew he understood that the land doesn't belong to humans, but is merely lent to them by God, so she was curious to see what he would do with the gum. She gave him a patient look.

The boy stuffed his hands into his pockets. "It's gross now, and I don't have a tissue to pick it up with. Besides, it should decompose completely within six or seven years."

"And in the meantime, what if a rare streaked horn lark finds it and gets sick?"

"That wouldn't be good." Using a dead leaf to pick it up, he said, "I'll put it in the trash can so the larks will stay safe."

Abby smiled her approval. She had never had children of her own—never married either—but at times like this, she certainly understood the meaning of motherly pride.

"While you're inside, would you grab my binoculars and bring them out with you?" she called after him. "A little while ago, I thought I saw a merlin."

Walking backward, with the leaf pinched gingerly between his fingers, Bobby asked, "Where are the binoculars?"

"If they're not on the table, ask Mary."

Abby watched in amusement as he raced across the backyard and up the wheelchair ramp to the house. It was remarkable how those scrawny little shoulders could support a head that carried so much information. If anyone ever doubted the existence of God, all Abby had to do was point to Bobby McDonald as proof of His amazing work.

Following in the boy's wake, she went to the upright post at the bottom of the ramp and retrieved the glass of ginger ale she'd left there earlier. As she sipped, she surveyed the work they'd accomplished today.

The bushes stood like stunted soldiers in a row, bordering a large yard behind the old farmhouse. On the other side was a recently plowed field awaiting the seeds that would transform it from a bed of brown dirt to lush green rows of corn, beans, peppers and tomatoes to fill the Stanton family's pantry and provide produce for their small organic farming business. Behind the yard, a well-traveled path led past alfalfa fields and down a hill to a stately stand of evergreens, and on to the rocky shoreline that spilled out into the sea.

Her parents would be pleased when they saw the tidy rows of bushes in their backyard. Although George Stanton was still active at age eighty-two, the backyard had become overgrown during the past few years. His issue was lack of time rather than lack of energy. Tending his crops, fishing from his boat and spending time with his family, he enjoyed all these activities and more. And when Ellen wasn't taking care of the home, she worked part-time at the Sparrow Island Visitors Center.

At any rate, the Stanton Farm, a common landmark among the island's 2,500 year-round inhabitants, had become quite weedy of late. And it had grown even worse after Mary's accident. Abby leaned her elbow against the post and imagined how the boundary bushes would look when fully grown, their branches splayed out in invitation for the shrikes, finches and grosbeaks to perch on or hide beneath while they sampled the sweet berries. The thorn-laden rugosa roses at the end of each strip of huckleberry would provide a sanctuary from the island's natural predators.

The back door opened and Abby heard the wheels of Mary's chair bump over the threshhold.

As she turned, the black and chrome conveyance streaked down the ramp, Bobby's dark brown hair and Mary's short silver locks ruffling in the self-made breeze. Mary's service dog Finnegan ran behind them, barking with glee. Bobby, sitting on Mary's lap, yelped a loud *"Yee hawww!"* as they whizzed past Abby. Startled, Abby clutched her heart.

The speedsters quickly came to a halt once they hit the grassy surface of the yard.

"That was fun," said Bobby. "Let's do it again."

Finnegan, a golden colored Lab-retriever mix, danced beside his mistress's chair, eager for another run. When none was forthcoming, he plunked his bottom down and swished the ground with his tail.

"Okay, but only ten or eleven more times. And you have to push me back up. I'm getting huge biceps from rolling this thing around." She flexed for him and he squeezed her arm, his eyes widening in affirmation.

Abby stepped in front of the ramp.

"You'll have to wait your turn," Mary said. "Bobby already called dibsies."

"Mary, you're fifty-eight years old. You could get hurt."

Her sister peered at her with a "duh" expression.

"You could get hurt *worse*. Do Mom and Dad know what you're doing out here?"

"No, and don't tell them. They'll want turns too." Mary winked at Bobby and he giggled.

"Well, even if you're not concerned for yourself, at least think of Bobby."

"Oh puddle ducks." Mary waved her hand dismissively.

Finnegan, interpreting the gesture to mean she wanted something, stood and followed her movement with his nose. Mary smiled at the dog's eagerness to please and scratched his soft yellow ears. "Bobby could get hurt worse when he climbs trees with you to peek at eggs."

"Shhh, don't say that," Bobby whispered. "She'll stop letting me go with her."

Abby supposed she should insist that her sister act her age. But when she considered all Mary had been through and still retained her vivacious energy and sense of humor, she couldn't bring herself to be a wet blanket.

"You know what your problem is?" Mary asked. "You think too much. Always gotta make things so complicated. It makes me glad I *don't* have a PhD in bird-ology. Or in anything else, for that matter."

"It's ornithology," Bobby interjected. "A brand of zoology dealing with the scientific study of birds."

"And quit turning the boy into an egghead."

"Actually, it's more of a pumpkin shape," he said, framing his head with his hands. "The hair in back that sticks up is sort of like the stem."

Both of the women turned and stared. He grinned, and it became clear that he'd accomplished what he intended—he made himself the center of attention.

Abby walked over to Mary and perched a hip on the wheelchair's armrest, braced her arm behind her sister in a conciliatory half hug and tousled the boy's "pumpkin stem."

"Want to help me move that big rock so we can plant the last bush?"

Mary answered for him. "Nah, let's go to the video store and rent a baseball movie."

"Yeah!" Bobby jumped off her lap.

Abby hesitated. "I'd really like to finish up today. It's just a little bit more."

She couldn't miss how Mary's eyebrows drew together. Her sister was right. She did sweat the details too much sometimes, unwilling or unable to rest until she'd seen things through to completion. But sometimes it was more important to set those details aside, as Mary often did, and look at the big picture. Like family. She and Mary had recently managed to put aside their long-standing differences. Perhaps Abby should focus on fostering the sisterly bonds of camaraderie that had tightened between them, and let God take care of growing the huckleberry bush that most likely would survive even if she did wait an extra day to plant it.

"Kevin Costner or Robert De Niro?" Mary persisted. "Can you think of a better way to spend your Saturday night?"

Abby softened. "How about Robert Redford?"

"He'll do just fine."

Abby stood and stuck out her hand. "Deal. But I'm still going to ask Dad to install speed bumps on that ramp."

IN CHURCH THE NEXT DAY, her sister and Sergeant Henry Cobb held hands and eyed each other affectionately throughout the service. It was too cute for words, and Abby was pleased that Mary and Henry had found each other.

After the last *Amen* was said, Abby shot out of the pew and down the aisle toward the front of the church to catch Ida Tolliver before she slipped away.

The young woman, barely twenty-four years old, had only recently started coming to church, and Abby had quickly befriended her. There was something about the girl that made

Abby want to protect her. Or help her. Or something. Maybe it was the faraway expression in Ida's eyes and the sweetness of her personality that snagged her attention. Whatever the reason, the two had instantly hit it off and Abby wanted to encourage her to keep coming to their church.

"Hey, Ida."

The girl looked up at the sound of Abby's voice and gave her a hug. "I wish I could stay and talk, but I have to hurry if I'm going to make it to work on time."

Abby's heart went out to her. The young woman had big dreams and a miniature purse, and she worked hard to try to make the two meet in the middle. "Poor dear. I'm so sorry you can't enjoy this glorious Sunday."

Ida pulled together her button-up blouse, covering a gold necklace and the uniform shirt beneath. "It's okay. Besides, the tips are better on weekends than during the weekdays."

"I know you're in a hurry, so I'll keep this short. We need volunteers to help with Vacation Bible School this summer. May I add your name to the list?"

Ida hesitated, her gaze averted. "I don't know. I—"

"Since you're a new member, we wouldn't ask you to teach just yet," she reassured her. "But what if I put you down as a snack lady? That's a fun position."

"Well, I suppose that would be all right."

"Wonderful. I'll let you know when the next planning meeting is scheduled."

She followed Ida outside. The day was promising to be as beautiful as yesterday, the sun having burned away the morning fog. Abby hoped the weather would remain dry until she'd finished planting the final bush in her parents' backyard.

With a tentative smile and a hasty good-bye, Ida practically sprinted across the parking lot to her car. When Abby turned to go back for Mary, she found her sister already rolling out the door, Finnegan right behind her.

"What's your hurry?" Mary asked, lifting her chin in a subtle show of irritation. "Got somewhere to go, or someone to get away from?"

Abby inhaled deeply, refusing to be drawn into old habits of conversation that led nowhere except to frustration. Things had changed a lot between them in the past months, and she didn't want to risk a setback.

"Where's Henry?"

"Gone to speak to Hugo Baron. Then he'll bring my van around to drive me home." Mary looked up at Abby. "If you don't want to spend time with me, you ought to just say so. I can take it."

Shoulders sagging, Abby stepped behind the wheelchair to guide her sister and the dog down the ramp and out of the path of worshippers exiting the building. "Of course I want to spend time with you. I just had to dash so I could catch Ida before she left for work."

Mary had been pressing her lips into a thin line, and when she spoke her voice was strained. "You always seem to be dashing off here, there or somewhere. I thought when you came back to the island to live, we'd finally have the time to reconnect and do some of the things we never did when we were kids, like talk and shop and ... well, just do stuff together."

"We talk."

"Talking about the flight patterns of migrating geese doesn't count. I meant sharing secrets and laughing about stuff that only we understand. And maybe even discuss, you know, men."

"Oh, that kind of talk." The kind of talk that she and Mary might have had in their youth, if only they hadn't been such opposites. More than their age had separated the sisters. While Mary had been out socializing, flirting with boys, involving herself in clubs and occasionally stepping a toe over to the wild side, Abby's activities had alternated between sticking her nose in a book and exploring Sparrow Island's plant growth and wildlife. Some of her fondest memories were of roaming the woods near the farm with her father as they tracked, photographed and logged journal entries of the many bird species that populated the island.

Such adventures, while wildly exhilirating to the ever-studious Abby, had held no appeal for Mary. Likewise, practicing the application of makeup and giggling over who said what at school had been of little interest to Abby.

But now things were different. Mary's automobile accident had bonded the sisters in a way that no amount of midnight whispering under the covers could have ever done. It had made them appreciate each other in a whole new way. In a sense, the accident, though tragic, was also a blessing. Her ordeal had taught them to grow closer in their relationship with each other . . . and with the Lord.

Abby steered her toward the parking lot, but then stopped and set the brake. Three years' difference in their ages didn't seem like much at this stage in their lives, but Abby had never quite lost the feelings of awe and intimidation that Mary had inspired in her since she was a toddler. Even after all these years, it was sometimes hard to meet her sister's intense gaze without glancing away.

Abby lifted Mary's hand and held it in her own. "We'll *make* time to spend together," she promised. "You're much more important than any dashing around that I might be doing. You've already been hurt once. I don't want to hurt you even more by falling into mindless habits and letting my schedule interfere with our friendship."

Mary's expression softened and she squeezed Abby's fingers. "Let's just do something fun and stop fretting about the past. Besides, you can't afford Botox to get rid of the worry lines."

Abby laughed and loosened the brake. "Then why don't you invite Henry to have lunch with us at the farm? If he sticks around long enough afterward, I'll put him to work moving the mini boulder that brought my shrub planting to a halt yesterday."

THE BOULDER TURNED OUT TO BE a large flat rock that wasn't as deep or as heavy as it had first appeared. And since Sergeant Cobb had been called away after church to help a tourist who'd locked his keys in his car, it was George Stanton who helped her load the thing onto the wheelbarrow and cart it to the wooded area at the edge of the property.

Although her father had wanted to dig the remaining hole, Abby had distracted him from overexerting himself by suggesting he prepare the final shrub for planting. While he busied himself with removing the green plastic growing pot from the roots and snipping the strings that held the branches together, Abby gripped the spade and positioned it over the ground where the final bush would go.

On the first stab, the spade struck yet another rock. Only, this one made an odd, hollow sound. *This might take longer than expected*, she thought. Abby widened the digging area, and the shovel went easily into the sandy soil. Another couple of prods into the earth and the metal "rock" came into view.

"What do you have there?" her father said, moving in for a closer look. "Does it look antique?"

Abby knocked the dirt and roots off the container, then sat down on the ground, the box in her lap, and traced the etched metal with her finger. The mass-produced artwork covering the box was that of a tree-edged inlet with what looked like a loon standing at water's edge. A heavy padlock held the rusted lid firmly shut.

"No, it's not antique," she said. "It looks like a plain old fishing tackle box, like all the other ones you can find at The Tackle Shop." She gave it a shake. A couple of hard objects rattled inside, but there was also a muffled noise, like that of paper or maybe plastic. She scrunched her face in distaste. "*Ew,* I hope that's not a ham sandwich in there."

Her father bent closer. "Or somebody's pet cat." He grinned at her horrified response. "Well, there's only one way to find out. I'll get the bolt cutters out of the shed."

"No! Dad." Abby got up and brushed the grass off the back of her pants.

He paused.

"This might be one time when it's best not to know all the answers."

CHAPTER ✿ TWO

MARY STOPPED HER wheelchair at the kitchen door at the Stanton homestead and waited for Finnegan to bound into the room ahead of her. Though he couldn't have known this was Monday, there was no doubt he knew Mary was taking him to the flower shop with her today.

Mary's parents, Ellen and George, were already seated, and Ellen was pouring herself a cup of coffee. The dog ignored them both, and even ignored Abby, who stood at the stove, stirring a panful of scrambled eggs.

Finnegan was trained not to respond to smells of human cooking. Instead, he tugged the leather strap attached to the cabinet door. Poking his head into the low cabinet, he picked up the half-full bag of dog food and carried it to Mary.

She chuckled and rubbed his knobby head, still amazed at Finnegan's skills after all these months.

"Here you go, Finnegan," she said as she leaned over and

poured dry food into his bowl. Finnegan had a strict feeding schedule which Mary always tried to adhere to.

From time to time, she and Abby would drive over from their house on Oceania Boulevard and have breakfast with their parents. Today was one of those times.

Mary rolled the top of the bag down and gave it back to Finnegan, who returned it to its rightful place. After a reminder from Mary to close the cabinet door, he rested his chin on her knee for an ear scratch and praises, which she lavished on him. He then began to eat.

Abby switched off the burner and scooped eggs onto five plates. She covered one with foil for Sam, her father's farmhand. "I'll fill Finnegan's water bowl in a minute."

Once they were settled at the table and George had said grace, Mary studied her younger sister from across the table.

Except for the squint lines at the outer corners of her eyes and some wrinkles that came from hours spent outside watching birds, she looked younger than her fifty-five years. Her slim figure gave evidence of the miles of walking through the woods along the shore in search of tanagers and murrelets or whatever other birds had caught her attention at the time. Unfortunately, her most recent haircut didn't do her face justice. Her short brown hair hung limp and seemed to drag her pretty features down. Even though Abby seldom wore makeup, her complexion usually looked rosy. But today her skin was pale, as if she hadn't slept well last night.

Mary would love to brighten up those inquisitive brown eyes with a green or purple eyeshadow. Maybe both . . . carefully blended, of course, so her conservative younger sister wouldn't immediately wash it off.

Mary wanted only the best for Abby. Which was why she

was determined to persist until Abby said yes to the plan she had in mind.

Abby looked up from her breakfast and self-consciously lifted a hand to her hair. "What?"

"Oh, nothing." Mary sipped her orange juice. "I was just wondering if you could meet me at the florist shop after work today. I want to make a decorative springtime wreath for our door, and thought it would be fun if we could come up with some ideas and shop together for craft supplies."

Abby nodded. "Sure, but I can't stay long. If we haven't found the owner of the box by this evening, I want to do some more checking around."

"Certainly that can wait," Mary insisted. "Besides, give Sam thirty seconds with a hacksaw and that should tell you everything you need to know about who buried the box."

Their father cleared his throat. "Speaking of Sam, has anyone seen him this morning? One of the cows seems to be favoring a leg. We'll need to get him to take a look at it."

Abby spoke up. "I saw him crossing the backyard as I was finishing the eggs. He'll probably be in after he makes his rounds at the barn."

Mary put down her fork. "And after we pick up the crafting supplies at In Stitches," she continued as if she hadn't been interrupted, "let's go to Willoughby Pharmacy and pick up a few things for you."

Abby scowled. "What kind of 'things'?"

"Some nail polish. A bit of mascara. Maybe even a home permanent kit to give your hair some pizzazz."

"Mary, I thought we had agreed to let the makeover idea drop."

Ellen finished off the last of her toast. "Sounds like a lovely idea," she said. "You could use a little perking up. Whoever cut your hair last time did something different. It doesn't have its usual bounce."

Abby touched her hair and made a face as if she, too, agreed. "I was pressed for time, so while I was running errands on the mainland, I tried a new stylist. Edmonia at the Silver Scissors will fix it when I go next month." Edmonia Lewis had been named after the nineteenth-century sculptor, and aptly so. Her gracefully crafted haircuts were like works of art.

"It's not as if you don't deserve some primping and beautifying," Mary told her. "You work so hard taking care of the birds on the island and everyone here at home. Let me take care of you for a change."

Abby gave her a regretful shrug. "Actually, I need to spend the rest of the evening finishing the incubator that Hugo and I started a week ago. We want to be ready at the conservatory for any emergencies once nesting season is in full swing.

"It won't be long now," Abby said. "Depending on the weather, the species of bird and their determination to reproduce, breeding could have started as early as late March and will continue through June or later."

Although the subject fascinated Abby, Mary wasn't concerned with that at the moment. "You're so pretty, yet you ravage your nails with all that sawing and hammering on the incubators," she persisted. "You should work on yourself and make the best of the attractive features God gave you."

"How about we buy some nail polish and bath salts for *you*. As for me, I'll leave preening to the birds."

Abby's voice was light, but there was a tone of finality in it. Even so, Mary would not let that stop her. Just as the prophet Nathan had advised King David where he was going wrong,

Mary would advise her little sister on how she could use a bit of self-improvement. In the long run, Mary was sure Abby would thank her for the help.

The back door opened and Sam walked in. He paused by the door and wiped his feet on the stiff straw mat. "I would have been here sooner," their farmhand announced, "but I wanted to stop by the barn and check on a cow's leg first."

George Stanton voiced his appreciation.

Sam seemed almost not to hear. He continud his explana-tion. "And before that, my neighbor, Thelma Rogers, had something go missing from her apartment. She was upset and said—" He paused abruptly, apparently disturbed by what had transpired between them. "Well, anyway, I stuck around for a while and tried to help her remember where she put it."

Abby pointed across the room. "There's a plate for you on the stove," she said. "What was Thelma missing?"

Mary stretched and pushed away from the table. "Oh, leave it be, Abby. Give the woman a day or two and whatever's missing will turn up in her refrigerator or under her bed or wherever else she might have left it in a moment of distraction. She's always forgetting something."

"Where are you going?" George asked her.

"To hide Abby's spyglass, pipe and deerstalker cap."

Ellen rose from the table and carried her dishes to the sink. "I didn't know you had a deerstalker cap, Abby."

Abby was finished with her breakfast, but it was obvious she was dawdling as she toyed with a remaining crust of toast. She shot Mary a lopsided grin as she answered their mother. "I don't. Perhaps she meant to say 'raincoat.'"

"Yes, that would be a good idea," Ellen said. "It looks like it could rain today."

Mary left the room to get her sweater, certain that Abby would fill their mother in on the joke. Finnegan followed her. He wasn't officially on duty yet, but he never was one for punching a timeclock.

In the living room, where she had deposited her things earlier, Mary maneuvered to the sofa and picked up her yellow cardigan with red tulips embroidered near the left shoulder.

"This looks quite springy, don't you think?" she said, holding it up for Finnegan to see.

Like most males, he seemed not to notice the mood-lifting effect of the colorful garment. It didn't help, either, that dogs didn't see color as humans see it. But when she lifted up his blue service coat, he recognized it instantly and came close to Mary so she could put it on him.

"Can't wait to go to work, huh?"

Finnegan pushed closer, and Mary leaned over the arm of her chair to slip the coat over his head. The blue fabric wasn't made to go around his front legs, so it wasn't truly a coat but perhaps more of a cape.

"Here's a cape for Finnegan the Wonder Dog." He lifted his ears and looked up at her with his deep amber eyes. "You're certainly a superhero to me," she confessed. "You're always there for me, no matter what."

Of course, God was always there for her, no matter what, and in a way that no animal or person could ever be. And for that Mary was grateful. But there were still moments when she felt a little lonely. Abby may have left her job in upstate New York and come home to the island to be with her and their parents, but sometimes—like this morning, when their conversation kept going back to that fishing tackle box she'd found—it felt like Abby's body was here, but the rest of her wasn't.

Whenever something puzzling like this captured her attention, Abby was like a dog with a bone and would not let go.

"It's okay," Mary said to Finnegan as she rumpled his ears. "When Abby gets this bee out of her bonnet, she'll come around. But in the meantime, she's in for the makeover of her life."

AS SAM SETTLED IN AT THE TABLE and dug into his breakfast, Abby quizzed him some more about Thelma's missing item. Although it was a long shot, she asked, "Would it, by any chance, be a tackle box that Thelma misplaced?"

Sam looked up from his eggs. "Uh, no." He hesitated for an uncomfortable moment before adding, "It was some money."

"Oh." The word came out as a chorus from Abby, Ellen and George.

Everyone knew about Thelma's "diva dollars." Whenever she had an extra dollar bill, or perhaps a five or ten, she set it aside in a special stash. Once the amount accumulated to a sufficient sum, she would treat herself to a "diva day" of pampering at the day spa at The Dorset, Sparrow Island's most exclusive hotel.

Abby cleared her throat. "It'll certainly turn up. Just give it time."

An awkward heaviness hung over the breakfast table and now Abby regretted having pursued the subject. Sam was a good man. However, at fifty-two years old, he carried a burdensome past that followed him like an ominous shadow.

In an effort to lighten the mood, she said, "Who knows, maybe it's in Thelma's refrigerator, just as Mary suggested. Why, just the other day, I was clearing out some old papers from my office at the museum when I forgot and left my birding journal beside a stack of trash to be taken out. Fortunately, I remembered it before everything was hauled away."

Such a loss would have been irreplaceable. So when she had found it again, relief and joy had flooded through her. Now that she thought of it, Abby supposed her own intense feelings were minor compared to her Heavenly Father's relief and joy whenever a lost sheep came back to His fold.

For many years, Sam had been a lost sheep. But no one would ever know it by the way he lived his life today.

"At any rate, if you ever need to keep your fishing tackle in a safe place," she continued with a laugh, "there's no need to bury it in the yard."

Sam lowered his fork. "What do you mean?"

Abby's eyebrows drew together. She had hoped finding the owner of the box would be a simple matter. Just ask the most likely people—those who had frequent access to the property—and very soon someone would claim it. Although she hadn't truly thought Sam would resort to hiding his belongings, she had hoped he might know something about how the tackle box came to be in her parents' yard.

At Sam's apparent confusion, George filled him in on their discovery of the day before. "We came up with a couple of possibilities of what might be inside," he said, "but there were no smells coming from the box, so we decided it's probably just what it appears to be . . . fishing gear."

"I don't have anything to hide from you," he told the Stantons. "Or from anyone. I'm a different person now."

Immediately, Abby felt contrite for having inadvertently put their friend on the hot seat. He'd been working for her parents for eleven years now, and never once during that time had he ever proved himself untrustworthy.

"Of that we have no doubt." Abby got up and retrieved the box from the top of the refrigerator, then carried it to him. "Actually, I was hoping this might be yours, so we could solve the puzzle of how it came to be buried in the backyard. Does it look familiar to you?"

"Abby's about to explode from curiosity," Ellen told him as she hovered nearby.

At that, Sam's moment of seriousness dissolved, and his mouth widened into a teasing grin. "What else is new?"

He turned the box over in his hands, running his work-roughened fingers over the raised-metal picture on the top.

"No, I haven't seen it before."

Abby sighed and felt her hopes deflate.

George reached over and tugged at the lock as if to test it. "I wanted to take a pair of bolt cutters to it, but Abby's concerned there might be a diary or something else personal inside that the owner might be embarrassed for us to see. So we decided to leave it intact until we do some asking around."

"It might be easier to remove the pins from the hinges," Sam responded. He was good at handling all things mechanical. "But that can wait until we do some more checking."

Ellen scooped up the rest of the dishes from the table and took them to the sink. A horn honked outside. "That must be Shirley. It's time for me to go to work at the Visitors Center. When the three of you solve this earth-shattering mystery, let me know so I can take it off my 'Things to Pray About' list." Abby knew that although Ellen was still as independent as she ever was, at her age her mother didn't relish driving. Shirley Farley took her mother twice a week to her part-time job in Green Harbor.

Ellen kissed George and Abby, then called a good-bye to

Mary and Sam before heading off to a morning of work greeting visitors and newcomers to Sparrow Island. With only half the rain of nearby Seattle, the San Juan Islands swelled with the tourists who each year came to sightsee, shop, whale watch and relax. The more adventurous ones enjoyed bicycle and kayak tours, hiking and climbing excursions, and fishing. Ellen often claimed, quite sincerely, that if given the choice of visiting only one of the islands, a smart tourist would choose Sparrow Island.

By now, Sam was scowling at the box in his hands. "Do you suppose Bobby buried it? Kids do that kind of stuff all the time."

"That's a definite possibility. I was planning to ask him about it after school today." Sure, Bobby had his own yard in which to bury things, but it made sense that he would perhaps hide special treasures at the Stanton Farm. Bobby spent many afternoons at The Nature Museum just down the road from the farm when his mother worked late. As a teacher at Green Harbor Public School, Sandy McDonald frequently stayed after to prepare for her next day's English classes or help students who needed extra attention. Bobby was a junior docent at the museum during those hours. "If it's Bobby's box, there's no telling what might be inside."

Indeed, the little rascal sometimes got the strangest notions. Since his brainpower was far more advanced than his maturity or experience, the Stantons often had occasion to help him develop a balanced perspective on life.

Sam set the box on the table and rose to get back to work. "What do you want me to do with this?" he asked.

Abby said. "I'll take it with me to work. It'll remind me to ask Bobby about it when he comes to the museum after school."

Even as Abby said the words, Sam flashed Abby an amused grin. They both knew there was no way she would need a reminder to ask the questions that would burn in her brain all day long.

As Sam and George headed out to finish taking care of the livestock and plan which garden plot to plant first, Sam paused at the door. "Let me know if there's anything I can do to help," he said. "I'm as curious as you are to find out who that box belongs to."

"Impossible," said George as he stepped out onto the back porch and into the early-morning fog.

And they both knew he was right.

FOR THE REST OF THE DAY, Abby tried to keep her mind on the tasks at hand. However, her thoughts kept going back to the tackle box that sat on her desk. Fortunately, there were enough things to do to keep her occupied and keep her mind off of the box. During the morning, Abby led a small group on a tour through the museum, then outside on a nature walk through the conservatory grounds to examine some of the island's flora and fauna.

Still early in the tourist season, the weather was chilly and damp, so Abby was surprised and pleased to have had any visitors at all today. This group, most likely a family on spring vacation, consisted of an elderly woman, a husband and wife who appeared to be about Abby's age, a young woman in her late twenties or early thirties, and a toddler . . . apparently four generations enjoying a family vacation together. Although the little girl's feet and hands stayed in constant motion throughout the tour, Abby was glad she could entertain the child's energetic curiosity by showing her an early-blooming crocus, the molted flight feather of a pileated woodpecker, and an empty snail shell.

Along the path through the conservatory, various indigenous plants and flowers were marked with small signs that listed their genus, species and a few facts about them. Abby noted a new cluster of toadstools that had sprung up in their midst.

As the family was preparing to leave, the wife said, "It's so quiet and peaceful here. It must be nice to live on this island, isolated from the world, where nothing ever happens."

Abby was happy for the opportunity to correct this common misconception.

"It's true that, in some ways, we have a slower pace of life on Sparrow Island." Abby steered the group back through the museum toward the tiny gift shop at the front of the building. "But, there's also enough excitement here to keep things interesting."

The couple exchanged glances as if they doubted anything exciting could ever happen on Sparrow Island, but Abby certainly knew better. Her thoughts automatically went back to the fishing box that waited for her on the corner of her desk in her office.

Later, as Abby worked on fitting the light sockets into the incubator she was constructing, she considered the eggs that would be warmed by the low-watt bulbs. Every spring, and sometimes into the summer with late-season clutches, tragedy would befall at least one nest. A parent bird killed by a wild or domestic animal might leave behind a nest of eggs that needed warmth and nurturing to survive. Or a newly hatched chick might fall out of a tree and require human help. Or it might not be a bird at all that needed assistance. Just last year Abby's supervisor, Hugo Baron, had come upon a nest of turtle eggs that had been raided by a hungry raccoon. Only a handful remained unbroken, so he had attempted to hatch the intact ones with the help of a chicken incubator borrowed from the Stantons. To everyone's surprise, most of them had survived and were returned to the wild.

Abby contemplated the mystery and possibility that existed inside each and every egg. Sure, she could gain a glimpse inside an egg with the help of a flashlight and determine whether it had been fertilized. But she could not know, until the chick pecked its way out of the shell, whether it would grow to become a hen or rooster, and whether it was healthy or weak. It would take longer still to learn the bird's individual personality. It was all fascinating to Abby and she never ceased to be amazed by what she discovered each and every day.

Abby wished she could hold a flashlight to the tackle box to peek inside. But she knew that its secrets, just like an egg's, would be revealed in God's time.

The light fixtures were now installed in the incubator, but the only bulbs to be found were too high in wattage. Much too warm for a delicate embryo. She'd pick up some smaller ones that evening when she took Mary shopping.

Abby sighed and ran a hand through her hair. Did she really look as bad as Mary had implied?

Hugo walked past her open door, backed up, then entered. He made himself comfortable in a side chair. He didn't slouch—he was much too dapper for that. He sat ramrod straight, as if he were conducting an interview. In fact, Abby found it amazing that he could wear starched white shirts while working with dusty museum artifacts and never look mussed. Today's look was green suspenders and a silk tie. His shoes, as always, gleamed as if he'd just finished polishing them, which was a definite possibility.

"Feast or famine, it is," he declared in the deep, melodious voice that commanded attention whenever he spoke.

Even when he was excited, as he was now, his words and tone held an air of refinement that sent delightful tingles down a person's spine. Or maybe it was just the ladies on which he had that effect. Abby pushed aside the possibility that perhaps this reaction was specific to her.

"Have you ever noticed, Abby, how things you want can elude you for weeks, months or even years? And then—*bam!*—right there is what you need. In abundance."

"You made a nice find?"

"Nice?" He twirled the ends of his thick white mustache for effect. "Today the good Lord led me to a stash of Native American artifacts that may be a couple of hundred years old or more. It was like manna in the desert. Only without the maggots."

Despite his sixty-five years, Hugo Baron had more energy than most people Abby knew, especially when talking about the passion that stirred his soul—remnants of Sparrow Island's rich history. Get him talking about the native Suquamish or Lummi Indians and their thousands of years of culture and tradition, and there was no "off" button for him.

"That's wonderful," she told him. "Tomorrow I'll block out some time to help you clean them up."

"They won't need much since they're in pretty good condition." Hugo leaned forward in the chair. "I was driving up Wayfarer Point Road, toward the lighthouse, when I noticed a woman—probably about your age—hauling baskets out to the roadside for the trash collector. Lummi Indian grain-threshing baskets, I tell you, with the most intricate patterns woven right into them. She was going through her grandfather's estate—

God rest his soul—and tossing out anything that was worn or broken. 'Junk,' she called it. Can you imagine?"

Actually, what Abby could imagine was Hugo's horror that anyone would ever throw anything away, whether functional or not. Fortunately, his philosophy extended to people as well as items. He believed that no one was ever too old or too broken-down to be of worth in this world.

"Lo and behold, she said the attic was overflowing with 'rubbish' and that I was welcome to take all I wanted."

Abby waited for the downside, which she knew was about to come because he was giving her a beatific smile, his endearing expression shining even brighter than his shoes.

"The only catch is that we have to move everything before the weekend."

We. "Of course I'll help. I'll be sure to wear my grubby clothes tomorrow."

Hugo eyed her as if she were a mule painted with stripes being passed off as a zebra.

Abby frowned. *Hmm, maybe Mary was right.* "Do you think I need a makeover?"

He rose from the chair and pointed toward her desk. "That looks familiar."

"The tackle box? You know something about it?"

She pushed the incubator aside and pulled the box to the center of the desk. Of course Hugo would know something about it. He was like a walking fact depository. No matter how trivial the information seemed to be, if it had anything to do with Sparrow Island, Hugo knew it. And he was always more than willing to share that information with anyone who wanted to listen.

"Yes, indeed." Hugo reached out to touch the embossed

metal lid. "My father had a small toolbox very similar to this. We spent many an hour together at his workbench, repairing household items or making Jacob's ladders to give to children at Christmas."

"Jacob's ladders," Abby said. "It's been years since I've seen one of those."

Hugo made a *pshaw* sound. "Kids nowadays are too high-tech. They're missing the joy of playing with a simple wood-and-rope gizmo and trying to figure out how it works. The rungs on the Jacob's ladders my father made flipped with precision, and the painting on them was like works of art."

"They sound lovely," Abby told him, "but I was hoping you knew something about this particular box."

He squinted at it, and his mustache slanted to one side. "Never saw it before in my life."

Then he proceeded to tell her at length how the world would be a better place if people would stop giving children electronic gadgets and encouraged them to play with simple toys of the past.

He never did say whether he thought she should get a makeover.

CHAPTER ✾ THREE

Y OU LOOK LIKE YOU COULD use Rev. Hale's sermon this week. 'Rest for the Weary.'"

Janet Heinz held the belief that, as Abby's friend, she could say whatever she wished. And she could. Her forthrightness was one of the many things Abby admired about her. Although Janet had graduated high school with Mary, Abby and Janet developed a friendship after Abby had returned to Sparrow Island for good.

"Why? Do I look tired?" Maybe she needed that makeover after all.

Janet set down the flyer she was folding, tilted her head and peered at Abby. "No, not tired. Preoccupied, maybe. Something on your mind?"

Given her tendency to gossip, anyone else might have thought Janet was on a fishing expedition, but Abby knew there was genuine concern, too. As secretary of Little Flock Church, Janet took her duties seriously. If she heard of a parishioner going through a difficult time, she alerted the prayer team. Or if she knew of someone in need, she would rally volunteers to donate their time, goods or money to help. In fact, this week when she discovered they were a few helpers short for the upcoming Vacation Bible School, she had taken it upon herself to type up a flyer to recruit more workers.

Abby showed her the fishing tackle box and filled her in on how she'd found it yesterday. Sure, the information she gave to Janet might "leak" to others in the community, but that was okay as long as the box eventually found its way back to its owner.

"Mom, Dad, Mary and I hadn't seen it before. And Sam is as clueless as we are." Abby continued folding flyers while Janet inspected the container as if it were the Hope Diamond they'd found. "When Bobby came to the conservatory this afternoon, I asked him about the box. He said it's not his."

"What about that girl who used to cut your parents' grass? You know, Al Minsky's daughter," Janet said, referring to the town mechanic and owner of Al's Garage.

"Eileen? I called over at her father's garage and she was there, thank goodness. But she hadn't buried the box and didn't have any ideas." Abby tucked a loose strand of hair behind her ear. "I even called the plumbers who had replaced a broken pipe in the yard a few years ago and asked if they knew anything about it."

Janet raised her eyebrows, looking hopeful.

"Nothing. In fact, they sounded like they thought I was some sort of quack."

Janet playfully rolled her eyes upward as if she were too pious to confirm what she knew to be true.

In return, Abby nudged her friend with an elbow. "So, seeing as how you know just about everything that happens on Sparrow Island, I came here and worked my fingers to the bone, folding flyers on the off chance that you could tell me you've seen this box before."

"Thank you for your help," Janet said, gathering up the flyers and tapping them on the table to even the stack. "And, yes, I have seen it before."

"Really?" Perhaps now she was finally getting somewhere.

"Yeah, The Tackle Shop over on Kingfisher Avenue has a million of them."

"Thanks. That narrows it down a lot."

Janet lifted her chin and pursed her lips. "Ooh, ooh, I know! It must have been Lawanna Porter who put it there. One day last summer, when Frank Holloway went to Paradise Cove, he came upon her digging near his favorite spot. He said she acted strangely and left soon after he arrived. Perhaps she went from there to your parents' house to bury the box."

"The movie actress? Don't you think you're being a little, um . . . dramatic?" Abby chuckled at her own joke. "Besides, Lawanna Porter probably just wanted some privacy at Paradise Cove, so when Frank showed up she left."

"Say what you will, but mystery absolutely swirls around celebrity types. They might be in the public eye, but there are secrets that even the tabloids don't know about them."

"Celebrities don't go around digging holes in strangers' yards when they're on vacation."

"They do if they have a good reason. Suppose the vacation was a story she concocted to cover up her true activities during her stay on the island? Open up that box and you might find diamonds and rubies inside. Or maybe the beaded purse she carried in her romantic movie *Quick Beats My Heart.*"

Janet shook the box and screwed up her face at the heavy, muffled *thunk* that greeted their ears.

"Or maybe a script. Yes, that's it! A script that she wrote and doesn't want anyone else to see because—"

"Are you finished?"

"I'm just getting started. Isn't this exciting? There's mystery and drama—"

"—and moments of comedy," Abby added as she considered her friend's wild imagination. No stone, however, was too small to go unturned. "I'll look into it."

She checked her watch. It was almost time to meet Mary at Island Blooms.

"Good, then you'll want to talk to Rev. Hale's wife. Patricia used to be an actress herself, you know."

Abby stood and picked up her things. She had no earthly idea what kind of help Patricia Hale would be able to offer, but Abby was formulating a plan for tracking down clues, and this tidbit would be on her list to investigate.

Janet walked with her to the exit near the church office. "Now that I think of it, a couple of years ago I saw a man walking away from town in the direction of your parents' farm."

Abby shrugged. "Primrose Lane is not the most traveled road on the island, but it's not that unusual to see people going for a long walk past the farm from time to time. Perhaps a friend of my parents had decided to visit them."

As they crossed the parking lot together, Janet laid a hand on her arm. "It stood out in my mind because he wasn't dressed either like an islander or a typical tourist. He seemed too stylish, out walking in shiny leather shoes. And your parents were out of town on vacation at the time."

Abby opened the car door. "Why didn't you say something then?" Abby asked, curious why Janet would wait until now to bring this up.

"Your parents didn't mention anything out of place when they returned. Besides, I didn't want to be a gossip."

Abby paused as she scooted into the driver's seat. At first she thought her friend was joking, but seeing the serious expression Janet wore, Abby thought it best not to bring the irony to her attention.

"Okay, I'll look into that too. Oh, and if you ask around about the box, don't mention to anyone that it's a tackle box. I want the owner to be able to describe it."

"I promise," Janet said and ducked back into the church.

Although she was grateful for the leads Janet had suggested, the possibilities seemed to be adding up to a series of random stabs in the dark. What she needed to do was start a list of the clues she'd collected so far, study them and come up with a step-by-step method for putting together the pieces of this puzzle. In fact, an idea was already beginning to form in her mind.

AT IN STITCHES THAT EVENING, the sisters had fun deciding which items would go with Mary's springtime project for making a wreath for their door. Pale green ribbons would transform sticks gathered on the island to a beautiful, circular shape. Mary would then add delicate painted leaves and a few small morning glory flowers. The final touch was to be a tiny bumblee figurine glued near the blossoms.

"When we're done here," Mary suggested, "let's go over to the soda fountain at Willoughby Pharmacy and spoil our appetites for dinner."

And our waistlines while we're at it, Abby thought. But rather than ruin Mary's good mood, Abby elected to keep her weight concerns to herself.

After they'd driven to the pharmacy, Abby rolled Mary past

the old-fashioned soda fountain where Ed Willoughby, resplendent in white coat and cap trimmed in red piping, pulled drinks and made ice cream treats for customers.

Carefully, Abby steered Mary's chair away from the cosmetics and hair products. Finnegan brought up the rear.

"I need lightbulbs for the conservatory's new incubator. Let's meet over at one of the tables by the fountain."

The search took a little longer than expected. The white bulbs were easy enough to find, but the colored ones took a little more searching. Abby could make do with white bulbs to provide heat for the incubator, but once the chicks hatched and were transferred to a brooder box, the dimmer light from colored bulbs would be easier on their young eyes.

After she had selected the sizes and colors she wanted, Abby made her way to the fountain. She found Mary positioning her chair at a small table away from the counter. It might have been Abby's imagination playing tricks, but it appeared as though Mary shoved something down in her lap.

"Let's have dinner here," Mary said, amending her earlier suggestion. "Then we won't have to cook tonight."

Abby smiled. "But my mouth is watering for a root beer float."

"Dessert, little sis." Mary took a straw from the old-fashioned dispenser and toyed with the paper cover. "Who said we can't have both?"

As Finnegan grunted and made himself comfortable under the table, Ed Willoughby came over, a pad in one hand and a stump of a pencil in the other, and wrote down their orders.

He returned a few minutes later with their sandwiches and chips. "I hear you're going to be giving a talk to the students over at the school later this week," he said as he slid a plate in front of Abby.

She pointed to herself. "I am?"

"Sure. You're going to be talking about trees and ecosystems, or something like that."

Mary straightened the plate in front of her. "You didn't tell me you were giving a speech."

"I didn't know it myself."

Abby racked her brain, worried that she'd forgotten to note the engagement in her calendar. But no matter how hard she tried, she couldn't remember any such conversation. It was understandable to have an occasional memory lapse, but it worried her that she was unable to recall the arrangement even after being reminded of it.

Ed put his hands on his hips and rocked on his heels. "Oh well, maybe they haven't gotten around to asking you yet. Margaret Blackstock was in here just before you came in and mentioned that she recommended you because one of the teachers assigned a leaf collection project."

"That would be Bobby McDonald's teacher." Margaret was the school secretary and, like Janet, she took an intense personal interest in everything that happened in her domain. In addition to their knack for chatter, the two women shared these and other interests in common. Perhaps that's why they were such good friends.

"You should do it," Mary said. "It'll be fun. I gave a talk there a couple of years ago about flower arranging. The little darlings had some good questions."

Ed didn't move from his position by their table. For a moment, Abby wondered if he was going to offer a suggestion for her upcoming talk.

"Have you found out who buried the treasure on your parents' property?" he asked.

Word sure traveled fast on Sparrow Island, especially when

Janet was involved. Abby had no doubt their mutual friend had fed Margaret the information. Perhaps Abby should buy stock in Janet's cell phone provider.

"No, we haven't. But if you happen to know of anyone who might have buried the box at the farm, I'd love to know so I can return it to them."

With a tilt of his chin to one side, Ed scratched his temple and contemplated. "No, can't say as I do."

"Or if you've seen any unusual people . . ."

He grinned and straightened his narrow red bowtie. It was obvious he and Hugo Baron didn't shop at the same place for their ties. Hugo's were made of silk, came in subdued colors, and he painstakingly tied them himself. Understated elegance. Ed's perky bowtie, although pristine and classic in a soda shop style, was a bold red to add contrast to the white jacket with red piping trim. The overall effect was quite cheerful.

"Who am I to call someone unusual?" he said with a laugh and went back to his station behind the counter.

Mary clasped her hands as a reminder to say grace before their meal. "You know, I don't think I've ever seen him when he wasn't smiling."

Abby bowed her head to ask a blessing on their food and for a cheerful heart like Ed's.

When they finished their meal, Mary shook open a handled tote bag and began filling it with items from her lap. She held the bag low, as if to keep Abby from seeing what she was doing.

Abby leaned forward to peek at what was going on. "Is that a home permanent kit?"

"Maybe. But you don't need to be concerned with that right now." Mary spoke to Finnegan, who got up and shook himself, then carried the tote over to the counter. Standing on his hind legs with front paws on the counter's edge, he allowed Ed to take the bag from his mouth and ring up the items on the old punch-button cash register.

In this case, Mary could just as easily have waited until Ed came over to clear their table to pay him for the items, but Mary was adamant about letting Finnegan practice his duties. Besides, the dog seemed to enjoy having a job to do and even acted proud of himself when he performed well.

"When did you decide to go auburn?" Ed called to Mary as he rang up the purchases.

She just shrugged and focused on putting bills in the small money purse for Finnegan to carry to the counter.

Abby had a strange feeling in the pit of her stomach, and she doubted it had anything to do with the club sandwich she'd just eaten. But she wouldn't worry about Mary's purchases now. There were more pressing things to think about.

For instance, who on the island had left the tackle box at Stanton Farm? And had Abby agreed to speak to Bobby's class and then forgotten about it?

For now, though, she was going to try to forget about what Mary intended to do with that auburn hair dye.

ABBY SPENT TUESDAY MORNING squeezed into a tiny, junk-filled attic with Hugo Baron. Of course, they didn't know that much of it was junk until they'd hauled it out and dumped it in a pile in the empty bedroom their benefactor had asked them to use.

The house stood on a small rise on the far side of Sparrow Island, beyond Mount Ortiz. The entire island was eight miles long and only three-fourths as wide, but it had still taken them some time to get to the house following the winding western path of Wayfarer Point Road. Of course, a stop to bird-watch along the way had added to their travel time. But both Abby and Hugo had deemed the stop worthwhile as they had pulled out their binoculars to observe a bald eagle soar to a rocky out-cropping where it had begun assembling a nest of sticks and leaves.

"Sneaky way to get us to clear out the attic for her," Hugo grumbled. "Baiting us with promises of historical artifacts."

Today he was dressed in a long-sleeved white shirt, olive jacket and khaki pants that were cuffed and crisply creased. His tie had come off more than an hour ago, and his sleeves were rolled up, but he still looked impeccable. Abby had no idea how he did it. Maybe it was the personality and erect posture, although today the personality wasn't quite as pert as usual.

"Have faith," she said, handing him the last of the boxes blocking their access to the far corner of the attic. "Perhaps there's something of historic value under this blanket."

She tossed the bedcovering to him and exposed a pedal-powered sewing machine.

"Look at this, Hugo. My mother has one like this at the farm."

But Hugo wasn't paying attention. His head was bent over the blanket she'd thrown to him, and at first she thought he was praying. But a second glance showed that he was examin-ing the patches on the quilt.

"I need to take this downstairs for a better look."

By the time they were ready to leave, Hugo had laid claim to an eighteenth-century spinning wheel, a box full of stone arrowheads and the quilt. And he practically salivated over the pottery and Indian tools and domestic items he found. Although he estimated the quilt had been crafted in the early 1800s, he planned to take it to Ana Dominguez, owner of

In Stitches, for a second opinion. Some of the pieces he found would go into the Early Settlers exhibit. As for the Indian artifacts, he was talking about creating a whole new display for them.

"I'm going out for a late lunch," Abby told him after they'd unloaded their haul at the museum. "Want to join me?"

He didn't bother to lift his head from the magnifying glass he was staring through to study the arrowheads. "No, thank you. I'll just get something out of the snack cabinet."

He waved a hand, and Abby made a mental note to bring something back for him since there were only a packet of peanut butter crackers, half a bagel and some empty plastic tubs in the cabinet.

At the Springhouse Café, most of the lunch crowd was gone. Only one waitress was to be seen, but Abby took a seat at one of Ida's tables anyway.

"She's not here." The waitress, her long brunette hair pulled back in a ponytail, wiped the table and filched a ketchup bottle from another table for her. "Had an appointment or something. Ought to be back in a few minutes, though."

"I'll wait," Abby said, hoping she wouldn't regret her decision. She had a lot of work left to do at the conservatory since she'd spent the morning on a treasure hunt with Hugo instead of performing her usual duties.

She gazed out the window at the back of the café and watched the activity on Randolph Bay. In the distance, a motorboat chugged past. Then a movement in the grass near the water's edge caught her eye, and Abby absentmindedly smiled at the sight of the feathered creature that waddled along the shore. From this distance, most people would assume it was a duck, but the white forehead and short beak gave evidence that this particular bird was an American coot. Abby smiled more broadly as she recalled the time her father had jokingly referred to himself as an American coot.

Abby refocused as the chair across from her was pulled away from the table, and Ida perched on the edge of the seat. She had once confided to Abby that the waitresses were only allowed to sit with customers if they kept only one "cheek" on the chair. Supposedly, the rule was to discourage idling.

"If I had known you were here, I would have hurried back sooner," Ida said.

"Your coworker mentioned you had an appointment." Abby reached over and touched her hand. "Have you been sick?"

"Oh no, thank goodness. The clasp on my necklace broke, so I took it to the jeweler on my break."

"Good." Then, realizing what she had said, Abby added, "That you're not sick, I mean. Not about the necklace."

Ida laughed, and her voice was high and bubbly. "I knew what you meant." She fidgeted on the chair as if the hard edge was beginning to bother her. "I'm so glad you showed up today. Ever since I heard about the box you found, I've been wondering how many gold coins are in there."

"Gold coins?"

"Yes, that's what the owner of Bayside Souvenirs said was inside. Almost everyone who came in today has been talking about it."

"Oh my, I don't know where anyone got the idea there are gold coins in the box. In fact, it hasn't even been opened yet."

"Really? What are you waiting for?"

"God's time."

Abby reached into her purse and pulled out the Vacation

Bible School flyer she'd saved for her young friend. "Here's some more information about Little Flock's summer day camp program. I thought you'd like to see what God has accomplished in the previous sessions and get an idea of how serving can make such a big impact on the children. Mary says the adult workers get as much out of it as the children do."

"Thank you," Ida said and tucked the paper into the apron she wore around her waist. "I'm looking forward to being a snack lady and seeing the little ones' smiles when we give them their treats. In fact, I've already been thinking how I can carve a watermelon into Noah's Ark and make animals out of marshmallows, raisins and other goodies."

"What a wonderful idea. Your enthusiasm is exactly why I knew you'd be a good person to work with the children."

Ida looked down and toyed with the fabric of her apron.

Sweet, hardworking, creative and modest, too. Abby had no doubt her young friend would be a good addition to the Little Flock congregation. She was certainly a good addition to Abby's circle of friends.

"About the box you found," Ida said, turning the subject back to one that was more comfortable for her. "When it's time to open it, may I watch? The suspense is absolutely killing me."

Abby laughed. "Certainly you may watch, though we both might be disappointed at the outcome. I'm beginning to think the box could be filled with dirty socks or something just as unappealing."

"It doesn't matter," Ida assured her. "In fact, I'd be happy to ask around and help you find the rightful owner. Every Sherlock needs a Watson. Imagine that. I could be like a character in a novel."

"Thank you." Abby unwrapped the napkin around her silverware. "I appreciate all the help I can get."

She liked Ida's company. Abby had made a mental list of some of the businesses in Green Harbor that she could visit and the people she could ask. Perhaps she could arrange to go at a time when Ida was off work so the two of them could investigate together. And they could use the time to get to know each other better.

Thelma Rogers had come into the café and was seated at a table near Abby's. Ida stood and went to get her drink order.

The woman said nothing to Ida. Instead, she pointed a finger at Abby. "That hired man of your parents' is up to no good," she declared. "There's two hundred dollars missing from the change tin in my apartment, and I have a good idea who took it."

Abby bristled at the slur against Sam. No wonder he had seemed disturbed by his encounter with her yesterday morning. Thelma was known for jumping to conclusions about people and their intentions, but this time she was bordering on slandering an innocent man. It was all Abby could do to respond in an even tone.

"It will show up eventually. Just give it time."

"Time for it to go missing for good." Thelma shook open her menu with a snap. "You know what he's done in the past and where he's been. It stands to reason the very same thing is happening again. But I'm not going to stand by and be a helpless victim."

Abby took a deep breath. There was nothing helpless about Thelma. And it took a lot of faith to remember that she wasn't hopeless, either.

"Would you like me to come to your apartment and help

you look for your missing money? Mary and I find that when we misplace something, it helps to have a fresh pair of eyes to look for it."

"I don't think so. You'd probably cover for him anyway. I wouldn't be surprised if my money is in that box you found." She turned her shoulder to Abby in a dismissive gesture and gave Ida her order. Ida then took Abby's order and headed into the kitchen.

Ten minutes later when Ida returned with Abby's plate and a carryout bag for Hugo, Abby leaned toward her and said quietly, "As you can see, that box could stir up some unpleasantness. Are you sure you want to help me search for clues? If you'd rather change your mind, I'll understand."

Ida shook her head and darted a glance in Thelma's direction. "There's more reason now than ever to help you find the owner."

CHAPTER ❦ FOUR

O<small>N HER WAY TO WORK</small> Wednesday morning, Abby went into the town of Green Harbor toward Primrose Lane. She drove past the newspaper building, which was still dark inside. *The Birdcall* was Sparrow Island's weekly newspaper of events, activities and even occasionally some news when it occurred. No cars were parked near the building, which was not a surprise given that yesterday's deadline duties had most likely kept the staff of four late at work putting the most recent edition to bed.

Almost a week until the next deadline. That would provide enough time for Abby to check into some other possibilities before taking her story to William Jansen, the paper's editor-in-chief.

As she drove east on Kingfisher Avenue, Abby noted that the grocery store and library showed signs of activity, but it would be another half hour or so before most of the tourist shops turned over the CLOSED signs in their front windows to read OPEN. However, fishermen were notorious for their early morning rising, so Abby was pleased to find The Tackle Shop's owner already in the store, sweeping the knotty pine floor.

Most people thought Brenda Wilson was just the owner's wife, but it was she who had started the business and was the true fishing aficionado. Her sun-bleached hair and lean physique gave evidence of her love of the outdoors. Mary had told Abby that ten years ago, when the quaint, hundred-year-old building at the north corner of Kingfisher and Primrose came available for rent, Brenda had snatched it up to start her tackle and fishing business, with her two teenage children helping out after school. Her husband Kyle handled the paperwork for her so she'd be free to do the part she loved most: talk fishing with her customers.

Abby waited, the tackle box in her folded arms, while Brenda put down the broom and pushed open the glass-paned front door.

"You're my first customer of the day. The early bird gets the worm." Brenda was dressed in jeans and a pocketed vest, as if at any moment she might decide to grab a rod and go fishing herself.

"Actually, I wanted to ask you about a tackle box." As Brenda started to lead her to a shelf loaded with various colored boxes, Abby added, "This one in particular."

She handed the padlocked box to the store owner. "I was hoping you might be able to tell me something about it."

Brenda shrugged as she turned it over in her hands. "I've sold a bajillion of them. The *Angler's Edge* is one of my best sellers. People seem to like the artwork on the top." She brushed a hand through her short blond hair. "I've seen folks use these suckers for everything from tackle boxes to lunch boxes, toolboxes and crafting supply boxes. One lady even bought one to use as a jewelry box."

"Oh dear. I was afraid of that. You see, I was hoping you might remember who bought this one."

The woman peered at Abby. "Are you the lady who found the buried treasure on her property? That's all people have been talking about for the past couple of days. But no one mentioned that it was in a tackle box."

Abby smiled. "Yes, I suppose what's inside is a treasure to the person who buried it. However, I would appreciate your not mentioning the fact that it is a tackle box. I want the owner to be able to describe it."

"No problem," Brenda said with a smile.

Abby leaned toward Brenda and turned the metal box over in her hands. "What about the numbers stamped into the bottom? Would that narrow it down to a production batch, or maybe tell you something about when it was manufactured?"

Brenda shook her head. "They're mass-produced at a factory in Ohio and shipped all over the country."

"Ohio." Abby heaved a deep sigh as she calculated the next move she would need to make.

"That's a fairly common padlock," Brenda said. "If you want, I have some master keys we could try on it. Perhaps the contents will give you the information you need."

"Thank you, but I'd rather save that option as a last resort. The person who hid it apparently didn't want anyone to see what was inside. So I'd like to honor that wish."

"That's very noble of you," she told Abby. "If it was me, I'd just open it up and save myself some trouble."

"It certainly can test a person's patience," Abby admitted. "Is there anything else you can tell me about this box?"

During her days as an ornithologist at Cornell University, Abby had found that one of her most helpful questions when interviewing people who had spotted a rare or unusual bird was an open-ended one. Oftentimes, people would offer information that she might not have thought to ask about.

The shop owner handed the box back to Abby. "Just that it's relatively new. The brushed-metal design was introduced about a year and a half ago, maybe two years at most. Before that was the gunmetal gray, but this one has sold so well that they discontinued the plain one."

Abby let this new information roll through her mind. So the box was buried no more than two years ago. That would help narrow her search tremendously.

"I'm sorry I couldn't be of more help," Brenda said.

"Actually, you've helped me much more than you know."

AT THE TIME that Janet had suggested Lawanna Porter might be responsible for burying the box on Stanton Farm, Abby had considered it a lead with limited potential. But since she now knew the movie actress's peculiar behavior had occurred within the two-year time frame of the box's manufacture, the likelihood of that possibility just went up a notch.

Recalling Janet's remark that Patricia Hale might know something about Lawanna Porter, Abby decided it was time for a call. That night Patricia was tied up with Wednesday night Bible study activities, so she suggested Abby drop by the parsonage the next evening. Since Ida wasn't scheduled to work that Thursday, Abby invited her along to the Hales' house.

It was Rev. James Hale himself who answered the doorbell. In his mid-forties, with sandy blond hair and boyish good looks, he was quite handsome in a Californian kind of way.

A miniature, towheaded clone of himself peeked from behind the reverend's knees and waved at the women. "Hi."

"Hey, Toby," Ida said and chucked the two-year-old's chin.

"Patricia will be here in a moment." The reverend invited them in and offered them soft drinks, which they declined. "That box you found was the subject of conversation at our Ministers with a Mission meeting today. The pastor at First Baptist has even decided to use the topic as a sermon this Sunday to go along with his message about the parable of Matthew 13:44." He chuckled and then recited part of the verse. "'The kingdom of heaven is like treasure hidden in a field.' Couldn't be more appropriate."

Ida's eyes widened as she turned to Abby and clutched her arm. "That's just like what you told me soon after we met . . . that there are verses in the Bible to address everything in our lives."

Abby agreed. "Absolutely. God's 'instruction manual' may be thousands of years old, but it's still relevant today."

When Patricia showed up, her husband excused himself, saying it was time to change Toby's diaper. He wrinkled his nose and whisked the laughing boy away as if he were an airplane zooming down the hall.

Although the boy had inherited most of his looks from his father, his eyes had come from Patricia. A beautiful redhead with cinnamon-colored eyes and the tall, slender frame of a model, she had no need to enhance her beauty by artificial means. Putting makeup on her would certainly be a case of gilding the lily.

"It's so good to see you," she said as Abby and Ida rose to greet her. "Please say you'll stay for dinner."

Abby looked to Ida for a response. Although she herself was

anxious to continue tracking down leads, she didn't want to deny her friend the opportunity of getting to know the Hales better if that was her wish.

Ida paused for only a moment. "Thank you for your generosity, but we have a lot of sleuthing to do this evening. I feel like a regular Jessica Fletcher when I'm with Abby."

Patricia sat down in a side chair. "I know what you mean. She has a knack for finding things that trigger curiosity." She turned to Abby. "Did you bring the box with you? I'd love to see what's stirred up everyone's interest."

"No, it's at the museum, locked in my desk drawer. I thought it would be safer to leave it there rather than risk forgetting it somewhere."

Patricia nodded, but they both knew the likelihood of Abby forgetting about it was slim. "I understand you're thinking the box may belong to Lawanna Porter."

"Yes. Janet Heinz seems to think that, since you were once an actress, you might have known Ms. Porter."

"Yes, I know her. I actually spent some time with Lawanna when she vacationed here last year."

"Could you tell us where she went and what she did while she was on the island? Do you think she might have had a reason to bury the box and leave it behind when she returned to Hollywood?" Abby leaned forward, elbows on knees, intent on getting to the bottom of this, and she noticed that Ida mimicked her action. "We don't want to pry into her personal business, but we also don't want to intrude on her time if it's not hers."

Patricia traced a finger over the swirl pattern on her chair. "We didn't really do much together. Just a couple of meals. She's really more a friend of my parents'. I was just doing them a favor by making her feel welcome and offering suggestions on some quiet places where she could go and relax."

Ida looked disappointed. "But I'd thought you and she would be close friends, since you both lived and worked in Hollywood. And you're both so glamorous."

Patricia smiled. "My father had a successful career as an actor and hung out with all the Tinseltown types. It only took acting in a few small roles—and later meeting James—for me to realize that showbiz wasn't my thing."

It was clear that Ida—a young woman who had grown up on the island and then had to support herself after her parents died when she was seventeen—had a few stars in her eyes about what life would be like elsewhere. Abby had wanted to tell her that all she ever needed was right here on Sparrow Island, but she knew Ida wouldn't believe her. She would have to figure that out for herself. Abby prayed that her young friend would soon find the Lord's purpose for her life.

Even so, Abby wondered if Patricia ever regretted leaving her life of glitz and glamour behind. "I heard that Lawanna was seen digging a hole at Paradise Cove," she said, bringing the subject back to the matter she and Ida had come to investigate. "Do you know if there might have been something she was trying to hide? Perhaps something that motivated her to ultimately bury the box on Stanton Farm?"

When no answer was immediately forthcoming, Abby added, "Or might she have been merely rehearsing a part for a movie, which was why her behavior seemed strange at the cove?"

Patricia leaned one arm on the chair and placed a finger to her mouth as she thought. "I'm a fan of her work, and my father usually keeps me posted on what his actor friends are doing, so I remember that last summer Lawanna was preparing to film a romantic movie about a Wall Street stockbroker and a showgirl from Branson, Missouri. I can't imagine how digging at a cove or burying a box would have had anything to do with the part she was playing."

"What about personal secrets?" Ida said, obviously getting into the swing of her role as Abby's Dr. Watson. "Something she didn't want the paparazzi to know about?"

Patricia made a sound that came out more like a snort than a laugh. "Lawanna Porter with secrets? She's more open than Oprah and Kathy Lee Gifford combined."

"So it looks as though her sole focus while on the island was to relax." Abby tentatively crossed Lawanna's name off the list in her head.

"I believe so." Patricia seemed truly regretful not to have been able to help.

"But you don't know for certain that she didn't have another agenda while on the island?" Ida asked.

Patricia shook her head.

Abby and Ida rose to leave, their investigation no further along than when they arrived. Then, remembering the success of her catchall question with Brenda at The Tackle Shop, Abby decided to give it another try.

"Can you think of anyone else who might know something about Lawanna's activities while she was here last year?"

Patricia walked with them to the door. "Why don't you ask the manager at The Dorset? That's where Lawanna stayed, and she once commented that the staff was very helpful in keeping away a few overeager fans who tried to monopolize her time."

In the car, as they headed east on Shoreline Drive, Ida was

clearly getting into the excitement of uncovering leads. "Suppose," she said, "they weren't just fans the hotel staff kept away, but people who knew something about Lawanna's covert activities and wanted to expose them?"

"Not to burst your bubble, but I doubt it's anything as sensational as that."

"Well, all I can say is, it's about time something interesting happened on this island."

"Good heavens, Ida, something interesting happens every time the good Lord sends us a new sunrise and fresh opportunities for a day to glorify Him."

"Yeah, I know I'm supposed to believe that, but sometimes it's hard to be content with my life. At least you've had the opportunity to live in exotic places. I'd love to go to New York and work there, like you did. But I don't know how to do anything other than wait tables, so I'll probably be stuck here for the rest of my life." She looked out the car window as they passed the Springhouse Café on the right. "Unless, of course, I marry a world traveler who has enough money for us to enjoy the good things."

Abby turned off Shoreline Drive onto Primrose Lane, then into the swank hotel's paved parking lot and pulled into a space near the front door. "Someday," she promised her friend, "you'll see that you already have 'the good things.'"

She doubted Ida would believe her anymore than Dorothy had believed that her destiny was right there on Auntie Em's farm. Instead, Ida would have to go on her own difficult journey before she could appreciate the treasure she already had.

In fact, Abby herself had needed to go on a personal journey of more than thirty years—earning her degrees, living in

New York and teaching and working at Cornell University—before her travels brought her right back here where she had started. And she had never been happier in her life. She prayed that Ida would find a similar happiness.

As they passed through the elegant lobby with its brass and crystal chandeliers and velvet sofas inviting them to linger and enjoy the luxurious ambience, Abby could easily imagine a movie star feeling comfortable in these surroundings.

Ida leaned toward her and whispered, "I feel so out of place. If I had known we were coming here, I would have worn something fancier than this T-shirt."

Abby patted her shoulder. "You're beautiful just the way you are."

The only thing gangly or awkward about The Dorset was the young man behind the check-in desk who obviously hadn't finished filling out. His wide, angular shoulders were little more than coat hangers for the crested jacket that threatened to swallow him up. The polished brass badge on his chest declared his name, though it wasn't certain whether it was his first or last: Cameron. Since the lobby was empty at the moment except for a smartly dressed bellman, they had his undivided attention.

He gave Ida an appreciative glance before quickly turning to what seemed like a well-practiced attempt at sophistication. "May I help you?"

"Yes, thank you," Abby said. "We'd like to speak with the manager if he—um, or she—is available."

"I'm sorry, but he's in a meeting right now. He'll be available in about an hour."

Although it was tempting to suggest they wait on the plush

covered sofa and admire the Persian rugs and polished cherry tables, neither of them had the time to spare. Not if they wanted to get home in time to prepare for work the next day.

Ida groaned her disappointment. Turning away from the hotel clerk, she asked Abby, "Do you suppose there's someone else here who might know something about Lawanna?"

"If you're referring to Ms. Porter," Cameron interjected, "maybe I can help you. A few times during her stay last summer, I was assigned to help ensure her privacy from all the lookie loos. Er, I mean well-wishers." He seemed proud of having been called upon to perform such an important duty.

Keeping the description of the events that brought them there as brief as possible, Abby explained about the box and said she had reason to believe it might belong to Lawanna Porter. At her mention of the box, his interested expression revealed that he was already aware of its existence.

"If you could give us an idea of where she went while she was here and some of the things she did, that could help us narrow down whether the box is hers."

"The staff is not allowed at any time to divulge the personal itineraries of its guests," he said as if he had memorized the words from the employees' policy and procedures manual.

Cameron glanced over his shoulder toward the bellman who had moved to the row of luggage carts and was rubbing fingerprints off the tall brass poles. He lowered his voice.

"If there's something specific you want to ask, I might be able to help. I just can't volunteer information."

"Understandably so," Abby said. She lowered her voice to match his, and Ida leaned in to hear. "Ms. Porter was seen at Paradise Cove, digging a hole by the beach. Did she perhaps mention why she was going there?"

The clerk smiled and spoke more loudly now, as if to prove to the bellman that he wasn't engaging in an indiscreet conversation. "Many of our guests inquire about shellfishing, and we recommend clamming as a peaceful way to spend an evening. We also direct them to Paradise Cove for fly-fishing." As an aside, he added, "Some people might not realize that the cove isn't the best place to find clams."

"Yes, of course. Clamming." Abby considered the likely possibility that Lawanna had gone to Paradise Cove with the intention of enjoying a quiet afternoon alone and, while there, decided to poke around to see if any clams turned up. "Thank you," she said. "You've been very helpful."

She turned to go, Lawanna Porter now erased from her list of possibilities, but Ida stopped her with a touch to the crook of her elbow.

"Just one more thing," Ida said to the young man. "Can you think of anyone else we should talk to about this? Someone who might know something about the box we found?"

Abby smiled for two reasons. One, because Ida was so into this investigation that she now included herself as a finder of the box. And two, because she had picked up on Abby's use of the one-final-question that often brought unexpected results.

Cameron paused and thought for a moment. "You could ask at The Bird Nest. One time last fall, they were trying to move a couple of their guests over here. Apparently, something about them bothered the owner."

Outside, Abby congratulated Ida on gathering that last bit of information.

Ida smiled, basking in the compliment. "Just following your lead," she said. "I'm learning a lot by hanging around with you."

"OH GOODY, YOU'RE HERE! Bobby McDonald has been bragging for the past couple of days that his friend Abby was coming to speak to his class." Margaret Blackstock put down the Friday attendance rosters she was using to key the information into her computer. "When I recommended you, I told Mrs. Quinn you know about everything that lives and grows on the island."

Abby set down the box she was carrying, balancing it on the arm of the guest chair in front of the school secretary's desk. "Thank you for your vote of confidence. I enjoy teaching children about the wonders of a world that most of us take for granted. Fifth graders are the perfect age, too, because they haven't decided yet that they're too cool to be excited about boreal toads and tree sap."

"You're right about that. I've heard about the surprises some of the moms find in their kids' pockets." Just a few years younger than Abby, Margaret had been unable to have children of her own, but her life with her husband—and "her kids" at the school, as she sometimes called them—was full.

"Mrs. Quinn asked me to be here at two o'clock," Abby said. "I'm a little early. Do you suppose I should go around to her class and wait there?"

"She's giving a quiz this period. If the students see you, they'll get excited and won't be able to concentrate. Why don't you sit here until the bell rings and give me an exclusive update on the mystery box you found?"

Her use of the reporting term elicited a laugh from Abby. As a close friend of Janet's, Margaret also loved to be in the know about everything that happened in Green Harbor and most of what happened on Sparrow Island.

"There's nothing to tell, really. But if you have any tips, I'm all ears."

"Well, actually . . ." Margaret drew the words out as if that were her intent from the start. "There are a couple of teenagers—brothers—who have a knack for finding trouble. And if they can't find any, they create it."

Abby toyed with the strap on her purse. "You think they may have buried the box?"

"I know they have the potential. Their history is pretty bad. Stealing, lying. Marijuana use by the older one." She shook her head. "It's a sad situation. If they were the ones who buried the box, there may be drugs or stolen goods inside."

Although Margaret loved to talk, Abby respected the fact that she hadn't mentioned the boys' names along with the bad report. Anytime there was good news, Margaret happily spread tales along with names. However, in sensitive cases like this, she tried hard to be circumspect. She wasn't always successful, but her heart was in the right place.

"In fact, things had gotten so bad at their previous school in Seattle that their parents moved the family to Green Harbor, hoping the smaller community would give the boys fewer opportunities to get into trouble." She sighed, her bosom expanding with the movement. "I tried to tell the mother that you can't run away from problems, you just take them with you. But she wouldn't hear it."

"That's something most people have to learn for themselves," Abby sympathized.

"The older son had been asked not to return to his old school. They couldn't handle him. And honestly, I'm not sure we can either."

"Hang in there. And remember, with God all things are possible," Abby said, shortening the popular verse from Matthew 19:26. "I hope that what you fear is not true. But it would be wise for us to keep our eyes and ears open, all the while praying for those troubled children."

Margaret gave a mirthless laugh. "I think God's tired of hearing from me about them."

"Fortunately, He never grows tired." The bell rang. Abby stood and picked up her carton of botanical samples. "Please keep me posted."

In the classroom, as the students settled themselves at their desks, Mrs. Quinn pulled Abby aside and thanked her for coming on such short notice. Then, without preamble, she said quietly, "I heard your parents found a bomb on their farm. Is everyone okay?"

"Did Bobby tell you that?"

"No, he said it was a box. But word has it the box was ticking."

Hmm, she hadn't heard that bit of scuttlebutt before. "No, there was no ticking. And even if that were the case, the box has been shaken and handled so much that I'm sure if it were a bomb the thing would have blown by now."

"Thank goodness. I was all set to call my uncle and ask him to safely detonate it for you. He handles the Fourth of July fireworks every year."

Mrs. Quinn was an attractive African American woman with a kind heart. Because she cared, she was often strict with the children. However, they thrived from her supportive attention.

"I don't think that will be necessary, but I'll keep your offer in mind, just in case."

After the bell rang, Mrs. Quinn introduced Abby to the

class, then took a seat at the back of the room to observe. Abby passed around some leaf samples, an insect cocoon attached to a twig like a balloon on a stick, and bits of lichen and moss. After a lively discussion about the creatures that depend on trees for food, shelter and reproduction, the children exclaimed over dried bits of mouse hair and bone that Abby held up, which they referred to as "owl barf."

From that point, their attitudes went from rapt attention to general silliness. Since Abby had finished covering the subject she had prepared, she raised one hand and *ahemmed* to regain their attention. Although most of her teaching experience had involved college students, she was glad to see that she still had "the touch" and that it worked on distractible fifth graders.

For the question-and-answer session, a couple of insightful queries were asked, just as Mary had predicted. But then their questions turned broader.

"Did you find a mummy in the box you dug up?" one child asked. "Maybe it was from King Tut's tomb."

Another said he'd seen an unidentified flying object once and wanted to know if a space alien was waiting to emerge from the container to take over the world.

"My, what imaginations," Abby said. Perhaps this would be a good opportunity to clear up the rumors, wild as they were, and encourage the children to think of real-life possibilities. It was about time to go public with the information anyway. "My guess is that one of the students at your school may have placed it at Stanton Farm. So if you know of anyone who can describe the box I found, please send them to me."

Bobby raised his hand. "Your parents' neighbors used to let their nieces come to visit every summer. Maybe one of them buried the box."

She smiled her thanks and wrote the latest tidbit on a notepad she carried in her purse. The leads were now growing more numerous, and she was running out of mental memory to keep track of them all.

After she had gathered up her things and was walking down the main corridor of the school, Abby came upon Bobby's mother, Sandy McDonald, on her way to the teacher's lounge.

Abby asked her if she knew of the boys Margaret had mentioned earlier, and expressed her concern that they may have been responsible for the box she'd found.

"It's possible," Sandy said. "One of them is in my English class. They've been full-time trouble since they registered for school. In the past month, their behavior has gotten a little better, but they're reasonable suspects for anything that might happen around here."

"How unfortunate. Do you recall when they moved to Green Harbor?"

"Yes. The date is emblazoned on my brain. It was in January, the first day of school after our winter break."

"This year?"

"Yeah, it's been only a little over three months, but it feels like three years."

Abby took in the information. "I don't know whether this is good news or not, but those boys didn't bury the box in my parents' yard."

CHAPTER ❦ FIVE

The following Tuesday at *The Birdcall,* owner and editor-in-chief William C. Jansen barely paused when he passed through the front office where Abby waited for him.

Thin, with sharp elbows and long limbs, William spent most of the time covering up his flustered feelings with a growly demeanor.

"Can't talk now, Abby. It's Tuesday, the deadline is looming and my lead story just fell through."

Ignoring his gruffness, she followed him into his office. He was often flustered about one thing or another, and on Tuesdays when the staff of four was scrambling to meet their weekly deadline, he was even worse. But his bark was truly worse than his bite.

"I have a story for you. About a box I dug up on my parents' farm. The whole town's talking about it."

"So I heard." William began riffling through the scattered papers on his desk. "A buried box is two steps below crop circles in news value. *The Birdcall* is a reputable newspaper, Abby. I don't want it to become a laughingstock because of following every cockamamy curiosity. I have to draw the line somewhere. Otherwise, we'll be printing articles about who stole a dress from Mrs. Dickerson's clothesline."

The last was a veiled reference to the previous owner and editor, an eighty-year-old retired librarian who had routinely put out the weekly newspaper with numerous mistakes—factual, grammatical and typographical. That had been before Abby's return to Sparrow Island, but the stories about it lingered on. There had been no crossword puzzle in the paper at that time, but townsfolk had made it a game each week to circle the typos and misprints and compete with other readers to see who got the highest "score" of errors detected.

The paper's readability had gone up since William bought it over five years ago, but that was all relative. It was well known that he'd always wanted to be a newspaper man, but his early efforts at reporting for the *Chicago Tribune* had failed and he'd been forced into the family business, Jansen's Essentials, a major name in baby products. Although he'd made good money as CEO of the company, he hadn't been happy about being unable to pursue his journalism dream and was depressed over being, what he called, a diaper pusher. So when he'd turned fifty, he put the family's business behind him, moved to Sparrow Island and bought the local newspaper. Even so, there were a few people in town who claimed he was still in the diaper business. After all, they said, didn't the paper serve the same purpose as a diaper when it was used to line the bottom of birdcages?

Abby actually enjoyed the paper . . . most of the time.

Unfortunately, when William was thick into playing the part of hard-bitten editor, he sometimes lost sight of what actually made for a good, public-interest story. Like now.

"You're in luck," she persisted. "This isn't a laundry story." Then again, if there were actually dirty socks in the box as she had joked, she might have to eat her words. "It's about buried secrets and possibly hidden dreams."

William stepped away from his desk and ran a hand through his bushy brown hair. "I don't know. We won't see if it's newsworthy until the box is opened. I don't want to get stuck with a Geraldo Rivera story, building the hype only to find a safe full of soggy papers. My reputation is at stake."

This was getting ridiculous. A newspaperman refusing to publish an intriguing discovery like this. "I understand your concern," Abby said, "but I won't be opening the box until I've exhausted all means of finding the owner first."

"Well, it's been nice talking to you," he said, ushering her toward the door.

"Same here." Abby retrieved the notepad from her purse and flipped it open. "Do you happen to know the deadline for the *Puget Sound Sentry*? Perhaps they'd be interested in running a feature article about my box. And then the story would go to all the San Juans, not just Sparrow Island."

William made an inadvertent raspberry sound with his lips. "The *Puget Sound Propaganda*, you mean."

Just as she had expected, the competition factor kicked in, and suddenly William's demeanor changed.

"Tell you what," he said, reaching for the 35mm camera by the door, "I'll take a picture of you holding the box and include a short caption with it."

"No, I want the person who comes forward to claim it to be able to describe the box. Running a picture would give away too much information."

He stared solemnly at her. "Okay, but it gets ten inches of print, no more. And you have to promise me an exclusive follow-up when you open the box."

"Fair enough," Abby said, and they shook on it.

THE SPARROW ISLAND VISITORS CENTER sat at the corner of Shoreline Drive and Primrose Lane, just across the street from The Complete Boater and within walking distance of the ferry landing. Though small, the center was airy and bright, with multicolored brochures and trifold maps lined up in neat rows in front of the pale ash-paneled walls.

At the moment, elderly twin sisters in matching bright pink jackets and purple visors stood at the counter, listening intently as Ellen Stanton described the whale watching tours.

A few minutes later, the ladies left clutching fistfuls of flyers and wearing enthusiastic smiles.

Abby stepped closer to the counter. "You were good at reassuring those sisters they'd made the right choice for their excursion."

Ellen Stanton smoothed her gray hair, which was perfect even before she touched it. Her light blue gaze settled on Abby and missed nothing. "What are you needing reassurance about?"

"I gave an interview to *The Birdcall* today. The story about the box will be out tomorrow."

"Good. After William's article helps you reunite the box with its owner," Ellen said, "perhaps you'll have more time to spend with your sister. She's quite excited about making you over."

Abby groaned. "I don't want to be made over. Why can't she find another way to entertain herself?"

Ellen leaned across the counter and gently tucked a wandering strand of Abby's hair behind her ear. "Mary is reaching out to you. Help her by meeting her halfway."

Her mother was right. Mary had been making an effort to find common ground between them, not an easy task given their differing personalities and interests.

"I'll see what I can do," Abby promised. "In the meantime, do you remember anything about your neighbors' nieces who used to visit them every summer? Bobby suggested they might have been the ones to bury the box at the farm."

Ellen touched a finger to her chin. "Yes, little Morgan and Melanie. They used to love to design clothes out of wrapping paper for their paper dolls. I wonder how they're doing now?"

"Didn't you see them last summer?"

"No, for the past three years the Flemmings have been flying to Virginia to visit them. Melanie must be close to a teenager by now. It's amazing how fast they grow up."

"*Hmm*. The box couldn't have been buried by them because it wasn't manufactured until just under two years ago. And Margaret Blackstock suggested it might have been put there by a couple of boys at school, but it wasn't them either. They didn't move to Sparrow Island until three months ago, but when I found the box it had at least a year's worth of vegetation growing around the rock that covered it.

"I even asked Mary to check with Nancy to see if her kids might have had something to do with the box the last time they were here from Florida," Abby said, referring to Mary's daughter.

Ellen glanced up, her brow furrowing. "They came that

week we had all that rain. They didn't have any chance to go outside and play at all when they were here."

Abby nodded. "That's basically what Nancy said."

Ellen picked up a cloth and busied herself with dusting. "It sounds like you're doing a good job of following leads."

"I am, if you give points for finding out who the box *doesn't* belong to. We know it's not Sam, that's for sure. Unfortunately, Thelma thinks he's responsible."

"She still hasn't found her 'diva dollars'?"

"No, and yesterday she received a letter in the mail, thanking her for a $225 donation to a children's charity. She's convinced it has something to do with her missing two hundred dollars."

"And with Sam?"

Abby gnawed the inside of her cheek. "And Sam."

ABBY'S MIND COULDN'T stop thinking about Thelma's situation the next day. It made no sense to think that someone would steal Thelma's money, then donate it to a charity with an additional twenty-five dollars. But people, Abby had come to know, didn't always make sense.

Birds, on the other hand, usually made plenty of sense. If a bird stole from another, it was because it was hungry. Or if it bullied another out of its nest, it was because the bird wanted to save itself the trouble of building its own. And even when a bird's behavior seemed bizarre, it could usually be explained by putting the pieces of evidence together and connecting the dots. In a couple of perplexing cases Abby had studied when she lived in New York, the feathered creatures' unusual activities had eventually been attributed to mild earthquake tremors or ingesting toxic runoff.

Hugo Baron looked up from the counter in the museum's workroom where they were sorting and cleaning the Native American tools they'd acquired last week.

"Good article in *The Birdcall*. Quite impressive that it made the front page, considering what you said about Jansen's reluctance to run the piece."

"Yes. Another article he'd planned didn't work out, so he must have plugged mine into its place. It's below the fold, but it's still on the front page. I'm hoping the mystery owner will soon step forward to claim the box."

"Indeed. And good thinking for you to suggest Jansen do a feature on our artifact find. It's good to bring the museum to the attention of both townsfolk and tourists."

"I'm glad he's following through," Abby agreed. She ran a steel brush over a bone awl to remove a crusted bit of dirt. "Perhaps the publicity will bring some extra visitors and donations to the museum."

"The timing was very good for bringing these things to light. And speaking of bringing things to light . . ."

He paused, letting his words dangle in the air until it was clear he had Abby's full attention.

". . . it'll soon be time to open the box."

The article hadn't even been on the newsstands for a full day yet. Abby wondered if he, too, had been bitten by the curiosity bug that had infected the rest of the islanders.

"You can't wait forever, you know."

"I thought I'd give it about a week, until the next *Birdcall* deadline. William said that if readers seem interested in this week's article, he'll do a short follow-up when I open the box. Then he said something about the value of stringing readers along with serial stories."

Hugo smiled, the corners of his eyes crinkling with amusement as he gazed at Abby.

"Ah yes. There is something to be said for the power of anticipation."

BY THE WEEKEND, William Jansen had apparently rethought his Geraldo Rivera comment. The phones at *The Birdcall* had been ringing off the hook all week, he told her. Two callers claimed to be the owners and another claimed to know who the box belonged to. Those he ran by Abby to see if they matched the description of the box.

They didn't.

Others offered their services—for a fee, of course—to dispose of the box. And then there were varying residents calling with wild speculations as to how the box got there. None of them panned out, however.

On Saturday, Mary told Abby she was spending the day at Island Blooms. She wanted to help her store manager Candace Grover with the weekend business. Mary also planned to put together planter pots and knickknacks to prepare for the Mother's Day business in a few weeks.

Abby had the day off, so she gathered up her shopping list and went to The Green Grocer. Business was heavy at the store. As she was searching for the freshest looking leaf lettuce—Mary had often said lettuce gives ladies a pretty complexion—Terza Choi sidled up beside her to reach for a glossy purple eggplant.

"What a surprise to see you here on a Saturday," Abby said. "I thought you'd be busy with a houseful of bed-and-breakfasters at The Bird Nest."

"Yes, a full house," the tiny, dark-haired woman said with a lingering trace of her Chinese accent. She held up the eggplant she'd been squeezing and laughed. "They all want to eat."

Abby laughed along with her. Originally from Hong Kong, Terza and her husband had suffered a difficult past, one which they did not talk about. After Cameron at The Dorset had suggested Abby and Ida speak to the Chois about the clients she had referred to them, Ida had filled Abby in on what little she knew about Terza and Martin. After losing their only child in an accident, the pair had emigrated to the United States, living first in Tacoma and later moving to Sparrow Island where they renovated a historic Victorian house into a beautiful and welcoming retreat for vacationers. Hugo, history buff that he was, had been thrilled to see the building restored to its turn-of-the-century finery. Now, seven years after the Chois had moved here, still very little was known about them. But what people did know was that they were upright, honest people who remained happy despite their past difficulties.

"Who's holding down the fort?" Abby placed the lettuce in her cart and turned her attention to the radishes.

"Rick's in charge. He can do anything." Terza swept a hand through the air to indicate his all-encompassing abilities. "That's why we call him a 'handyman.'"

Rick DeBow was known throughout the community for his jack-of-all-trades skills. In addition to working at The Bird Nest, the former stockbroker also did maintenance chores for the church, and he repaired and overhauled boat engines at the marina.

"Terza, do you recall a couple of guests who came to you last fall that you referred to The Dorset?" Abby pushed her cart to stay alongside Terza as she moved over to examine the oranges.

The woman's dark brown eyes clouded over in an expression that was rare for her. "I didn't like them," she said unapologetically. "They had secrets."

"Really? Do you know what kind of secrets?" To let Terza know she didn't intend to pry, she added, "I found a box on my parents' farm. Do you think they might have buried it?"

At that moment, Martin Choi walked up and placed a pork loin in their cart.

"I don't know," she said. "I just know I didn't like them. Always, 'whisper, whisper.'" Her thumb and fingers moved to mimic someone talking.

Martin smiled at his wife and seemed to know exactly who she was talking about. "Of course they whispered. They were on their honeymoon." Martin did the thumb-and-fingers movement as well, and said to Abby, "Sweet nothings. That's all."

Terza scowled. "They weren't nice. Talking loud all night, and taking things that didn't belong to them."

"Oh yes, the embroidered towels," Martin said as if he had pushed the negative memory from his mind.

"You don't be all kissy-kissy in front of other people like that."

Abby certainly understood her feelings in the matter. Although it was obvious to anyone who saw them together that Terza and Martin were very much in love, they showed it in ways that didn't involve much bodily contact. A lingering glance, a gentle word, an adoring smile. And occasionally holding hands. All of these made it clear that, despite their decades of marriage, they too were still honeymooners.

Martin shrugged and nodded agreement. "They were—how do you say?—out there with it. But it's not illegal to be rude."

Abby couldn't help laughing at his observation. "If it were, we'd have more jails than restaurants."

They said their good-byes, and as the Chois moved on to the dairy section, Abby checked yet another prospect off her list. There was still no one to come forward and claim the box.

Soon it would be time to open it. If that didn't bring the owner's name to light, then the contents should at least offer some new information to analyze, as well as new possibilities to pursue.

THE NEXT MORNING, Abby prayed in church about whether now was the right time to open the box. She had been praying at home, too, but church prayers and woodland prayers seemed to her to be more potent, perhaps because the atmosphere in church and in nature was more meditative and less distracting.

The answer didn't come to her in words, but rather as a sense of knowing. It was a comfortable certainty that in opening the box now she'd be going in the right direction . . . at the right time. God's time.

But even with the spiritual go-ahead, Abby put off the unveiling until Monday because Ida had to pick up the Sunday evening shift in addition to her own lunchtime hours when another waitress called in sick.

Abby arranged to open it at Monday night dinner at the Stanton Farm, which seemed only fitting since that was where the box had been found. Mary had offered to help cook the evening meal, possibly because she was anxious to hasten dinner so they could hurry and break into the box. Although Ellen welcomed the chance to turn the cooking over to her daughters, she still insisted on preparing a loaf of crusty garlic bread to go with the eggplant lasagna.

That night, Abby, Mary, George, Ellen, Ida and Sam were crowded around the weathered table in the farmhouse kitchen. Lying on the floor a short distance away, Finnegan watched his mistress, at the ready in case she should need him.

Sensing the family's impatience, Abby hurried to dish out the main course. The savory scent of oregano, olive oil, tomatoes and cheese seemed to calm their restlessness.

"Where's Bobby?" Mary asked. She scooped some salad into her bowl and passed the dish to Ida. "I didn't think there was any way Bobby would miss the big unveiling."

George helped himself to a slice of bread. "He's finishing chores that he neglected to do earlier. His mother called a few minutes ago and said to go ahead and start eating. She'll drive him over after he's done sweeping the porch. She's making a point." The elder Stanton chuckled. "It must be sheer torture for the little guy. But he probably won't dawdle with his chores again in the near future."

Ellen and Mary, the mothers in the group, exchanged glances. For a brief moment—no more than a flicker of a second, actually—Abby felt left out. She had no regrets about her life. In fact, she'd experienced plenty of mother-like moments of her own, first with the students she'd supervised at Cornell who occasionally needed a maternal style of guidance, and now as Bobby's friend. So when that flickering feeling sneaked up on her, as it had just now, she put it in perspective by remembering that she had followed the path that was intended for her, and then she moved on.

George led them in a short prayer. "Lord, we ask Your blessing on this delicious food, on the hands that prepared it and on everyone gathered in Your name around this table. Help us, Father, to find the owner of the box, and please shed Your grace and kindness on that person, whoever it is."

A low chorus of *amens* arose from around the table.

"Where's the mystery box?" Ida asked as she dug into the lasagna.

Sam looked up from his plate. "Over there on the counter by the stove."

Next to the tackle box sat a ring of master keys lent to them by Brenda at The Tackle Shop.

Ida turned in her chair to look over her shoulder where Sam pointed. As she opened her mouth to say something, air apparently went in the wrong way and she launched into a fit of coughing.

Finnegan rose from his sentry point, waiting for an instruction from Mary. He received none because her attention, like everyone else's, was focused on Ida.

Abby reached over to pat her on the back as Bobby let himself in the back door.

"Let's give her the Heimlich," the boy said, positioning himself behind her chair.

At that, Abby stood and steered him to the empty seat beside Mary. "The Heimlich maneuver is only used if the airway is blocked. Ida's breathing fine. She just needs a moment to collect herself."

Ida nodded gratefully, gave a final couple of coughs and wiped the tears from her eyes. When she could speak again, she said, "I was expecting something that looked more like a treasure chest. Or perhaps even a simple cigar box."

Mary spoke up. "Abby didn't let it get around that it was a tackle box because she wanted the person who claimed it to be able to correctly identify it."

Ellen had already gotten Bobby a plate and the boy was swiftly devouring his food. Mary placed a hand on Bobby's forearm, effectively stilling his fork. "Slow down. The box will still be here when you're done eating."

After everyone had finished and the table was cleared, they all moved outside to the weather-beaten picnic table to watch the opening of the box. Ida hovered beside Abby, making it clear she didn't want to risk losing her prime position to see everything.

Abby tried each of the master keys while Sam stood by with a heavy pair of bolt cutters.

When all of the keys failed to open the lock, Sam silently picked up the box and moved several yards away from the eager crowd. George followed him to hold the box in position on the ground. The rest of the group fell silent as well, waiting reverently as if the pair had picked up the Olympic torch and were carrying it on its final leg before the games were to begin.

"Don't come any closer," Sam told the rest of them, "just in case some metal goes flying. And, George, you might want to turn your face away when I make the cut."

With that, he braced his short muscular frame over the bolt cutter handles. His arms shook for a mere second and the curved rod popped. He repeated the movement on the other side, and the padlock fell to the ground.

While Sam examined the cut marks on the lock, George picked up the undamaged container and carried it to Abby where he placed it in her lap.

She rose from her seat on the picnic bench. "You should open it, Dad. It was found in your yard."

He shook his head. "If you hadn't taken it upon yourself to enhance the farm with these beautiful—" He paused and glanced behind him at the bare, stick-like shrubs that were just beginning to show evidence of green leaf buds. "—with these soon-to-be-beautiful bushes, this box might have stayed hidden away for years or even decades more. Please. You do the honors."

Aware of six pairs of eyes upon her, she carefully placed the box on the edge of the picnic table. The air had turned chilly as the sun settled lower on the horizon, but she barely noticed the need for a jacket.

"Any last guesses as to what's inside?" she teased as she dragged out the moment.

"Open it!" Bobby urged, and Ida seconded the motion. Heads nodded in agreement.

Carefully, as if there might be a toy snake inside to leap out at her, Abby stepped back and eased the lid up.

Nothing leaped out.

She raised the lid the rest of the way.

As the contents of the box came into view and registered in Abby's brain, she felt her chest squeeze tight, shutting off the air to her lungs. For a brief moment, a hazy feeling of stunned surprise threatened to overwhelm her.

CHAPTER ❦ SIX

Even with the contents spread out on the table before them, Abby found it hard to believe her eyes. Six thick bundles of bills, mostly fifties and hundreds, tied together with string. A woman's gold ring. And a map of a nearby island with an area of it circled in blue ink.

"We're rich," said Bobby.

Abby laid an arm around his small shoulders. "You're right. We're rich with God's blessings."

"You mean the money isn't ours?"

She shook her head.

"That ring is pretty," Mary said with interest. A sea of gold swirls encircled a lovely aqua and pink opal.

Sam stood away from the crowd at the table, watching with a flat expression, the bolt cutters dangling from one hand.

Abby rubbed her eyes, pushing away the sense of unreality. "We need to see if the owner's name is written anywhere inside."

Ida, who seemed as dazed as Abby felt, picked up the box

and stared vacantly inside it. "I don't see any markings," she said at last, "but there's a key wedged into the corner."

Abby stepped closer. Sure enough, the edge of a key had found its way under an uneven bit of metal where the pieces of the box came together. She waited while Ida worked it loose and handed it to her.

"Maybe it fits the lock," Bobby suggested.

Mary leaned over in her chair so she could get a better view. "It looks like my bank key."

Abby slid her glasses closer to the bridge of her nose. "There's a word that looks like the company that made the key." She flipped it over. Unfortunately, the identification number had been ground smooth.

Her father leaned in. "Somebody didn't want anyone to trace this key."

Ellen rubbed her arms. "Let's go back inside and get warm."

Bobby jumped up and down where he stood. "Let's go back inside and count the dough!"

Sandy McDonald's car pulled into the drive. Ellen scurried over to greet her.

As they went inside, Ellen followed them in. She retrieved Bobby's coat and handed it to him. "Sorry you can't stay, but your mother found another chore that you forgot to finish."

His shoulders drooped, but he didn't argue, which said a lot about his upbringing.

Abby hugged him. "I'll let you know tomorrow just how much it is," she promised. Then she whispered into his ear, "Next time, think about Ecclesiastes 9:10. 'Whatever your hand finds to do, do it with all your might.' Things always turn out best when you do."

He nodded forlornly. As she watched him trudge across the yard toward the car, it was all Abby could do to refrain from calling out to Sandy and asking her to reconsider her decision.

"So do you still think it's a kid's time capsule?" Mary asked as Abby and the rest gathered in the kitchen.

"Maybe it's someone's life savings. Maybe they were saving for the future . . . like a down payment for a house," Ida ventured. "Maybe they didn't trust banks."

"But there's a bank key in the box," Mary challenged.

Abby settled herself at the table and untied a string from one of the bundles of money. "We don't know that for certain."

Mary watched as Abby's counting reached the thousands. "I think you should turn everything over to Henry."

"I think you're right." She placed the counted bills in her hand next to the others. "But didn't you say he won't be back at the Sparrow Island Sheriff's Station until tomorrow afternoon?"

Mary gave an affirming nod. "You could give it to one of the deputies on duty tonight, but I'd feel better if Henry was the one in charge of it."

Abby agreed. Henry would be a safe steward of the stash until the owner was found.

"I wonder if it's counterfeit," she mused, holding one of the bills to the light.

Sam moved away from the table to stand by George who also was examining a fifty. All evening Sam had said very little, positioning himself away from the cash. When he finally spoke, his voice rang clear and bold.

"The money is stolen."

THAT NIGHT, Abby returned the contents to the box—the ring, the key, the map and what had turned out to be a staggering

$115,000 in cash—and took it to the museum where she put it in the heavy waist-high safe that sat in Hugo's office.

Sam hadn't been able to give any solid evidence to confirm his assertion that the money was stolen. Because he had only a "funny feeling" to prove his claim, he insisted they should proceed as if the money had been gained by illegal means.

Even though the stash was now carefully locked away, Abby had an uneasy feeling about having carried it around with her for the past two weeks. Her sleep was broken with dreams of either losing the money or being chased for it. And in one particularly troubling one, Sam was furiously digging a hole while dressed in a black-and-white striped jumpsuit. Her dream image showed a heavy black ball chained to his ankle. Abby woke up the next morning groggy and ashamed that she had dreamt such things about Sam. She knew for certain he had turned his life around and she was upset that her unconscious mind painted him as a crook.

In spite of the disturbing dreams, Abby's overworked brain had come up with a new plan. She had only the beginning steps of the plan, but it was a solid start that would bring her closer to unraveling the mystery behind the hidden loot and finding out whether the money in the box was just a curiosity or whether it was from a crime.

Unfortunately, before she could make it up the steps to Green Harbor Bank to find answers to the two questions she had, William Jansen met her as he was coming out. *The Birdcall* was approaching another deadline, and William looked determined to grill her for everything she knew. Abby paused to consider whether to give him a full disclosure and hoped he would be satisfied with some generalities instead.

"You opened it already, didn't you? I can see it in your eyes."

Abby looked from side to side. "Can we talk about this somewhere else?"

He stepped aside and led her to a low stone wall that separated the bank's property from the post office next door. "It's not a dud, is it? This is a real story."

"I think it would be best to wait until later today or tomorrow to talk to you. After I turn the box over to the Sparrow Island Sheriff's Station, that is."

"The sheriff's department. We *do* have a story!"

He would soon get the information from Henry anyway, and the paper wasn't due to come out until tomorrow. So it shouldn't do any harm to give him the basics now.

"You promised me an exclusive," he reminded her.

"Okay, but all I can tell you is that there was a piece of jewelry and a wad of money." She thought it best not to mention the key or the map. The true owner, if he or she decided to come forward, should be able to identify the box by naming the amount of cash and describing the ring. And if they mentioned the other items, that would be even further proof.

"A large sum of money?" By now, he had fished a notepad and pen out of his pocket.

Abby waited a moment too long before answering.

"A lot, huh? Where is it now?"

"In a safe place."

And it would be in an even safer place after she took it to Henry this afternoon.

INSIDE THE BANK, the account representative who handled The Nature Museum's finances patiently answered Abby's questions. Abby let her think it was because she wanted to know how to prevent accepting a counterfeit bill if they received one at the museum's gift shop.

"All you have to do is make a tiny mark on the bill. If it's real, the ink will be an orangish color. If it's counterfeit, the mark will turn black." She demonstrated on a real dollar, then reached across her desk to hand the marking pen to Abby. "Here, go ahead and borrow this until you buy one for the museum. You can never be too careful. I've heard of fake bills as small as fives making the rounds."

Abby thanked her and tucked the pen into her purse. "Fifties and hundreds would be more common?"

She nodded.

"Do you have a sample of a counterfeit bill that I could look at?"

"No. If someone should show up with one, we're required to confiscate it and turn it over to the Secret Service.

"But if you do encounter a questionable bill, look closely at it to see if the tiny lines on the president's head are clear and consistent. Fakes look sort of watery, like the lines have faded, or they have a dot matrix effect. And the stamp in the lower right corner might be the wrong color."

"Just one more question," Abby said. "I recently came across a key that might fit either a post office box or a safe deposit box. Is there some way you can tell by looking at it if the key is from your bank?"

"I'm more likely to be able to tell you if it's *not* from our bank."

THAT SAME AFTERNOON, Sparrow Island was hit with one of the roughest spring rainstorms the island had seen in several years. So vicious were the wind and rain that the dead Douglas maple at the northeast corner of the conservatory came down with a creaking groan and a muffled crash. That one, having died within the past year, had already been tagged for removal, but now Hugo had been spared the trouble. Abby only hoped it didn't create too much damage to the nature trail.

With all the lightning and booming that had taken place, Abby—even though she was safe inside the museum—felt like the prophet Elijah witnessing a panoramic display of God's special audio-visual effects. As a child, after having read Elijah's story in I Kings, she had never again been afraid of thunder or lightning. Instead, she now saw the natural phenomenon as a reminder that God was in control and that there was something He would soon reveal to her in a gentle whisper. Today's storm was a reminder of God's power and glory. What she needed to do was pay attention and listen to hear His message.

Abby was just about to go outside and check out the conservatory grounds as well as the nesting boxes she and Hugo had recently set up when the phone in her office rang.

As tempting as it was to ignore the jangling sound and let the call go to her voicemail, Abby resisted the impulse and lifted the handpiece from the cradle. "The Nature Museum. Abby Stanton speaking."

It was Ida.

Abby listened for a few minutes as Ida described the situation, and it soon became clear that her problem was urgent enough to warrant immediate intervention.

"Don't touch a thing. I'll be right there."

IDA FOLLOWED ABBY as they made their way up the stairs to Ida's small apartment. "I came home from work shortly after the rain stopped and was walking to my apartment when I noticed something in the tree line near the side yard."

She held the door open for Abby, who clutched a small brown bundle in her arms. Ida was still wearing her waitress top and navy khakis, and was talking faster than usual.

"It wasn't anything I *saw* that drew me over there. It was more like I *sensed* it. Something just didn't seem right."

Abby waited while Ida moved a stack of junk mail and flyers from the coffee table in the living room. Taking great care not to jostle the nest any more than necessary, Abby set the well-crafted nest on the table. Three speckled eggs lay inside. A fourth had landed on the ground, crushed beyond help.

"It's a good thing you went to check. If these eggs had gone much longer without warmth, they would have been goners for certain." Abby plugged in the electric heating pad that stayed in her car for just such emergencies, turned it to the lowest setting and placed the nest on top. "Even so, it's questionable whether these will make it. It all depends on how hard the impact was felt when they hit the ground, how well the nest insulated them from the cold and how well they respond to our rescue efforts."

"And it depends on God," Ida added.

"Yes, of course. We'll do what we can to save them, and pray. The rest is up to God."

Ida left the room for a minute and came back with a hand-towel for Abby to place around the eggs to trap the warmth. "What kind of eggs are they? Something rare and exotic?"

"How about something common and ordinary like a house sparrow? Also known as the English sparrow."

Ida's shoulders drooped. "Oh, is that all? The eggs are so pretty. How do you know they're not from an endangered species, or even a bird with beautiful, bright-colored feathers? Maybe even a bluebird?"

"Simple, my dear Watson," Abby said with a teasing grin. "You merely gather the evidence, put it together and look at the whole. In this case, the nest is made of grass, bits of debris, feathers and twigs. Oh, look. There's a bit of fur woven into it."

Abby gingerly lifted one tiny speckled egg, only to reveal that its underside was already broken open. Fluid from the egg seeped out into the nest.

"Oh, what a shame," Ida said. Despite her obvious disappointment that the eggs weren't rare, she seemed truly saddened by the loss.

"The other way you can tell about the breed is from the size and coloring," Abby said. "These are about an inch long and three quarters of an inch wide, which indicates small parent birds, and the light green overall color with gray and brown dots near the larger end suggests a house sparrow."

"That's amazing," Ida said. "It's like putting together clues in a mystery."

The second egg showed signs of a faint hairline crack. Abby set it on the towel anyway. The final egg appeared to be intact, so she added it to the towel as well.

"The cracked one is questionable as to whether it will survive," she explained. "If it's just a surface fissure, the egg might remain viable. But if it's too deep, the opening could introduce air and bacteria to the baby bird inside, which would stop it from growing."

"What about the other one?" Ida asked. "The one that's not damaged."

"If it was very recently laid, the shell may not have finished hardening before the storm came. And the slight sponginess could have offered a little give when the nest hit the ground."

"I hope it survives," Ida said. "But it would have been more interesting if it were a bluebird or a yellow warbler instead."

"There's no shame in being ordinary," Abby said. "Just look at all the stories in the Bible that show how God uses ordinary people. Moses, Gideon, Esther. They all were ordinary folks until they became involved in God's work. It was their faith that made them special."

Ida sighed and sat on the couch beside Abby.

Sensing that her friend was hurting, Abby knew it was about more than the eggs.

"What's really bothering you?" Abby asked. Now that the eggs were warming on the heating pad, there was no particular rush to get them into an incubator at the conservatory.

Ida sighed. "Most of the time I feel like a plain old house sparrow. You've seen one, you've seen 'em all."

"Ida, dear, you are a precious child of God. What could be more unique than that?" It pained Abby to know that Ida saw herself as less than interesting. "You've heard the song, haven't you? 'His Eye Is on the Sparrow.' Well, His eye was on these sparrows, and He used you—*you*—to rescue them. How else can you explain being aware of them when you didn't actually see the nest from where you stood?"

"That's true," Ida admitted. "I didn't see them. But God did. And at least these little birdies will get to live in a new place. Which is more than I can say for myself."

Abby understood Ida's frustration and didn't want to discount her feelings. "If the eggs hatch and the birds survive to fledgling age, they'll be returned to the wild to rejoin their flock. Do you feel like you're searching for your flock, Ida?"

At that, the girl smiled. "Yeah, and my flock is out there somewhere—anywhere but on this dull island—living a life of glamour and excitement."

"Personally, I don't think life gets much more exciting than this. Do you realize we're making the difference between life and death for these little creatures?" Abby reached into her purse and withdrew the felt marking pen she'd gotten at the bank today. Ever so carefully, she marked a tiny X on each egg, rolled them over and drew an O on the opposite sides.

"Right. And as you speak, you're so bored you resort to playing tic-tac-toe on the eggs."

Abby laughed out loud. This was what she enjoyed about Ida. Even when she was feeling blue, she still found a way to make a joke. "Actually, the eggs will need to be turned twice a day to warm them evenly. The marks let me know which side should be up."

She settled the towel back over them to hold in the warmth.

"You know, lots of people who grow up in a small town want to get away and see what else the world has to offer. They assume that bright lights and fast living make for a more interesting time. But the truth is that life is the most exciting wherever we're involved in God's work."

"My boyfriend is from Seattle, and he has lots of fun and excitement in his life. But I'm stuck here, waiting tables, while he's following his dreams."

"Oh, so that's what this is all about," Abby said gently. "Feeling a little lonely, huh?"

Ida leaned back and put her feet on the coffee table, taking care not to rest them near the eggs. "Frustrated is more like it. Ryan works in sales, which means his schedule doesn't allow him to visit very often. So we're staying in touch mostly by e-mail. We've talked about marriage. Sometimes, when I'm doodling on a scrap of paper, I practice writing my name as if I were already married." She moved her hand through the air as she mimicked the motion. *"Ida Tolliver Landau.* Sounds classy, doesn't it?"

Abby smiled. "You're plenty classy, just as you are."

Ida blew a breath, and a wisp of her blond bangs moved

against her temple. "Ryan says he likes it on Sparrow Island, and he even encourages me to write and tell him what's going on around here, but his crazy hours and all the traveling don't give him much chance to write back."

"Perhaps this is an opportunity for both of you to practice patience."

"Or maybe it's a message that I should move to Seattle where we can spend more time together and I can make something of myself in a new and interesting career."

"Only you and God know that for certain."

"I don't know anything for certain."

"Just ask, and listen for the answer. He'll let you know."

Ida removed her feet from the table and stood over the eggs. "Would it be all right if I keep these guys here? I could turn them and make sure they stay warm and safe."

"Their chances are better at the conservatory's lab where we have a generator in case the power goes out. But you're welcome to come by any time you're off work and help care for them. In fact, why don't you come with me now and help get them settled in?"

"Sure, I'd love to." Ida moved across the room to retrieve the jacket she'd worn earlier.

"Afterward, if you want, you can come with me to take the box to the sheriff's office."

CHAPTER ❦ SEVEN

MARY HELD THE TACKLE box in her lap as Abby guided her down the hall to Sergeant Cobb's office. On the drive there, Abby had told her about the marking pen she'd borrowed from the bank, and that she'd tested some of the money in the box. All authentic. She wondered if it really was stolen, as Sam had suggested.

"I thought your sidekick was going to join us," Mary said.

Abby wasn't sure, but it sounded like her sister was a little miffed. "Ida? She decided not to come after all."

Mary sat ramrod straight in front of her. "So I guess I'll do in a pinch."

Okay, so Mary was miffed. Abby was about to say something in response when Sergeant Cobb stepped out of his office and greeted them. The tan shirt and dark green tie and slacks, along with the gold seven-pointed star on the left side of his chest, gave him an air of firm authority. He bent and kissed Mary on the cheek, then clasped Abby's hand in his.

Almost six feet tall and of stocky build, he looked as capable of apprehending a thug as any officer half his age, and the strength in his hand made her glad they were both on the same side of the law.

"So what's this big surprise you two ladies have for me? Something to do with that buried box you found?"

"Indeed," said Abby. She waited until they were settled in his office, then let Mary do most of the talking as they filled him in on all that had transpired since she'd unearthed the box over two weeks ago.

"A hundred and fifteen thousand dollars, you say?" He thumbed the bills and gave a long, low whistle.

"And a few extra for good measure. They're real," Mary said. "Abby checked them with a counterfeit testing pen."

"You don't do anything in a small way, do you?" Henry shot a teasing grin toward Abby and turned to the computer on his desk. As they relayed the details and answered his questions, he took their information and wrote a brief description of how the box came to be in their possession.

"I've asked around," Abby added, "but none of the leads panned out."

Henry's gaze grew serious. "Considering how thorough you are, that tells me this won't be an open-and-shut case."

When he was done typing in the information, he promised to let them know if there was a reward involved.

All in all, turning over the box was much less eventful than Abby had anticipated, perhaps because there were still so many unanswered questions. In fact, the whole process was decidedly anticlimactic.

"Will you keep us posted as you receive updates on the case?" Abby asked as they left his office.

Sergeant Cobb followed them out into the hallway, the box tucked securely under his arm. "I can't make any promises. This is a police matter now."

OUTSIDE, MARY WATCHED as Abby climbed in the passenger side of her van. There was nothing at all pretentious about her sister. The only statement her casual slacks and pullover shirt made was that she was too busy to be bothered with what she considered unnecessary trappings. Her face, however, made plenty of statements.

Mary turned the key in the ignition. She'd noticed the look of disappointment on Abby's face when Henry wouldn't promise to feed her information as it came to him.

"Henry wasn't trying to put you off," she said. "He was just doing his job."

"I know." Abby leaned back and laced her fingers behind her head. "He's a professional. That's why I'm glad he's handling the case."

And now that the box was in Henry's capable hands, her sister could finally wash her hands of it and let him do all the probing and investigating. Mary smiled. And now that Abby wouldn't be so distracted, perhaps they would have more time together.

Silence blanketed them until they reached Oceania Boulevard. Twigs, sticks and leaf debris—remnants of this afternoon's thunderstorm—littered the road. Mary steered around the larger pieces, then pulled into her driveway.

"Mary, is something wrong?" Abby asked. "Are you upset with me?"

Mary maneuvered into her usual spot in the garage, leaving plenty of room beside Abby's car for her to get in and out.

Previously, when there had been tension between them, they had both tiptoed around the issue and pretended it didn't exist. Or worse, they'd sometimes get into tiffs over minor problems that were totally unrelated to the real problem that sat unresolved between them.

But they didn't do that anymore, for which Mary was glad. It was sometimes uncomfortable to confront the situation directly, but doing so always worked out best in the end. They'd both grown up a lot since Mary's accident and, as a result, it was a pleasure to see their relationship grow to a whole new level.

"No, I'm not upset with you. I'm just ready for us to spend more time together."

Abby lifted her purse from the floorboard and set it on her lap where she toyed with the clasp. "After the accident . . . while you were adjusting to your new way of life and getting used to the wheelchair, I tried to be close to you," she said softly. "You said I was hovering and that you wanted to be independent. So when Finnegan came and you devoted a lot of time getting to know him, I backed away."

On hearing his name, the dog rose from his bed in the back of the van and nudged his nose between the two front seats. Mary rubbed him above his eyebrows.

"You seemed relieved when I eased back," Abby continued. "So I thought that's what you wanted. More space."

Mary rested her hands on the steering wheel. More space. She'd certainly gotten that when her house was renovated and the furniture rearranged to accommodate her wheelchair. That kind of space she had needed. And she had even needed emotional space at the time. But now the space between her and Abby seemed to have widened to an uncomfortable distance.

"That's what I wanted at the time. I needed to know I could

do things for myself," Mary admitted. "But now the pendulum has swung too far away, and I'm missing you."

"I've missed you too." Abby let go of the purse and reached past Finnegan's inquisitive nose to hold Mary's hand.

Mary squeezed her fingers and smiled at the dog's jealous nuzzling. "Good, then let's swing that pendulum back to the middle where we can both be comfortable together."

"You won't get any argument from me. Hey, let's stay in tonight and do something fun."

Mary smiled again and felt her heart warming. "Sure," Mary said. "I would like that very much."

AT BIBLE STUDY on Wednesday evening, Abby focused on the stained glass windows. In the settling dusk, their colors gleamed deeper and richer than in the midday sun. Inside, the overhead lights were also dim, which lent a sense of calm and reverence to the room.

She had looked forward to a time of meditation and prayer in the beautiful sanctuary where she would release the matter of the tackle box and its contents to God. She was still curious, but it seemed that it was time for her to step back from the case now so she could turn her attention to Mary.

Tonight, at Janet Heinz's request, the plate was passed for a special collection. The money was to be given to a young family whose house had been damaged by a fire resulting from one of yesterday's lightning strikes.

With an unsettling sense of anticipation, Abby recalled Elijah's encounter with God in I Kings 19:11–12.

Then a great and powerful wind tore the mountains apart and shattered the rocks before the LORD, but the

LORD was not in the wind. After the wind there was an earthquake, but the LORD was not in the earthquake. After the earthquake came a fire, but the LORD was not in the fire. And after the fire came a gentle whisper. . . .

So far there had been a storm with thunder and lightning that knocked the nest out of the tree near Ida's apartment. Then a fire followed, temporarily displacing a family until the repairs were made. Too often, people wanted to blame God for the unfortunate things that happened in their lives, but it said right in the Bible that the Lord was not in those things. It also said that after such tragedies, He would be there for them . . . speaking in a quiet whisper. All they had to do was listen for it.

A shiver of goosebumps crawled down Abby's arms.

She and Mary both dropped as much as they could spare into the offering plate, then Abby passed it to Sam sitting next to her, who did the same.

A couple of rows behind them, someone stirred noisily in the pew and a woman's angry whispers could be heard. Abby turned to see what was the matter and found Thelma pointing in their direction.

In her early seventies, Thelma was still a pretty woman. Slim almost to the point of looking unhealthy, all her clothes were bought in sets so they would coordinate perfectly, and she never mixed and matched her skirts and tops for variety the way Mary did. Her thin gray hair had been dyed blond and permed like a cotton puff to cover the bare patches in her scalp. And her purse, though overlarge and bulging, was jammed securely under one arm the way a running back guarded the football as he sprinted across the field.

Abby paused to pray, first for the family that had been

displaced from their home, and then for Thelma. It was hard for her to feel like praying for Thelma, but she did it anyway and then asked God for a loving heart in herself.

And it was a good thing she did, because right after the service was over Thelma marched up to the usher to insist that he put the money in safekeeping right away.

"Just because people are in church doesn't mean they can be trusted," she said, directing a pointed stare at Sam.

To stop her before she got really wound up and starting calling attention to herself, Abby walked up to Thelma with a smile frozen in place, looped an arm through the older woman's and walked her to a relatively quiet corner of the foyer.

"Thelma, I know you and Sam have had your differences," Abby said, her voice steady despite the inflammatory nature of their discussion, "but what you're doing is slandering an innocent person."

"Innocent, my foot." Thelma pulled her arm away from Abby's grasp. "He's got all of you Stantons bamboozled. You may be willing to turn a blind eye to his misdeeds, but I most certainly will not. I'm no fool."

"No one's calling you a fool. All I'm doing is asking you to be very careful what you say about a person's integrity. Especially when you don't have all the facts."

"I have enough facts to know that the man's fingerprints are probably on every speck of money in that box you found."

Her voice had now reached a shrill pitch, and others in the church were turning to see what the noise was about.

"Thelma, could you please keep it down? You're going to have the whole church thinking the worst about Sam."

"They already do," she declared. "I told them all about my

missing money. And everyone I talked to agrees the box must be his."

"PEOPLE DON'T AGREE WITH THELMA," Hugo assured her the next day. "They just nod and let her talk. Eventually, she'll see that she was mistaken, and everyone will have forgotten about it because she's always getting fired up about something. Soon it'll be as if nothing ever happened."

The countertop in the museum's workroom was cluttered with brushes, picks and bottles of solvent for cleaning. A window nearby was open to let in fresh spring air, and also brought in the scents of plants and flowers and the slurred *chee chee* of a Wilson's warbler.

Abby sighed. "You sound very confident."

"I am because I know what the people on this island are like. Most of them consider the source and then cut the person some slack. And they do the same thing for Sam. The ones who know he hit some rough patches in his past also know that he's a good bloke."

"Bloke?" Abby grinned and nudged him with her elbow. "Veddy British today, aren't we, chap?"

"Would you rather I say he's an 'all right dude'?"

Just hearing the slang phrase come out of impeccable Hugo's mouth—with an ever-so-proper inflection, of course—was enough to give Abby a case of the giggles.

Hugo set down the pottery bowl he'd been working on and joined in the laughter. After a moment, he wiped away a tear of laughter from the outer corner of his eye and turned to Abby. "So, now that you've turned the box over to Sergeant Cobb, you must have a surfeit of time on your hands."

"Not exactly. Ida's eggs weren't the only casualties of the storm. In addition to monitoring the incubating eggs, I'm working with an injured bufflehead duck. Poor little guy somehow broke his leg. It's a good thing a tourist saw it or he might have become seal bait. Both the eggs and the duck are doing well in the lab."

She wiped a cloth dampened with a mild solution over the beaded breastplate that she was cleaning.

"And on the homefront, Mary and I have been poring over catalogs. She keeps pushing me to buy clothes with bright colors, which is ridiculous for birding. Some mammals may not see colors, but birds do, which means it would be impossible to walk through the woods without stirring up entire coveys and alerting the whole forest of my presence." She gave another dab at the vest. "Besides, it seems silly to pay so much money for fancy clothes when there are plenty of like-new bargains at the thrift store."

Hugo leaned on one elbow and stared directly at her. "Maybe Mary's not talking about you going birding in the colorful clothes. Perhaps she's setting you up to go out and kick up your heels. Dancing, maybe. Or to a party." His fingertips gently thrummed the table. "Ever have a hankering to do that, Abby?"

Suddenly the distance between them seemed very close. "Uh—"

In the blink of an eye, Hugo resumed his square-shouldered posture and went back at the textured bowl with a crevice brush. "While you've been catalog shopping, I've been interviewing with *The Birdcall*. In fact, that's where I was earlier this morning. Mr. Jansen tells me our find is quite newsworthy."

That wasn't what he'd said when Abby had first asked him

to run a story about the found box. But she was glad he was astute enough to recognize the value in Hugo's discovery.

"That's wonderful! Will it come out in next week's paper?"

"That's the plan. Jansen will come by in the next few days to take pictures of the tools and household items we found in Mrs. Nygaard's grandfather's attic. I've already mapped out space in the museum to include these Native American artifacts.

"God willing, these magnificent pieces of history will attract attention from tourists and interested residents, and possibly even inspire a benefactor or two to donate to our cause. Imagine all we could accomplish here at the museum if we added a well-heeled patron."

To anyone who didn't know Hugo, that might have sounded like a crass focus on the monetary gain from the artifacts. But Abby knew that Hugo's first and foremost priority was to preserve historical items and the stories behind them. Next to that, he treasured opportunities to educate people about the history of the islands and to get them as excited about the enthralling cultures of its inhabitants as he was.

Hugo cleared the clouds from his eyes. "It's probably just as well that my feature didn't run this week. The buzz about the money you unearthed could have wound up dividing the readers' interest."

Abby smiled as she considered his words. Only Hugo would assume the general public would be equally as interested in historic artifacts as they were in a box containing over a hundred thousand dollars.

"By the way," he said, "Jansen thinks there's a chance your article might be picked up by one or more of the mainland newspapers. The man is practically calving, he's so excited by the prospect."

Abby paused, taken aback by the unusual image. "Oh, you mean he's 'having a cow'?" she said, paraphrasing a popular slang term.

"Yes, exactly."

She considered the implications of *The Birdcall* editor's joy. "This is certainly a good news, bad news situation. If there was no crime involved with the box, then the additional newspaper coverage will be good news for the owner because his property will be returned to him."

She set the breastplate down and leaned a hip against the counter where they worked. Her hands were beginning to chap from the water and cleaners they'd been using.

"But if it *is* crime-related, then it's bad news because I worry we might be tipping off the criminals by letting them know what's happening with the box."

Hugo passed her a clean rag from his pile. "The good news is that you don't have to fret over the matter anymore."

"Unfortunately, I do. Although people in town may not take Thelma's comments seriously, the authorities will. Sam shouldn't have to go through that kind of scrutiny. Not now. Not after all the changes he's made in his life."

"You said Sergeant Cobb is handling the affair. He knows Sam wouldn't have anything to do with a crime."

"He knows Sam, but he's also very serious about the law. He'll investigate any reasonable suspect, friend or not. You know how by-the-book he is."

"Yes, you're right about that. The man is the virtual personification of duty and honor." He rose from his seat at the workbench. "It appears as though this case is not done with you after all. I trust you have a plan?"

"Well, up to now I've been focusing on the most likely possibilities of family and friends, as well as some random leads that didn't go anywhere. But now that we know what's inside the box, that opens up new directions."

She stood and paced the floor. "So now I'll be focusing on who among us has access to that kind of cash. And then there's the rest of the stash in the box to consider as clues."

"Excellent. I have a couple of names for you to look into. Not as a way of pointing fingers, mind you, but as a way of seeking the truth."

The names he mentioned were already on her list, but she thanked him anyway.

"Do talk to Sam first, though. He'll appreciate knowing you're in his corner. And perhaps between the two of you, you'll come up with the answer to Thelma's missing money."

She nodded her agreement. Hugo had confirmed her fear that Sam was a likely suspect for law enforcement officials to investigate. She, however, believed he was innocent.

Unfortunately, in some people's eyes, Sam did have reasons for them to doubt him.

CHAPTER ❦ EIGHT

THE WEATHERED BOARDS on the Stanton barn were rough and faded from the many years' exposure to sunshine and the island's moisture-laden air. It was time for the evening milking, and the farm's two dairy cows knew it. Their lowing carried on the breeze that floated across the yard.

Inside, the warm, rich smell of hay teased Abby's memory and her nostrils. The pungent scent brought back recollections of many an afternoon spent in the hayloft as a child seeking the stillness of the barn to read or just to think. Sam went about the twice-daily process of cleaning the cows' udders and then placing the stool and milk bucket in position. Though Friday heralded two days off for most people, his job did not cease on the weekends.

Instead of immediately sitting down to the milking, Sam rested an arm on the animal's hip. He bent his forehead down to his arm and stayed like that for a long moment.

Abby frowned. Was the cow lame? Perhaps he was watching the way she held her weight on that hoof. Curious, Abby walked closer, rustling her nylon jacket as she pulled it tighter around her.

Sam started at the sound. In reaction, the cow—his armrest—shifted in the confined space, her head held steady by the rope tied to her halter. It was only then that Abby realized Sam had allowed himself a quiet moment.

"Is there something I can do for you?" he asked.

"Send a few of those prayers my way. That's always a help," she said. It seemed that he enjoyed the solitude of the barn, just as she had so many years ago. "This is a good place for praying. Nice and calm."

"*Any* place is a good place for praying."

Sam had a tendency to come across as gruff sometimes, which casual acquaintances occasionally misread as grumpiness. It was just his way to say exactly what was on his mind and not worry whether it was phrased delicately enough for the listener's ears.

"Actually, I was hoping I could help *you*," Abby said, referring to his earlier question.

He sat down and placed his fingers expertly around the cow's udders. The milk hit the metal container with a soothing *pish-pish* sound. "People are going to talk about whatever's on their minds at the time," he said. "I can't stop it. You can't stop it. The best thing to do is just ignore it."

"Sometimes you can't ignore it. Even if someone is ill-informed and has a tendency to engage their mouth before their brain is in gear, they can still damage your reputation."

Sam looked up from his task and gave her a sad smile. "Thelma Rogers can't do anything to my reputation that I haven't already done myself."

"But she's wrong," Abby insisted. "You didn't take her money. And I know you didn't have anything to do with the cash in that tackle box."

He shrugged. "She knows I did some petty thefts when I was younger and eventually graduated to breaking and entering. She also knows I spent some fifteen years, on and off, at the prison in Walla Walla. Who could blame her for thinking I've picked up and started again?"

"Nobody's blaming anyone," Abby said. *Except Thelma*, Abby thought. "I just want to help set the record straight."

"Abby, the record *is* straight. The good Lord cleaned all that up a long time ago. I have Him to thank for the good life I'm living now, and for leading me to your family. I wish everyone believed in me the way the Stantons do, and I wish folks didn't think of me as an ex-con. But even if they don't believe in me the way you all do, that's okay because I know I'm right with the law, and I'm right with God."

"He is merciful."

"And I'm living proof of that. God was good enough to forgive me for my poor judgment," he said. "It's only right that I should forgive others when they make mistakes in their judgments about me."

Abby gave Sam a heartfelt smile of admiration. Not many people would be so understanding.

"But, to make sure I don't give 'em a reason to misjudge me, I do my best to stay away from shady situations."

"That's why you stood at a distance after the box was opened, isn't it?" she asked. "You didn't want to give the appearance of being overly interested."

He nodded.

"Would it be all right if I ask you some personal questions?"

She began filling the second cow's trough with sweet-smelling clover hay.

"There's no need for you to bother yourself with me. As I said, people are going to think what they want."

She leaned over the stall partition and met his gaze directly. "Not if I can help it."

He turned back to his work. "Is stubbornness a virtue?"

Abby picked up the teasing jab and tossed it right back at him. "It is if it's done for the right purpose." Abby leaned her forearms against the stall divider. "Have you stayed in touch with any of your friends from . . . er, that other time in your life?"

Sam snorted. "Those weren't friends. They were fair-weather acquaintances. And no, I haven't made any effort to stay in touch with them."

"Do you think any of them might have had a grudge against you? A reason to hide the box here so they could set you up to take the fall?"

Sam shook his head. "I doubt they even know where I am. My friends—the true ones—used to give me updates on what they'd heard about them until I asked them to stop. But the last I heard—which was at least five years ago—some were in prison, some dead. Others are still running. It's a rough existence. I hope at least a few of them got away from it, like I did."

"Me too. The world would be a better place if we had more people in it like you." To keep from embarrassing Sam with what he would call "mushiness," Abby quickly changed the subject. "This is a hard question for me to ask, but please understand that I'm doing it with your best interests at heart."

He slanted a glance at her but gave no indication that he wanted her to leave him alone.

"Do you know anything about Thelma's missing money, or that strange letter she got for a charity donation she says she never made?"

"No, I stay as far away from her as I can."

"That's exactly what I thought."

"She always looks at me funny, like she thinks I'm going to swipe her poodle. If someone's uncomfortable because of me, I just steer clear of 'em."

"Yes, of course. I understand." It looked like it was time for that "one last question" again. "Sam, do you have any idea who might be responsible for that box showing up on the farm? Perhaps someone who has access to a lot of money? And I don't know if Thelma's situation is related, but if you've seen anyone go into her place, whether she was there or not. . . ."

He lifted his hands palms-out and stepped away. "I know your intentions are good, Abby, but I'm not going to point fingers. I've had that done to me, and there's no way I'm going to pass it on to someone else."

Abby smiled, proud to know such a good and honorable man. His past had haunted him long enough.

THAT EVENING ABBY FILLED MARY in on the day's events. They went together into the living room, where Mary picked up the remote control from the coffee table. Abby was headed for the foyer and the stairs to get ready for bed, but paused there at the entrance of the living room while they finished their conversation.

"I love Sam like a brother," Mary said, "but I have to admit, there's a teeny-tiny part in the back of my mind that wonders if he could have some involvement in the recent goings-on."

Abby gasped.

Holding up her hand in defense of what she had said, Mary attempted to explain. "It's not that I *believe* he's involved with either the tackle box or Thelma's missing cash. Rather, it's like there's a discerning part inside of me that says to slow down and consider the facts."

With a press of her thumb, she lowered the volume on the television. "And my heart tells me Sam is exactly what he presents himself to be. A reformed man."

"'Wisdom reposes in the heart of the discerning,'" Abby said. "Proverbs 14–"

"Wait! Let me me guess. Chapter 14, verse 33."

Abby smiled. "Bingo. You're right that we are to use our God-given reason to determine the difference between good and evil. And when all is said and done, I still believe Sam is innocent."

"As do I. But I also understand that others in town need to weigh for themselves what they believe to be true. And you'll most likely be helping them with that." Mary flipped the station to her favorite sitcom. "I saw Henry today. He's going to see if the serial numbers from the money can be traced to a bank robbery."

"A bank robbery, huh? That could explain why there are so many bills in large denominations. But it still doesn't explain the ring. The map, on the other hand, could point to a hiding place for more money."

Finnegan sat facing Mary, his tail giving an occasional swish across the floor. It looked as though he was waiting for her response to Abby's theory.

"Nope. They already went to the island and dug up various spots in the area that was circled on the map. They got nothing but sore muscles."

"Well, I'm glad they're checking it out thoroughly." Abby edged into the foyer. "Do you want me to get you anything before I go to bed?"

"Why so early to bed for you? Come sit with me."

Abby crossed the room and bent to kiss her sister on the forehead. "Thanks, but I'm planning to go birding first thing in the morning. I need to go early if I'm going to be able to watch the early bird get the worm."

Mary stiffened and pulled away. "I know you love your birds," Mary told her, "but I have to confess I'm feeling like the last one on your dance card again."

Abby took a seat in the overstuffed chair next to her. "Mary, you're far from last in my heart." She pulled the throw blanket across her lap as she settled in for an evening of television viewing. "Tell you what. I'll watch the show with you if you'll go birding with me this weekend."

Mary smiled and patted her arm. "Sure, if you'll help me push this chair up Mount Ortiz."

"There's no need for that. The nature trail at the conservatory is accessible. I know of a spot where we can watch shorebirds fish for their breakfast."

"Delightful."

Abby had to agree that the prospect of sharing a peaceful hour or two in the company of both her sister and the birds was an irresistible combination.

Mary leaned over and stroked Abby's hair, letting the strands fall between her fingers. "You know, I could show you how to style your hair so it looks fluffier. Until your next appointment with Edmonia, of course. After she fixes the cut, I'm sure it'll return to its usual bounce."

Abby started to protest, but Mary cut her off.

"It's not a makeover," she insisted. "Just a different way to comb it. If you don't like what I do, you can brush it all out, and your hair will be just the same as it is now." She paused, waiting for Abby's consent. "I promise."

Abby had her misgivings, but she got up and retrieved the things her sister said they would need for her "new look." A brush, a handheld mirror, hairspray and a rattail comb. Then she moved the small chair from the front foyer and placed it near Mary.

"Don't worry!" Mary said. "Good heavens, you should see the look on your face. All I'm going to do is lift your hair at the crown and backcomb it a little."

"You mean you're going to 'tease' my hair. Go ahead and admit it."

Mary lifted a shoulder, indicating she wasn't going to quibble over terminology. "I'm not going to give you a beehive, if that's what you're asking. Backcombing is the latest thing now. That actress did it too." She pointed the comb at the television screen. "You can tell because her hair is so soft it wouldn't stay like that without a little help. She just backcombed enough to keep her hair from lying plastered to her head."

Abby took in the image of the young brunette. The beautiful actress's hair fell in soft, wavy locks, almost to her shoulder blades. Abby touched her own hair.

Flat.

"I tried wearing my hair like that once. When I was in my twenties. It was inconvenient then, and it would look plain silly now."

Mary waved the comb at her, waving away her resistance. "Just because we're older than they are doesn't mean we can't use some of their beauty tricks."

She continued fluffing and spritzing. Finnegan sneezed and moved away from the smell. Although Abby had her misgivings about what might come of this styling session, she did enjoy the easy camaraderie that swirled like hairspray around them.

"Voilà!" Mary handed Abby the mirror for a look at her handiwork.

Abby leaned closer to the light that fell from the end table lamp and twisted her grip on the mirror to better see the surprising picture in front of her.

"Wow, this really looks good."

Mary beamed. "I told you it would. Now maybe you'll pay more attention to what your big sister tells you in the future."

"You're right. I will." Abby touched her hair and was surprised that it didn't move. "It feels like a helmet. When I style it myself, can't I just backcomb it and forget about the hairspray?"

"Not if you want it to stay."

Abby gazed at her reflection in the mirror. "That's too bad, because I doubt I should walk around outside with all this hairspray. Bees might be attracted to the smell."

Mary pressed her lips together and poked them out as she thought. "You raise a good point. Your hairstyle should fit your lifestyle." She reached out to touch Abby's hair, and the whole thing moved like a floating forcefield around her head.

Abby giggled. Cupping a hand under the right side of her hair, she lifted it and her entire hair shifted to the left. Then she did the same thing on the other side. "Hey, look, I'm juggling."

Mary joined in the laughter. "It's like a giant hairball." She held the comb in both hands and pretended to swing at Abby's hair. "Batter up!"

In the next moment, the two of them were laughing so hard that Mary's cat Blossom padded over to see what was going on.

"Stay away, Blossom," Mary called, "or you'll be next."

The image of the white Persian cat, with her long fur fluffed, teased and sprayed until she looked like an electrocuted cartoon cat sent the two of them off into renewed gales of laughter.

When they could finally catch their breaths, Mary slumped back in her chair and flung her arms out on either side.

"Thanks for the effort," Abby said, her voice still bubbling with laughter. "It really does look good though."

"If you really like the way it looks," she said, a speculative gleam in her eye, "I could give you a home permanent. That should give your hair some lift—without hairspray—until you get a chance to let Edmonia fix the cut."

Abby had been resisting Mary's idea of a makeover, but now that she had seen how nice her hair could look with a little tweaking, she felt more encouraged to give the perm a try. "Are you sure it won't kink up?"

"It's a body perm. All it will do is give you more fullness."

Abby grinned at her sister. With a swivel of one shoulder and lowering her voice in a corny Mae West imitation, she said, "A gal can always use more fullness."

"Good, then we'll do it this weekend."

Abby frowned. "This weekend is already booked up."

"How about next weekend?"

"Okay, but no color."

CHAPTER ❦ NINE

Tᴴᴱ ᴠᴀᴄᴀᴛɪᴏɴ ʙɪʙʟᴇ School planning meeting on Saturday lasted until mid-afternoon, but Abby didn't mind because her spirit had already been replenished with a morning of bird-watching with Mary.

Though Abby enjoyed it all, even down to the less showy horsetail plant and the various ferns, mosses and mushrooms, Mary had showed a definite preference for the flowering plants. They had gone to watch for birds, but their focus had quickly switched to scouting for plants after Mary had spotted an inside-out flower whose white funnel-shaped blossoms looked like an umbrella blown backwards. Her sister's favorite was the starflower, with its pink star-shaped petals, rising from a bed of large green leaves.

While they were out, Abby had collected some miner's lettuce to take home for lunch. The strong peppery taste of the leaves easily took their salads from bland to exciting.

After returning home for lunch, the two of them had played fetch in the front yard with Finnegan, who enjoyed the opportunity to romp. Abby had enjoyed the romp, too, and it had given her some ideas for games the children could play at the church's day camp this summer. Some were games she hadn't played since Mary's children were small, so a refresher on the rules would be helpful now.

In the meeting room at church that afternoon, Patricia Hale was wrapping up the meeting and about to close with prayer when Abby raised her hand to speak.

"The ideas suggested here today are excellent," she said. The others around the table nodded in agreement. "We're a little behind schedule in collecting the rest of the lesson plans and other materials, so may I suggest we order them this week? That should give us plenty of time to pull everything together before school lets out for the summer and our Bible day camp begins.

"I'm planning to go to Bellingham next week to pick up some things for the museum," she continued, "so I could buy the Vacation Bible School items at the same time."

Patricia shifted her gaze to Rev. Hale, who cleared his throat. "Thank you for the offer," he said, "but I'm afraid we'll need to wait another week or two before making the purchase."

He acted as if he wanted to just leave it at that, but now everyone had turned toward him, watching curiously as he obviously weighed the matter in his mind before speaking again.

"Usually by this time of year, the donations for our Vacation Bible School fund have been collected and earmarked for distribution. However, this year the treasury is suffering a significant shortfall." At the alarmed reaction from the group, he hastily added, "There's plenty of money in our church budget to cover the costs. We just need to wait to make the purchase until the finance committee can meet to approve the transfer of funds. That's all."

Sounds of relief swept through the room, but to Abby a problem still existed. What had happened to the Vacation Bible School money?

THE MATTER OF THE Vacation Bible School money would have to wait. Rather than probe into the matter now in front of the group, Abby would make some discreet inquiries later.

But before she turned her attention to the unexpected financial shortfall, Abby decided it was time for some solitude and serenity. Paradise Cove was the perfect place for that. Even on a Saturday afternoon, one of the busiest times at the retreat area, she should be able to find a quiet spot.

At the cove, Abby parked her car near a half-dozen others. After retrieving her binoculars and bird journal, she walked past a car with a vanity license plate she recognized: NEWS-4U. Just the person she needed to see.

Wrapping her jacket tighter against the stiff breeze that came in off the strait, she passed a young man in the clearing who was struggling to get a kite airborne. After it stabilized on the gusty breezes, he handed the string to the older of two children with him. The kite immediately took a nosedive and crashed to the ground. "Do it again, Daddy!" the smaller one shouted. Considering the now-mangled condition of the kite, Abby had her doubts whether it would see the sky again this afternoon.

Moving through the brush toward the craggy shoreline, Abby saw a handful of people trying their prowess at fly-fishing. Off to one side, William Jansen leaned forward on a rock that jutted out toward the sound.

Tucking her journal in her jacket pocket, she clambered across the rocky terrain. William reached out a hand to give her a steadying arm.

Remembering that he was right-handed, Abby took a seat to his left to stay out of range of his casting. "Except for the waders you're wearing and the mustache, you remind me of a maiden on the front of an ancient sailing ship."

He grinned and lifted a hand to his clean-shaven chin. "Then perhaps it's time to let the beard grow too."

They sat in companionable silence for a while, William casting to a shady spot under a nearby madrone tree and Abby taking an informal tally of the waterbirds that roamed the shore.

The weather today hovered in the sixties. Except for the occasional gap winds that danced in from the choppy waters farther out in the sound, a jacket might not have been needed.

The cove provided a break in the winds and current, creating an idyllic sanctuary, not only for people but also for terns, gulls and other shorebirds that she'd already spotted. The narrow sandy strip served as a bed for clams, sand crabs and other burrowing creatures, and as a breakfast bar for the curious birds.

It was Abby who broke the silence. "Hugo is thrilled about your interest in his Native American artifacts. He's been working like a beaver on the new display he's planning for the museum."

"It'll be a good exhibit," William said. "I met with him and took some excellent pictures yesterday. I've set aside a page and a quarter for the article and shots in this week's paper."

"I'll be sure to look for it." Abby's pencil made quiet scratching noises as she shaded her drawing of a Brandt's cormorant that had just come ashore from diving for fish. Now perched on a rock, the glossy blackbird held out his wings to dry.

"I have a question for you . . . of the newspaper variety."

"Shoot," William said, never taking his eyes off the line running from his rod to the water.

"Why were you initially so reluctant to run an article about the box I found?"

"I told you at the time, it didn't seem newsworthy."

"It was as newsworthy as the salamander Mrs. Nachman found in her bathtub."

"At least she knew what was *in* the bathtub," he retorted.

"I'll grant you that."

William drew in his line and tossed again. "Why the questions, Abby? I'm the one who's supposed to do the interviewing."

She closed her journal.

"I want to put to rest the suspicions surrounding the money in the tackle box so that people can get on with their lives."

"I heard that your parents' hired man is getting the once-over from folks in the community. Too bad about that."

"Indeed, it is." She paused, considering how best to broach a subject that could be touchy for him. "William, you used to be the chief executive officer of your family's business, dealing in baby products. Yet you left that lucrative position to come to Sparrow Island and head up a tiny newspaper. That could raise a question about your motives in some people's minds."

"Are you asking me to air my dirty diapers?" He laughed, but it was not a happy sound. He gazed past her, a faraway look in his eyes. "I always wanted to be a journalist. A newspaperman of the ilk of Horace Greeley who founded the *New York Tribune* in the eighteen hundreds. But my family was against it. They wanted me to continue the legacy of Jansen's Essentials."

He heaved a long sigh, reinforcing to Abby that he

suppressed a lot of frustration over the matter. "And you did work in the family business," she said. "For a while, anyway."

"Not at first. My first job was as a reporter at the *Chicago Tribune.*"

Although the overall quality of *The Birdcall* wasn't bad, neither was it of the caliber that one would expect from a former reporter at one of the nation's top newspapers. She already knew about his time at the *Chicago Tribune,* but she said nothing, her silence encouraging him to continue . . . and perhaps fill in a bit of information she didn't already know.

He frowned, and his bushy brown eyebrows tented up between his eyes. "It didn't work out," he said, a brittle edge to his voice. "So I went into the family business until I couldn't stand it anymore. And now here I am, loving what I do."

She nodded, fully understanding the kind of satisfaction he must feel at doing the kind of work he loved.

"You're wondering if the box you found is mine, aren't you? Or that the cash was taken from my family's business?"

She didn't deny that the scenario he suggested was a possibility that had crossed her mind. "There aren't many people on the island with access to that much money."

"True, but there are others. Rick DeBow, for one. How else could you explain a former stockbroker—a millionaire, I hear—who supposedly gave it all up and then came here to work as a handyman?"

The Chois's employee was one of the first people she'd considered when compiling her list of possible owners of the box. She would look into Rick's circumstances, but at the moment it seemed William was very quick to direct attention away from himself and toward another.

"And there's someone else that you wouldn't even want to

think about. Someone you might want to protect. It could even be that your 'evidence gathering' is merely a ruse to deflect attention away from him. Or him and you."

"I would do no such thing." Abby stood to leave. "My intent is to uncover the truth, no matter who's involved."

"No matter if the one in question is your very own boss, Mr. Hugo Baron?"

REV. HALE'S SERMON SUNDAY was about the tenth commandment. Coveting. Abby couldn't help thinking that if the items in the tackle box were stolen—and it seemed very likely they were—it may have all begun with a covetous heart.

Their pastor had a certain flair for delivering his messages. With his dynamic stage presence and engaging style of speaking, it was hard not to pay attention. But today, try as she might, Abby could not keep her mind from wandering to the two subjects that burned in her brain.

The first, of course, was the question of who had buried the box on her parents' property and now seemed determined to remain anonymous. And the more recent was the issue of the shortfall for this year's Vacation Bible School.

Even with the registration fees, it took a lot of money to run a day camp. Not a tremendous amount, but enough to cause some juggling of the church's general budget to cover this year's unexpected deficit. There was the cost of lesson plans and craft supplies. Also, games, music CDs and decorations. Then there were the "invisible" expenses, such as repair costs for the sports equipment and grounds and insurance to cover the possibility of injury. And, of course, the ever-popular snacks.

The finance committee knew how much it took to run the

Vacation Bible School. Why, after all these years of running the day camp, was the church now faced with a financial shortfall?

After the sermon was over and greetings exchanged, members began returning home to begin cooking their Sunday dinners. Abby found Janet in her office, stuffing her cross-embroidered bag with her Bible and Sunday school lesson book.

"What's up?" Abby asked, knowing Janet would understand exactly what she meant.

Janet motioned to the door, so Abby closed it.

"This is about the budget problem that was announced yesterday, isn't it?"

Abby nodded.

"One of our members—and you may know who, so I won't mention his name—has always given us a big, fat check every year to be used for Bible camp."

Abby knew exactly who she was talking about. After seeing how much his own children had enjoyed the Bible camp, Vince Emory, a well-to-do professional man, had taken a personal interest in assuring that it was never without funding and had even made it his personal mission that no child who wanted to attend camp would be left out. Although he preferred to remain anonymous, a few people in the church were aware that the day camp project was so close to his heart. As far as Abby knew, this was one juicy tidbit that Janet had not spread far and wide.

"Anyway, there's tension going on at home, and this year he didn't come through with his usual hefty donation. We should have known better than to plan our Bible school budget around one person's donation. It's just that he's been doing it for so many years that no one ever thought it would stop."

"But it did. I wonder what could have caused him to change his mind so abruptly."

"He didn't say." Janet leaned closer. "Don't tell anyone, but his wife thinks he's going through a midlife crisis. She's worried he may be having an affair."

"Oh no." Abby's heart hurt for the pain Cheryl must be going through. At the same time, she wondered if Vince might be diverting the money normally earmarked for Bible school and spending it instead on a young chickadee. And could the money in the tackle box be his? He wouldn't be the first person to siphon money from the marital coffers and hide it in preparation for divorce.

She needed to proceed carefully. Her mission was to clear Sam's name, not offer up a new scapegoat.

ABBY CROSSED THROUGH The Nature Museum, past the brightly lit floor-to-ceiling displays of sea creatures indigenous to the San Juan Islands, the small gift shop at the front of the building and the reception desk. The oversized calendar on the wall behind the receptionist declared today was Wednesday, May 4.

Abby took the exit to the conservatory grounds. Ever since last week's storm, they'd had to take visitors on an alternative route along the trail. The Douglas maple that had blown down during the storm had taken a smaller pine with it—complete with its newly installed nest box—and now lay across the fine-graveled path, its brown-leafed branches blocking the path and crushing the wildflowers and ferns. Today Hugo was out at the back section with Rick DeBow, overseeing removal of the downed trees.

Abby had only walked a quarter of a mile when she met Rick coming back toward the museum.

"That's one of the thickest maples I've seen in quite a while," he said. "I'm going to need to buy a new chain for the saw." He swept a hand down the trail. "Hugo's still down there, trying to decide how much of the tree to leave to show your visitors how a tree decays."

"We appreciate you working us into your schedule," Abby told him. "I know you've been incredibly busy since last week, helping other people with their storm damage."

"I like staying busy." He made a move to go past Abby, but she remained where she was.

"That's what has me curious about you," she said. "The busier you are, the better you seem to like it. But you left your job as a stockbroker in Dallas, living a high-action lifestyle, to come here and stay just as busy as you were there."

Rick smiled and hooked one thumb through a belt loop on his sawdust-covered jeans. "What you mean to say is, I'm working just as hard here as I did in the stock market and I'm earning a fraction of the income. What idiot would do that?"

"Well, I—"

"It's okay. Everybody wonders that."

Just a few years older than Abby and standing about the same height, Rick didn't look like what one would expect of a high-powered stockbroker. Deeply tanned, with curling grayish-brown hair and light green eyes, he wore faded jeans, a green plaid shirt and a waist-length corduroy jacket. Mud caked his thick-soled workboots. This man would look alien in a three-piece suit and a penthouse suite. It was hard to imagine him ever having lived that way.

Placing his hands on his narrow hips, Rick laughed, the sound cracking the air like a gunshot. "I'm your latest suspect, aren't I? You're wondering if the money in that box you found is from illegal investments."

Abby considered how best to respond to that. "It did cross my mind."

He bent and braced his hands on his knees. "*Hoo*, that's a doozy! Thanks for the laugh."

"Rick, this could be serious."

"Not to me, it isn't. Hey, tell Hugo that if I don't have a spare chain in my truck, I'll be back after a trip to Holloway's Hardware." He jogged down the trail toward the parking lot.

Abby turned and walked the rest of the way to the far end of the trail. It was possible that Rick's dismissive reaction was a cover. She wouldn't erase his name from the list just yet.

When she found Hugo, he was standing with his back to her, one hand raised to his head as he apparently pondered the fate of the tree. Although Abby had learned to walk quietly through the woods, he seemed to sense her presence. He turned slowly, placing a hand in his coat pocket.

"What do you think, Abby? You're the expert on these things." He pointed at the tree that sprawled across the path. "Should we salvage it as a refuge for rodents, birds and snakes, or haul it out of here for firewood and keep a tidier display?"

"How about both? We could ask Rick to cut away and remove the section that fell across the path. Then keep a portion of the top for a small animal hideaway. Same for a portion of the trunk and roots. Eventually moss will cover the log, insects will bore into it and fungi will grow from it. Our visitors will be able to see nature in action as it uses the death of a tree to provide life for other plants and creatures."

"Excellent plan."

"But we should fill in the hole left by the root ball. There are plenty of mosquito breeding areas without adding to them."

"Yes, indeed. And we'll move the nest box to a tree that's currently vertical."

Abby passed along the message from Rick and summarized her meeting with William Jansen over the weekend. "I don't think he was being malicious in mentioning you and Rick." She didn't bother to say William might have called attention to them to keep from being a suspect himself. "But what he said has an element of truth. Both of you do—or have had—access to large sums of cash. Rick with stock investments and you with donations to the museum."

Hugo seemed distracted as he scanned the area where the work would be performed. "So Jansen has taken up fiction writing now? What did Rick have to say about the notion of him carrying on such nefarious activities?"

"He laughed."

"As well he should. By the way, you're welcome to look at the museum's books anytime you want. You'll find everything in nice, tidy order, just the way you like it."

"Hugo, I wasn't saying you—"

"Of course you weren't, my dear. Only someone with an overactive imagination would—" He abruptly interrupted himself with a laugh. "That would describe you, wouldn't it? Come, let's go to the lab and check to see if those eggs of Ida's are starting to hatch yet."

As they walked back to the smaller building on the grounds —separate from The Nature Museum—that housed the conservatory's lab and equipment, Hugo seemed more interested in the large spread in this week's newspaper than he was about the fact that the publisher had suggested he might be pilfering funds from the museum.

"Have you seen the article yet?" Hugo asked. "I bought several copies. You may have one if you like."

"Thank you. I'll take a look when we get back to the museum." Abby slowed her pace as the building came into sight. "It amazes me how men can so easily shrug off situations like this and not hold it against the other."

"Situations like Jansen saying the money might be mine or Rick's?" He made a sound that was too elegant to be called a snort. "Holding a grudge for something like that would be a waste of time. I have better ways to spend my time than being angry with someone for expressing his opinion. You don't have to defend Rick or me or Sam or anybody else. The truth will out itself."

"I know. I just don't like having unanswered questions. Especially when those questions make my friends look bad." She stopped and picked up a stick that had fallen on the path. "Hugo, are you familiar with Dorsal Island?"

"Besides that it's shaped like a dorsal fin and is so small it attracts only the hardiest visitors?"

"Right." Abby already knew that with no ferry service to the island, the only access was by motorboat or kayak. The place was completely natural, with no buildings and few trails. "The name wasn't written on the map in the tackle box, but the drawing was clearly of Dorsal Island."

"Is that right? What else was on the map?"

Using the stick she'd picked up earlier, Abby sketched what she remembered, including the circled area near the northernmost curve of the dorsal shape. Then she relayed what Mary had said about Sergeant Cobb and his deputies going over to investigate.

"They didn't find anything," she said.

"I imagine not. As I recall, that's one of the rockiest areas on the island. Not much going on there. Kayakers and other adventurers prefer to go to the southern end to see the waterfall."

"Interesting." It was too rocky to bury anything there, but it was also away from the sole attraction on the island. "I think I might go over there myself and take a look."

"Uh-huh." Hugo held the door open for her, but gauging from the distracted look in his eyes, his thoughts had already moved on to other matters. "I'm thinking of asking Ana Dominguez to repair the quilt that was given to us for the museum."

Ana would, of course, be able to repair it. Abby supposed Hugo's true concern was whether she was skilled enough to mend the delicate fabric of the antique heirloom. "Good luck getting her to work it into her busy schedule."

"It will need to be cleaned too. I think I might go over to In Stitches this afternoon and see what she can do with it."

"I'll come along with you if you'd like. I want to look at her selection of embroidery flosses."

He followed her through the door and walked with her to the lab. "Your company would be most welcome," he said. "But do me a favor and ease up on your questions about the tackle box. I'm concerned people may start avoiding you."

"I can't make any promises," Abby said. In fact, In Stitches was next on her list to continue her investigation.

CHAPTER ✿ TEN

Ana Dominguez exclaimed over Hugo's antique quilt and rushed to put on a pair of white gloves before handling it. Abby, interested in flosses and strings, strolled over to the colorful cacophony against the white wall. Ignoring the thick yarns, she concentrated on the durable floss. She was deep in thought when Hugo called her to join them.

"Mrs. Dominguez was just telling me that the blueberry accents on this quilt were common to early settlers in this region."

Ana hovered at his elbow, excitement dancing in her cocoa brown eyes. Her smooth brown skin contrasted beautifully with the white ruffled blouse and full tan skirt she wore. With a flip of her black braid, which was amply laced with gray, she pointed to a small stain near the center of the quilt.

"I know a cleaner that specializes in old wedding dresses," she said in her soft Spanish accent. "Don't let just anybody clean it, or it will come back with holes and rips. This is too *precioso* to let just anyone handle it."

Then, as if she were concerned that Hugo might, in fact, take the quilt to someone who would desecrate it, she offered to put it at the top of her overflowing list of projects.

"I'll get it back to you *muy pronto*."

When Hugo was done turning custody of the quilt over to Ana, she directed her attention to Abby. "What can I help you with?"

"I'm looking for a thick black string with silver fibers."

"For crochet?"

"I don't really know. It would probably be more like thread than yarn."

Ana walked back to the wall, waving her to follow, then picked up a spool of multicolored floss. "Like this?"

"Close, but more like a string than a floss. Like this." Abby reached into her pocket and pulled out a black string with a hint of glittery silver woven into it.

"Oh yes, we have something like that. Come over here." She led the way to an aisle with colorful beads and thin leather strips. Reaching past boxes of miniature safety pins, she retrieved a small skein of rough-textured thread. "The little girls love this stuff."

"Really, what's it used for?"

"Anything. Necklaces, *anillos*." She pointed to her finger. "Rings. They tie them like macramé and wind beads or different colored threads into them to make their initials or a word. For the longest time everyone wore bracelets that said 'W.W.J.D.' What Would Jesus Do? But now that craze is over, and they've moved on to other things."

"Actually, I was looking for this exact thread. It seems to have a more silky feel to it."

"I have thread *like* that, but not the exact color."

"Have you ever sold this particular style in the past?"

"No, I've never seen that color combination before today. If I knew where to find it, I'd stock it. Teenage girls would go crazy for that pretty black and silver. They think they're too grown up for pink and purple."

Abby thanked her for her time and turned to follow Hugo and return to the conservatory. As they walked out into the sunshine, he asked to see the string she carried. He held it up and squinted to see what all the fuss had been about.

"Considering your intense interest in this, I can only assume it has something to do with the tackle box you found."

"This is one of the strings that were tied around the bundles of money."

"Careful. You may be tampering with evidence."

"No, this one was overlooked when we were returning the money to the box. It turned up when I swept my parents' kitchen floor the other day, but I intend to give it to Sergeant Cobb the next time our paths cross."

"Did you learn anything that will help you solve the mystery of the box?"

Abby considered his question. "Only that this type of material is often used to make casual jewelry. But there was an expensive ring in the box I found, so it doesn't make sense to create your own jewelry when you own something like that."

Hugo closed the passenger door behind Abby, then walked around the car to the driver's side.

"Something tells me you'll figure it all out," he said. "It's just a matter of time."

THAT EVENING MARY WAS WORKING late at Island Blooms to help prepare for the upcoming Mother's Day rush. So when

Ida's shift at the Springhouse Café ended at 4:30, Abby joined her young friend for an early dinner before Wednesday night Bible study at Little Flock Church.

Over a sumptuous meal of pecan-crusted Dungeness crab-cakes for Abby and fried shrimp and onion rings for Ida, Abby brought her up to date on the information she had tracked down since the day of the storm when they'd last been together. Her conversation with Sam. The leads she'd followed to William Jansen, Rick DeBow and Hugo Baron. And the futile investigation at In Stitches. However, she withheld the bit about Vince Emory, partly because his donations to the church were between him and God, but mainly because she wanted to investigate this one privately since a marriage was possibly at stake.

They still had a half hour before Bible study began. So Ida suggested they walk across the street to Beach Bag Books and take a look at the latest fiction offerings.

"How are the sparrow eggs?" Ida asked. "Business is picking up at the café, so I haven't had time to come by and see them."

Inside the store, they both faced the row of books at the front of the shop featuring the latest hardcover best sellers. The selections ranged from slash-and-hack murder stories to tell-all celebrity biographies to true and fictional tales of family dysfunction. Uninterested in those books, the two women continued moseying their way to the back of the store.

"The egg with the hairline crack didn't make it," Abby told her.

Ida's pretty, bow-like lips turned down, and a shadowy mist clouded her eyes.

"Fortunately, the embryo in the other one appears to be growing," Abby said, hoping to cheer her with this good news.

"How can you tell?"

"When the egg is held up to a light, it's possible to see shadows of the chick's body. The liquid portion of the egg reduces as the chick grows to fill the shell, and what I've been seeing is that the shadowy part is getting larger."

"That's fascinating," Ida declared. "I can't wait until it hatches. You know, since our little bird's tumble out of the tree proved the law of gravity, I think we should name him Newton, as in, Sir Isaac."

Abby laughed. "Newton it shall be."

"Shouldn't it be hatched by now?"

"I would have thought so. They usually incubate for about ten to fourteen days. Since it's been a little over a week since you found it, I have to assume the mother bird had laid the egg right before the storm hit."

"Well, please let me know when the time comes. I'd love to be there to watch the miracle take place."

"I'll be sure to let you know."

Ida had gravitated to the romance section and was now glancing at the blurb on the back cover of a book that pictured a handsome couple cradling a smiling infant.

Abby watched the expression on her friend's face soften into wistfulness as she turned the book over and stared at the cover picture. Considering Ida's devoted attention to the sparrow egg and her reaction to the picture on the book, it seemed clear that she yearned for romance and a family of her own.

Curious, Abby picked one up and read the story description on the back. The main characters were younger than herself, but the story tapped into a wish harbored by so many women, regardless of their age—to be loved unconditionally.

Abby already had that kind of love, a pure and heavenly love from God. As Ida grew closer in her spiritual walk with the Lord, she would come to understand just how precious that love was. But Abby also understood the desire for a human companion with whom to share unconditional love. There were times, even now with a life that felt perfect in so many ways, when Abby sometimes wondered what her life would have been like if she had married one of her former love interests.

"I don't know why I'm even looking at these," Abby said. "I don't expect to have much time to read for a couple of months, at least."

Ida tucked the book into the crook of her arm. "Everyone should make time to read. It opens the imagination and makes you consider new possibilities that you might never have dreamed of otherwise."

Abby smiled and laid her hand affectionately on Ida's shoulder. The girl's violet eyes smoldered with a fire that was beyond that of the average reader. "Do you write, Ida?"

She shrugged, apparently embarrassed to have the attention turned from the books back to her. "Other than long, descriptive e-mails to my boyfriend? No. I guess I'd rather live a life of glamour and excitement than write about it."

"Glamour and excitement aren't all they're cracked up to be. Personally, I'd rather live the life I have and wear jewels in a crown after I enter eternity."

Ida looked at her with an expression of wonder. "You amaze me. You're one of those people who'd probably be happy even if all you owned were the clothes on your back."

"If that's where God wanted me to be, then yes. He can show us the joy in whatever situation we're living. We just have to look for it. And ask Him to guide us."

They had finished perusing the romance section when Ida

said, "Let's go look in nonfiction. Perhaps there's a book on how to find someone who doesn't want to be found."

"Good thinking, Watson."

The nonfiction section was quite small, and most of the selections were histories of Washington State and the San Juan Islands, information about local Indian tribes and books about the area's plant and animal life. It took Abby only a moment to ferret out the bookseller, a woman of indeterminate age with a becomingly slim figure and short, thick dark hair.

"I can't promise that I have anything on how to find people," she told them. "Most of our sales are fiction for beach reads or the top-selling self-improvement books."

She checked the shelves anyway and came up empty-handed.

"The last time anyone showed an interest in a subject like this, it was for a book on how *not* to be found." She pulled one off the shelf and handed it to Abby.

"Really? This doesn't seem to be the typical vacation reading material."

"Actually, it's a humor book on how to avoid people you don't like. Most of it is pure silliness, but there is also some factual information on how to disappear without a trace."

"Do you remember when this happened? And who bought the book?" Now Abby was really intrigued, and it seemed that Ida's antennae had gone up too.

"It was a year or two ago, and he didn't buy it. He tried to shoplift the book, but I caught him before he made it out of the store. Since no harm was done, I let him save face by pretending to believe it was a mistake on his part.

"The weird thing is, he had the money to pay for it. When he pulled out his wallet to buy the book, he had plenty of cash."

Abby looked at the price printed on the paperback book. "It's not that expensive," she agreed. "Just a few dollars."

"And what was weirder still was that when I asked him for his ZIP code to ring up the purchase, he changed his mind and decided not to buy the book."

"His ZIP code?" Abby supposed the customer himself didn't want to be traced.

"Yeah, I ask for ZIP codes because it gives me an idea of where our customers come from and what selections I should stock." The woman laughed as she recalled the customer. "That guy was probably going to steal the book and then disappear without a trace so I couldn't track him down."

"You and who else?" Ida wondered aloud.

A thought occurred to Abby as she pieced together the information she'd learned over the past few days. Had Vince Emory been planning, even then, to hide his money and then slip away with his paramour?

"Can you describe the shoplifter? What he was wearing, the color of his hair, his facial features?"

The woman shook her head. "All I remember is how weird it was that someone who could easily have afforded a six-dollar book was trying to steal it."

"You don't remember if he had brown hair with a bit of gray, or if he was perhaps in his forties?"

Ida jerked her attention to Abby.

"Just a hunch," Abby explained.

"I see so many people in this store, they all blur together in my mind after a while." The bookseller gestured toward Ida's romance and the how-to-disappear book that Abby still held. "Do you want to buy those?"

They followed her to the checkout register, and while the

woman was ringing up their purchases—complete with ZIP
codes—Abby considered her next move.

A ferry trip to Bellingham on Friday might provide the
change of scenery she needed while she worked out her plan.

MARY SWITCHED OFF THE BLOW-DRYER to check the curl on the
perm rod in her sister's hair. "Hold still. I'm almost finished."

Mary should have waited until tomorrow night to do this.
A Friday night perm would still have given Abby a day to work
with her hair some before being seen at church on Sunday. But
when Abby had eased her resistance to the makeover, Mary
knew she'd better strike now, before her sister had time to
change her mind.

The animals had left the kitchen an hour ago to avoid the
chemical smell and the noise of the dryer, and Mary suspected
Abby would have liked to do the same. But she wasn't about to
let her get away just yet. Once Abby saw how much better her
hair looked with the help of a do-it-yourself kit, Mary was certain she would want to continue the process.

"Are you sure you're not giving it too much curl? I already
have enough birds to take care of without worrying about
wrens nesting in my hair."

"Okay, I think we're almost ready to put the neutralizer on.
Hold this a sec while I check the instructions." She left Abby
by the sink, holding the bottle of neutralizing solution while
she wheeled over to the kitchen table where she'd left the box
earlier.

"I don't want it too curly. Maybe I should go ahead and
start now." Abby uncapped the bottle.

"No, it's not about how long you leave the solution in, it's
about how fast your hair takes the perm." Mary came back

with the box on her lap. "See, the strands are supposed to separate like it's shown in this picture. After we neutralize it we'll rinse you, then take the rods out before your hair has a chance to conform to the bend of the roller too much."

In order to get a better reach, Mary positioned her wheelchair so that the left side was to the front of the sink. Then she had Abby balance herself front-side-down across the arms of the chair with her head over the stainless steel basin. Taking care to squirt the neutralizer evenly over the rollers, Mary did as much as she could reach, then directed Abby on the rest.

"What if my hair took the perm too fast?" Abby asked.

"You worry too much." Mary pointed out a roller they'd both missed, and Abby aimed the nozzle to cover that area. "But even if it did grab the perm too fast, you'd just wash it sooner than the two days that's called for in the instructions, and the hair will relax a little."

Abby turned her head and peered at her as if she wasn't sure things would go as simply as Mary promised.

Mary leaned farther toward the sink and nudged Abby's head under the faucet to begin rinsing. To take her little sister's mind off the disastrous hair images that were surely flitting through her mind, Mary changed the subject to something she was sure Abby would be interested in talking about.

"I spoke to Henry earlier today. He said his men are still working on the case, but they haven't made much headway."

"Much? So they've learned *something*?"

"I suppose. He didn't say what, though."

Abby sighed, and Mary wondered if she shouldn't have brought up the investigation after all. With no real information to share, she should have known that would only frustrate her sister.

"What about you?" Mary asked. "It sounds like you might have found a suspect at Beach Bag Books last night. Were you able to find out who the guy was that tried to shoplift the book?"

"No, but I'm still working on that. Today Ida and I went to Holloway's Hardware to pick up some materials for a brooder box to put the sparrow in after it hatches. Frank Holloway's grandson Aaron waited on us."

"That kid is so quiet it's painful," Mary commented.

"That 'kid' is a year older than Ida." Abby turned her head to let the water flow over the other side of her scalp. "Someone had suggested that Aaron's quiet ways might actually be secretiveness, but it has nothing to do with the money."

Mary had no idea who might have suggested the boy was hiding something. Abby and Janet were getting to be as tight as ticks lately, and though Janet gossiped about *some* things, she would never accuse Aaron of hiding the box.

"So what did you find out?"

"That he's absolutely smitten with Ida." Abby turned off the water and stood, wrapping a faded brown towel around her head, curlers and all. "He was so tongue-tied around her that we could barely make out what he was saying."

"Is that so? Here, I'll help you take those rods out."

Mary pondered the possibilities. Despite the fact that Ida had lost both of her parents and been on her own since her senior year in high school, she was somewhat naïve and innocent for someone her age.

"Maybe we should try to get them together," Mary suggested. "Aaron's a sweet fellow, and Ida's rather quiet herself. They might just hit it off."

"Not a chance. Ida didn't seem the least bit interested. Besides, she already has a boyfriend."

"You don't say."

Mary reached to remove the first rod and was about ask about the boyfriend when they heard Finnegan scramble to his feet in the next room, a growl rumbling deep in his throat.

"I wonder what's got him all stirred up."

Abby didn't wait for Mary to find out. She strode quickly to the living room where Blossom was now darting from the room, her long white tail fluffed out like a bottle brush.

Finnegan had his front feet on the sliding glass doors where he tried to push the vertical blinds aside with his nose to look out.

"Finnegan, honey, what's going on?" Abby placed one hand on Finnegan's head and tried to see what had stirred the dog's interest. She had just had a quick peek out when he took off to the window in the dining room. In his frustration, the dog alternated between growling and whining, so Abby followed him to that window.

Mary came into the room and switched off the light just as Abby crossed the room. With a loud ferocious barking that startled both of the women, Finnegan leaped toward the window, his claws scratching at the sill. Outside, Abby heard a hasty rustling and a thump.

It all happened in the space of a second, or maybe two at the most, that Abby pulled open the blinds and caught a glimpse of something—or maybe someone, she wasn't quite sure—scrambling on the deck just outside the window. In the next instant, it was gone.

But that didn't matter to Finnegan. The golden dog raced to the sliding glass doors, barking so loudly that the sound bounced off the walls as he begged to be let outside to take care of the intruder. Abby's heart pounded so hard she thought it might leap out of her ribcage.

With a hand to her chest, she stepped away from the window and turned toward Mary.

"It was a man, I think," Abby said. "A Peeping Tom." The glimpse was so brief and the prowler gone so quickly, she wondered if she had imagined seeing him. But the snapshot image of dark brown hair still burned in her brain. Then again, she supposed it could have been fur.

Mary snapped her fingers. "Finnegan, come." The dog immediately quieted and went to her side. He assumed his working position beside her chair, but kept glancing over his shoulder at his mistress as if to ask if she wasn't sure she'd rather let him chase down the trespasser. "It was probably just the tomcat that's been hanging around here lately," Mary said. "He was probably wooing Blossom."

"No, I *think* this was a person," Abby said. She went to the phone and picked up the receiver to call the emergency number. "I saw something dark, with a white stripe. It could have been part of a jacket."

"You sure it wasn't a skunk?" Mary said with a nervous giggle.

"I don't know anything about his personality," Abby retorted while the phone rang on the other end, "but I do know I'm going to take this seriously. I'd rather act now and be mistaken than do nothing and be sorry later."

CHAPTER ❧ ELEVEN

THE BOAT TRIP TO Bellingham was a long one, but the view of the islands and the appearance of an orca whale acted like a natural tranquilizer on Abby's nerves. A heavy fog hung over the channel this morning, and Abby and the pilot of the small pleasure craft both wore protective rain gear. Mary had been kind enough to check with her boat-owner friends until she found one with whom Abby could catch a ride to the mainland.

Last night's encounter with the Peeping Tom had made Abby edgy for the rest of the evening, and the feeling had carried over to this morning. At the time of the call last night, Henry had been on another of the islands he regularly patrolled, so a deputy had been dispatched to the house to take the report.

Since Finnegan had calmed down almost immediately and then acted as if nothing had happened, Mary had shared her theory that the prowler may have been merely a Peeping Tom*cat*.

The deputy had seemed to prefer that explanation to Abby's. Although his low-key response may have been meant to reassure Abby, it actually had the opposite effect, and Abby now worried that the matter would be swept aside as a woman-scared-by-noise call.

To make matters worse, all the commotion had caused both her and Mary to forget about the perm rods in her hair. By the time they took them out, her hair had dried in tousled ringlets around her head. Mary had been delighted by the result, saying she looked like a young country music star, but Abby thought she looked more like a young Shirley Temple with her sausage curls.

Washing and blow-drying her hair this morning had lessened the corkscrew effect, but Abby just knew she didn't look like herself.

In an attempt to change Abby's mind about what she saw on the deck, Mary had compared their situation to a scary movie she'd seen and asked, "If it really was a prowler, wouldn't he have waited until we went to sleep and then have come back for us?"

And Abby's reply had been that he had taken one look at the curlers in her hair and was too scared to come back.

Today, staring out from under the boat's canopy at the drippy scenery, Abby recalled Mary's reaction to her joking retort. Her sister really wanted Abby to like the new hairdo as much as she did. For that reason, Abby would hold off making an appointment with Edmonia at the Silver Scissors to try to straighten her hair. At least for now.

She checked her watch. When the boat finally reached the Port of Bellingham, she would cross the railroad tracks into town and head north on Victor Street toward the Bible Resource Store. Once there, she'd pick up the lesson book and some craft supplies to get a head start on her summer Vacation Bible School preparations. Abby would have liked to pick up the entire order today, but she certainly understood the church's need to handle the financial aspects of the purchase through the proper channels. After the Bible Resource Store, she would enjoy a salad with chicken and poppy seed dressing, then browse the consignment store. After that, she would run a few more errands and finally meet her ride to return to Sparrow Island.

After thanking her new friend for the lift and confirming this afternoon's departure time, Abby pulled her all-weather coat tighter around her waist and raised the umbrella over her head. Reacting to the humidity, her hair coiled even tighter.

By the time she got to Victor Street, the pedestrian crowd had thinned and Abby was able to pick up her pace. Ahead of her a man bent his head against the misting rain and pulled his coat collar up around his ears. Something about him looked familiar. As Abby closed the distance between them, she realized it was Vince Emory.

His job at the sheet metal company was in the opposite direction from where he was going. Since he was walking in the same direction as she, Abby supposed he might also be going to the Bible Resource Store. She smiled, thinking that perhaps he'd been able to come through with the donation to the church's day camp activities after all.

She quickened her step, intent on saying hello to him. She had almost caught up to him when he turned right, one block before the store.

Puzzled, she stopped at the intersection and watched him hustle east on Madison Street. Janet's comment nagged at the back of Abby's mind. Vince's wife suspected him of having an affair. Was he on a rendezvous to meet his mistress? Curiosity got the better of her, and Abby followed him.

At the end of the block, he turned into a plain gray stucco office building. About twenty-five feet behind him, Abby reached the glass front doors just in time to see him step onto an elevator. She went inside just as the elevator doors closed.

She pushed the button and watched the indicator lights overhead. It stopped on the fourth floor, and again on the seventh before returning to the lobby. Ignoring the opened doors, Abby walked over to the directory and scanned the listings to see which businesses were located on those floors.

A counseling facility. An executive search company. An upscale matchmaking service. And an accounting office.

Abby took the notepad out of her purse and jotted an entry as she tried to put the pieces together. If he was coming to visit a mistress, wouldn't he meet her at a hotel or perhaps her own residence?

Hmm, maybe that would be too obvious, she thought. At any rate, she hadn't seen him with a woman, and for that Abby was grateful. That didn't mean he *wasn't* having an affair, but Abby was relieved that she hadn't been the one to confirm it.

What she *did* know, however, was that Vince Emory wasn't where he was supposed to be, namely at work.

SINCE IT WAS FRIDAY NIGHT and Mary had a date with Henry, Abby didn't feel rushed to return home by a particular time. The museum staff was leaving just as Abby got back from her trip to Bellingham, and Hugo had left early to do some research at the library. So now she had the building to herself. She could stay as long as she needed to complete her research.

The first few times she'd stayed late to work by herself, the experience had been eerie. Without the visitors and staff talking, the phones ringing and audio portions of the museum's displays explaining the various exhibits, even the smallest sounds seemed loud. The movement of air through the vents gave the impression that a person was passing through the next room, clothes swishing as he or she walked. But after a few months of becoming accustomed to the odd crackles and snaps that punctuated the silent evening, Abby had learned to differentiate between the building's usual sounds and those that warranted closer attention.

Even so, she was somewhat jumpy tonight. Probably because Henry had called her on her cell phone today, just to follow up on the report she had filed last night.

Abby called up a search engine on the computer and typed in the key words that would help her find the information she wanted. When her phone rang a moment later, she leaped in her seat, causing the rolling chair to slide away from the desk.

She loosened her shoulders and shook her arms to get rid of the tension that suddenly befell her. If it had been the museum's main phone ringing, she'd let it switch over to voice mail to give the caller their hours and other operating information. But the ringing of her office phone meant it was someone calling specifically for her.

She picked it up on the second ring.

"It's Ida," said the voice at the other end. "I'm outside on my cell phone. The door's locked."

Abby went to the main door to let her in.

"Oh," Ida said and stared openly at Abby's hair.

"It was Mary's idea." Abby raised a hand to her hair. "She promised me it will relax eventually."

Abby suspected even a Caribbean vacation wouldn't relax these curls.

Apparently recovering from her surprise at the unexpected sight, Ida quickly turned to the point of her visit. "Your car was in the parking lot so I knew you were here. Have you turned Newton yet?"

"Not this evening. Why don't you do the honors yourself?"

Ida knew the way to the conservatory building, having come so often to check on her adopted little one. She went straight to the lab where the bufflehead with the splinted leg struggled to rise on his good leg. Out of concern for the wary duck, Ida walked along the opposite side of the lab to the incubator where Newton waited, O side up.

Taking great care not to jostle the incubator, Ida lifted the clear plastic lid and slowly rotated the egg so the X now faced up. "I wonder if he gets dizzy when we do this."

Obviously, it was too soon to know whether the chick was male or female, but they had begun referring to it as "he," probably because that gender best fit the name they had given it. Abby watched as her friend gently closed the lid.

"If anything, he's probably relieved to move to a new position."

Ida pushed a stray strand of hair behind her ear. "He should have hatched by now, but I don't see any signs of cracking in the shell. Could there be something wrong?"

Ida truly cared about the chick. Abby wanted to give her the good news she sought. But she also needed to be honest.

"It could have stopped growing. That happens sometimes. No one knows why."

Ida clenched her jaw as she moved away.

"But there's still that chance that it was very young when you found it. Give it a couple more days. And have faith."

Ida gave her a sad smile. "His eye is on the sparrow," she said, echoing Abby's words from their earlier conversation.

Once again, she skirted the bufflehead's cage. The small wire enclosure kept the creature from thrashing and possibly doing more damage to itself. The waterbird settled back down as they left the room. Abby locked up the building and they headed back to The Nature Museum.

In Abby's office, Ida lounged in a chair by the desk while Abby sat in front of the computer. "Do you want to go get something to eat?"

"Funny you should mention eating out," Abby said. "My sister has a dinner date tonight with her boyfriend, and she offered to fix me up to go with them."

"Matchmaking, huh? Is that why she did your hair?"

Abby paused as she considered the possibility. "I don't know, but after I told her about our visit to Holloway's Hardware, she was sure interested in fixing you up with Aaron. I told her you're already seeing someone."

Ida lowered her gaze and picked at the pink nail polish on her thumb. "Aaron's a nice guy, but I don't see him as my type."

Abby had a feeling she knew what Ida meant. "Too close to home?"

"I guess. Ryan has everything I'm looking for. He hangs out with really cool people, he goes to parties and leads a glamorous life, and . . . well, he spoils me." She sighed dreamily. "Ryan is always telling me how much he loves me. He even gave me a promise necklace. I'd show it to you, but I haven't taken the time to get it back from the jeweler after the clasp was repaired.

Ryan's going to give me an engagement ring to match it as soon as he doesn't have to travel so much for work."

"Aaron would have a hard time competing with that."

"It's not just about lifestyle. Ryan and I e-mail each other almost every day. He can't come to the island as often as he'd like, so I write and tell him about everything that's going on in my life. It's like we connect on so many levels."

Abby typed some words into the search engine and hit Enter. "He sounds like a great catch."

Ida's violet eyes darkened. "In most ways. He's not much of a churchgoer, but he has so many good things going for him that it's hard to hold that against him. Besides, after we're married and settled into a nice place on the mainland, I'll encourage him to go to church with me. That should smooth out his rough edges."

Abby paused, her fingers poised over the keyboard. She hesitated a moment, wondering how much she should say about this to her young friend. A Bible verse seemed to shout itself in her mind, and Abby felt as if God was urging, "Tell her."

Turning to her bookshelf, she pulled down a well-thumbed black Bible and opened it to II Corinthians 6:14. She handed the book to Ida.

"Having never been married myself, I don't claim to be an expert on the subject," Abby said, "but the Good Book has some excellent advice for those thinking of entering into the state of matrimony."

Ida read the words aloud. "'Do not be yoked together with unbelievers.'" She gasped. "Does this mean I shouldn't marry him?"

"No, it just means that you should encourage him to develop a relationship with God . . . *before* you marry."

"Oh." She let her gaze travel over the passage she'd just read. "There's more. 'For what do righteousness and wickedness have in common? Or what fellowship can light have with darkness?'" She set the book on her lap. "Ryan's choices are a little shaky sometimes, but I wouldn't call him wicked."

"Nor would I. But it's good advice to think about. Imagine, if you both have God as your North Star, you'll move together through life in tandem. You'll be evenly yoked, so neither will be pulling ahead or holding the other one back. And that will make you both a stronger team for raising children."

Ida's cheeks pinkened at the mention of children. "Okay, I get it," she said with a laugh. "We should become birds of a feather before we decide to flock together."

Abby laughed with her. "Exactly!" She was heartened that her young friend was so open to hearing God's Word. She silently prayed that Ida would now apply it to her life.

Ida cleared her throat and leaned forward to see what Abby had typed on the screen. "What are you looking up?"

Her attempt to change the subject was less than subtle, but Abby let it pass. She had no desire to hammer anyone over the head with preaching. All Abby could do was follow God's leading to share what she could, and know that He would continue to work in Ida's mind and heart long after their conversation was over.

"I'm checking to see if there's a posting about the money. If it was stolen, the owner may have put something on the Internet in hopes of getting it back."

Not wishing to scroll through a half-million entries about how to earn more than $100,000 a year, Abby narrowed her search parameters and tried again while Ida moved her chair around to see the computer monitor.

"I think we have a hit," Abby said, clicking on a link that took her to a Seattle area newspaper article dated September, almost two years ago. "Oh my goodness."

"What is it?"

"Listen to this. 'An undercover police officer, posing as a drug buyer, and a civilian bystander were critically wounded in an exchange of gunfire yesterday when a drug bust went sour. The suspect in the shooting who was identified only by his street name, "Jellybean," had been under surveillance by detectives for several months while they collected evidence. As officers were preparing to close in for the sting, Jellybean allegedly fired at police before escaping with more than $115,000. Police refused to comment on whether he was working independently or through a syndicate.'" Abby clicked the mouse to print a copy of the article.

"Jellybean," Ida said, looking worried. "Without a real name, this article won't really help find the guilty party—and clear the innocent."

Abby was touched by her concern for Sam. "No, but it will give Sergeant Cobb some new leads to check, and that may ultimately direct him to the real perpetrator."

Two pages emerged from the printer. Abby folded them and tucked them in her purse to take to Henry. Since he was off duty tonight, she didn't want to ruin the happy glow of his date with Mary, so she would take the article to him at the sheriff's substation tomorrow afternoon.

It was always a possibility that the article might not be about the box she'd found, but the amount of money seemed too similar for it to be a mere coincidence.

CHAPTER ❧ TWELVE

BOBBY MOVED THE COOLER to the center of the metal skiff and rested his waterproof boots on it. In the water nearby, a rhinoceros auklet surfaced from a dive, noticed the pair in the boat and quickly paddled away. Abby noted the white streaks behind his eyes and the hornlike ridge on its upper bill that indicated the bird was in breeding season.

"Abby, I did my chores 'with all my might' this morning. That's why Mom let me come with you for lunch on Dorsal Island."

"Excellent, Bobby! I'm very proud of you, and I'm sure your mother is too."

Sitting at the back of the small boat she'd borrowed from her father, Abby steered the aluminum craft to the shore of the tiny island. Sunbleached drift logs littered the narrow strip of beach, and black oystercatchers poked their long red beaks into the rockweed, looking for food. As the boat approached, Abby shut off the outboard motor and raised it to keep it from dragging the bottom. The oystercatchers scattered briefly before regrouping on the far side of the secluded cove.

When they got out of the boat, Bobby ran to the front and helped Abby pull it out of the water so that the tide would not creep up and claim it. The cooler would keep their food safe from inquisitive wildlife until they returned for it later.

"Why do birds hang around in groups like that?" Bobby asked, pointing to the oystercatchers. "If I was one of them, I'd want to go off by myself sometimes and do some exploring."

Abby shrugged and headed off in the direction of the spot that had been marked on the map. "They have things in common," she said. "Like us. We like to do some of the same things together. And then there's safety. The birds look out for each other."

"Me and you don't need to look out for each other. We can take care of ourselves 'cause we know about being in the woods."

"*You* and *I*," Abby said, feeling like Margaret Blackstock for correcting his grammar. "Sure, we know about the woods, but it's nice having someone with you who'd help you if there was an accident."

Bobby puffed out his chest. "I would look out for you if you got hurt."

"I know you would. And I know that you would protect me from those who might try to hurt me. The oystercatchers know that other creatures would love to make a meal out of them, but they're safe with their own kind."

He nodded. "That's why Mom tells me to hang around with good kids. Because I won't get into trouble with them the way I might with the troublemakers."

"Your mom is a very wise person."

"That's why we go to church too. To hang around with people who value the things we believe."

"Yes, and so we can encourage each other to do God's will."

Pushing through the weedy underbrush, she and Bobby walked for about twenty minutes before they reached the apex at the far end of the island. Since Dorsal Island was too small to build on—especially at high tide when easily a fourth of the island disappeared under water—and was lacking in some of the grander sights of the neighboring islands, it attracted only the most outdoorsy visitors. For this reason, there were few footworn paths to follow. But it also meant there was little carelessly dropped litter, and the features of the land were relatively unaltered by humans. Abby suspected that, other than Sergeant Cobb and his deputies, she and Bobby were the first to come here since the previous tourist season.

The spot she sought was very tiny. And it was hard enough to reach so that only the most devoted birder or fisherman would bother trying to get to it. It was secluded, indeed.

There wasn't much of a cove to speak of. Mainly just a tiny clearing surrounded by jumbled rocks and the most determined trees growing among them. As she walked, Bobby amused himself by searching for sand crabs where the water lapped against the pebble and sand covered shore. When he tired of that, he turned to examining the dead jellyfish and dogfish egg cases that had been abandoned by the receding tide.

Abby paced the perimeter of the clearing, noting several freshly dug spots among the grasses and wildflowers. Henry and his men must have considered them likely spots for someone to bury their loot.

"Abby, look at me. I'm a king sitting on a throne!"

Among the piles of rocks, Bobby had found a large one that

served as the seat. Behind him and on either side, upward jutting rocks formed convenient back and arm rests. Taking a closer look at the beaming boy, she saw that he had fashioned for himself a crown made out of a shooting star plant. The stems were tied together around his head, and the purple and yellow blossoms that reminded her of badminton birdies dangled over his forehead.

She made her way over the rocks to join him. It was a tight squeeze, but she slid in beside him, causing Bobby to erupt in a fit of laughter. "You're the queen," he declared, tapping her shoulder with a stick that served as his scepter. "Sorry, I don't have a crown for you."

"It's just as well. I'd rather let the wildflowers grow."

Bobby tucked his chin, and his dark-lashed eyes got big. "Oops. I forgot."

Abby patted his knee. "That's okay. Just try to remember next time."

She leaned back and relaxed against the rock backrest. Sitting on the rocks like this reminded her of William Jansen at Paradise Cove, and she imagined he would enjoy fishing here. With only one person sitting on the "throne," there would be room for his fishing gear beside him. From this vantage point, a person really could feel like a king or queen.

"Are you hungry?" Bobby asked, his hazel eyes hopeful.

"Yes. Let's go back and have a picnic."

Still wearing his king's crown, Bobby picked his way over the rocks, back to where they had arrived at the small clearing. Taking her time, Abby rose from the royal seat and surveyed their glorious surroundings.

A pair of belted kingfishers dipped past, chattering as they flew. Farther out, standing in a low tidepool, a blue heron balanced himself one-legged on a kelp bed.

She made a mental note to come here again sometime, when the weather and her schedule allowed.

With care, so as not to twist an ankle, she stepped over a loose rock. Something glinted on the ground. She made her way to the other side of the rock and stopped to pick up what appeared to be a drink can tab. But when she reached for the shiny object, she found blue feathers attached to a metallic hook.

A fishing fly. It looked like someone had already discovered this idyllic fishing spot. If she left the fly where it had been dropped, a bird might find it and get the hook caught in its throat.

Abby stopped in her tracks, balancing her weatherproof boot against the jagged edges of rock, and studied the object in her hand.

Many commercial fishing flies were created from man-made products. This one, however, had been hand tied using real feathers. At first glance, the feathers appeared to be from a bluebird, or maybe even a lazuli bunting. But upon closer examination something seemed different about them. Abby picked up the fishing lure and tucked it in a small zippered pocket on the front of her jacket.

After they got back to the landing at the opposite end of the island, she and Bobby ate a lunch of peanut butter sandwiches, apples and homemade brownies that Abby's mother had prepared. Their time together was punctuated with laughter, and Abby said a prayer of thanks for her young friend.

She had hoped to find a clue—anything—that would lead her closer to uncovering the identity of the person who'd buried the tackle box on Stanton Farm. But now she was no closer to solving the mystery than when she'd awakened this morning. Even so, she didn't consider their trek to the island a waste of time. Rather, Abby saw it as a wonderful opportunity to enjoy Bobby's company.

As for the fishing fly, on Monday she would take it to the lab at the conservatory and compare it with her collection of feather samples.

BACK AT THE STANTON FARM, Bobby helped Abby put the skiff away, then climbed into her car, still wearing his shooting star king's crown. Calling a thank you to her father for letting her borrow the boat, she got into her car to drive the boy home.

After she pulled back out onto Primrose Lane, a sheriff's department car appeared in her rearview mirror. It was hard to tell who was driving, and after a moment the rooftop lights lit up and the siren sounded a brief command for her to pull over. Abby looked down at the dash. Her speed was good, so it couldn't be that.

"Uh-oh," Bobby said.

Rather than pull over to the side of the narrow road and risk blocking traffic, she drove to the nearest place with a parking lot, the Green Harbor Public School. Fortunately today was Saturday, so the school children would not be witness to her encounter with the law.

She was rolling down her window when Sergeant Cobb walked over and asked for her driver's license.

"Abby! I didn't know that was you." He bent down for a closer look, his eyebrows furrowing into a concerned crease. "It looked like someone else was driving your car."

The hair. He was staring at it like she'd grown a beaver on her head. An electrified beaver.

"Hi, Sergeant Cobb," Bobby said.

"Hi Bobby. Well don't you look . . . interesting."

Bobby smiled and adjusted his crown.

"Wait here, Bobby." Abby pushed open the door and got out. Resting a hip against the fender, she attempted to finger-comb the curls into a more ordered mess. Judging from Henry's boggled expression, she hadn't helped matters any.

"Mary," she said, as if that one word explained it all.

He shoved his hands into his pockets. "She finally caught you, huh?" He squinted and took a closer look. "It actually doesn't look bad."

She shook her head and felt the curls bang against the top of her neck. "A lot of people would like this style," she agreed. "It's just not . . . me."

Henry chuckled. "I thought someone had stolen your new car."

When Abby first returned to Sparrow Island, she had borrowed her mother's Lincoln. Just recently, Abby had purchased the gas-electric hybrid she now drove.

"Thanks for looking out for me."

"You can count on me—and the deputies—to look out for you. It bothers me to think of someone prowling around the house."

Now Abby felt sheepish for having called the deputy about whatever it was that she thought she had seen the other night. "It was so dark that I'm not really sure if it was a some*one*. It might have been a some*thing*. All I saw was some movement and a quick flash of color."

"It doesn't matter. We'll be stepping up patrol by your house, just to make sure."

Abby appreciated the caring concern that was so evident in his tone and in his expression. "Actually, I'm glad we met up today. I was just on my way to the substation to talk to you about the investigation."

"I've been interviewing a number of people on the island," he confirmed.

Abby thought she detected a dark glimmer in his gaze, but the expression was so fleeting that she couldn't be sure.

"It turns out you beat me to several of the subjects."

There was one he didn't know about—Vince Emory—but she didn't want to implicate him unless there was actual evidence to prove that he was involved. And now that the Internet article had provided more insight, she believed what Vince may have done was immoral rather than illegal. "I didn't mean to step on your toes. It's just that I was worried about Sam." Abby and Henry moved further away from the car so Bobby's inquisitive ears couldn't overhear.

"I've spoken with Sam." He must have noticed her look of alarm, for then he added, "I hope he's not involved either, but we have to look at all possibilities." Then, almost as an afterthought, he said, "*The Birdcall* article—the one that mentioned the money you discovered—got picked up by a mainland newspaper. Seattle."

"Really?" Seattle was where the drug bust had occurred. "With that much publicity, it'll be interesting to see if the quail is flushed from its cover."

"What makes you think the thief's from Seattle?"

"Last night Ida and I searched the Internet and found an article about a botched drug bust."

As she filled him in on the contents of the article, Abby concluded that he was already aware of this information.

"I'm impressed with what you've found," he said. "You don't miss much, do you?"

"We were hoping it might help with your investigation."

Henry cleared his throat. "I appreciate your wanting to help. It's time, though, for you to step back and let the sheriff's office handle the rest."

He wasn't a man who was easily concerned, but today his attitude seemed unusually subdued.

"The money in the tackle box is from the drug bust, isn't it?"

Henry hesitated a long minute. "Yes, it is."

"How did you know?"

He paused again, and Abby knew he was assessing how much he should tell her. Always circumspect, he was careful to adhere to official protocol, no matter that he was dating Abby's sister. "Let's just say the serial numbers from the money in the box matched up with the cash the undercover detectives used to buy the drugs."

A sense of elation swept over Abby as the news sank in. Abby grabbed Henry's arm. "This is wonderful! Sam's off the hook."

He covered her hand with his own and patted it distractedly. "Abby, I don't want to ruin your good mood, but I need to remind you the box was found where Sam works." He watched as she drew her hand away from his arm and took a step back. "He's not off the hook yet."

But Abby would not be easily deterred. "Find this Jellybean guy," she said. "Once you catch him, it will be clear that Sam is innocent."

"For Sam's sake, I hope so. But more importantly, you and

Mary need to take precautions. Keep the doors locked. Take care not to be alone at night."

"Of course, Henry." Abby slid back into her car. "We're always careful to take reasonable safety precautions."

He gave her a tight-lipped nod and pushed the door closed behind her. With a flick of his thumb, he pushed down the lock.

"Stay alert," he said. "Good-bye, Bobby."

Bobby saluted as Abby drove off.

SINCE THEIR REGULAR Sunday school discussion leader had gone to Olympia to visit her mother for the weekend, Patricia Hale was filling in this morning. The lesson was on Matthew 5:23 and 24, in which Jesus taught that a worshipper is to leave his gift at the altar and make amends with his brother before proceeding with his sacrifice. It seemed like a strange lesson for Mother's Day until Patricia explained that our earthly parents can't enjoy their celebration day gifts if there's discord among the children.

Abby thought about the thread of tension that had woven its way between her and Mary recently. George and Ellen hadn't seemed to notice, but it was still something that she and Mary needed to resolve. As Ellen used to say during their Saturday morning cleaning sessions, dirt under the carpet is impossible to sweep away. It has to come out into the open before it can be removed.

She leaned over and whispered to her sister, "We need to talk."

Mary gave a small smile and silently nodded her agreement.

The class was almost over when Patricia reminded them of today's special offering for teen mothers. Vince Emory had been the one to bring to the church's attention the home for young mothers, and directing their gifts there seemed appropriate, given that this was a day to honor mothers.

Abby left the classroom and paused in the chapel to write a check to help with the home's mission. As she was signing her name in preparation for dropping it in the offering plate during the worship service, Vince moved past her to join the others who were gathering in the pews.

Recalling today's Bible lesson, Abby knew that Vince was a "brother" that she needed to get right with before offering her gift in church. By keeping silent about his activities in Bellingham, it was as if she was keeping a secret along with him. By not talking about it, she felt as though the guilt covered her as well as Vince.

Quickly, before he could get away, Abby shoved the check into her purse and called out to him. "May I speak with you for just a moment?"

They moved to a less busy area in the back of the church. In his mid-forties, Vince was a handsome man. His silver-edged brown hair was neatly trimmed in a business cut and his features, though marked by the remnants of battles with teen acne, were compelling in their firmly defined angles. If his wife's suspicions were true, Abby could see how he might turn another woman's head. She hoped Cheryl was wrong, but the signs didn't look good.

"First, I want to thank you for bringing the Grace Girls' Home to the church's attention. Cheryl said that your job in the public relations department of your company brings you into contact with a lot of worthwhile charitable organizations. I'm just glad we have the opportunity to help this one."

His eyes darted to the right, and Vince seemed discomfited by her comments. "Thank you. Uh, if that's all. . . ."

"Actually, it isn't." This was the hard part. How did one confess to tiptoeing behind a person as he went about his day? *When in doubt, blurt it out.* "I went to Bellingham Friday. I saw you there. At the Monroe Building."

He frowned and made to move away, but Abby sidestepped to indicate she would not let him casually slip out of dealing with this issue.

"I don't know what you mean," he said.

"I think you do." He could play dumb all he wanted, but God knew the truth. "As I see it, you've had some changes in your life lately. Vince, God wants to lead you in your decisions. Turn to Him, and let Him help you through this."

Vince rubbed the heel of his hand across his eyes. "Please, Abby, don't say anything to Cheryl."

His distress was evident, and Abby felt bad for having put him through it. She knew that confronting him was the right thing to do, but there were limits to how involved she should become. "It's not my place to speak to your wife about the thing that's troubling you."

His shoulders eased down, and Vince tilted his head back in a gesture of thanks.

"You need to talk to her," she continued. "If not today, then as soon as possible. Go to Rev. Hale first if need be, or talk it over with Henry. They're both good advisers."

Vince mumbled something unintelligible. They paused as an elderly church member moved slowly past, leaning on a cane.

"However you choose to do it, Vince, you need to come clean. I can't carry your secret any longer."

CHAPTER ❧ THIRTEEN

ABBY DECIDED THE feather couldn't wait until Monday. After a special Mother's Day dinner after church with her folks and Mary, she stopped by the lab briefly to research the feather used in the fishing fly. What she found was enough to send her on an immediate trip to Orcas Island.

Known throughout the San Juans and even across the country as *the* place to go for specialty fishing items, the Rod 'n' Reel shop on Orcas offered not only tackle and gear of the highest quality, but also expert advice from the owner and employees who frequently entered and won fishing competitions.

The outside of the shop looked like a medium-sized Victorian-era business, but the inside more closely resembled a warehouse, with canoes, kayaks, rods, reels and everything in between stacked from floor to ceiling. Abby located the owner, conveniently named Rod, and showed him the fly she'd found.

"Oh yeah, I remember that fly. We special ordered the feathers from overseas for one of our regular customers. They're from a Damar flycatcher," he said.

That part she already knew from her research at the lab this afternoon. What he didn't bother to say, for obvious reasons, was that the Damar flycatcher was a protected species in eastern Indonesia. And that fact alone had prompted the trip here today.

"This particular fisherman considered the name to be good luck. Others think a bright color will attract more fish. Personally, I think a common brown turkey feather would be just as good."

"Really?" Abby said. "Why is that?"

"The striation—that is, the rippled stripes—on the feather is what attracts the fish's attention. Solid colors, even if they're bright, aren't always as effective."

Rod reached for the lure, and Abby handed it over to him. Using a thumb to push aside the feathers, he examined the thick foil strip covering the quills. "We may have ordered the feathers for Max, but we sure as the dickens didn't tie this fly. Looks like a farmer trussed it up for slaughter."

Abby resisted the urge to tell him her father was a farmer, and that he could tie flies as well as the next person. The watermen in this area, being proud of their skills in fishing and boating, sometimes referred to less knowledgeable landlubbers as farmers. But though the comment was issued as an insult to this Max fellow's tying skills, it wasn't meant as an insult to farmers themselves.

"See, the foil creates drag and interferes with the action of the spoon." Rod examined the curved metal tab fastened to the rig. "The spoon here is supposed to wobble through the water, like the swimming movements of a distressed insect or baitfish. But the way the foil is bunched on here, it would have set the thing spinning, which would defeat the purpose."

Sergeant Cobb had suggested she should step away from the case. Although Abby had a hunch this lure was somehow connected with the drug bust since it was found in the area marked on the map, it could also be nothing more than a fly that had been poorly tied by someone who didn't know better—or maybe didn't care—about the shady market for feathers from rare birds.

"This Max you spoke of...he might want this lure returned. Do you know how I can get in touch with him?" Abby wasn't actually going to return the fly since it was possible that it was illegal to own such feathers. She'd have to look that up when she returned to her computer. What she wanted to do was inform him that using these feathers was further endangering a vulnerable bird species.

"I can't give you his personal contact information," Rod said, "but you shouldn't have any trouble finding Max Rigolo. He's a big-time businessman on the mainland. Everybody knows who he is. I'm surprised you haven't heard of him. Big spender. Max is a great customer. I'm gonna have to teach him to tie better flies though."

"Thank you. That gives me a place to start. I have one more question," she said as he handed the fly back to her.

"Fire away."

"How is it possible to buy these feathers when the Damar flycatcher is on the vulnerable list?"

Rod stared at her for a long moment, then looked away as if he was hoping someone would rescue him from her probing question. "You're that Bird Lady from Sparrow Island, aren't you? I haven't done anything illegal."

"I'm not saying you did. It's just surprising that these feathers are available on the open market."

"The way it was explained to me, you're not supposed to buy and sell the birds. But if kids find fallen feathers in the woods and want to sell them for some extra cash, then that's okay." Rod crossed his arms over his chest. "The way I see it, we're actually helping to put food on the table of some poverty-stricken family. So our policy is that by giving them our business for found feathers, we're also doing a good thing for them. It's a win-win situation."

Abby was convinced he meant no harm. But he obviously wasn't aware of the repercussions of his well-meaning actions. She lowered her voice and spoke carefully because she wanted to educate him—not browbeat him—into changing this aspect of doing business.

"You may be inadvertently giving those poverty-stricken kids an incentive to capture or kill the birds so they'll have more feathers with which to meet the demands of the market. So you may want to rethink your policy."

Rod fidgeted under her gaze and lifted a hand to smooth the hair at the nape of his neck. It seemed obvious that he'd rather be talking to someone more interested in fishing than in bird conservation.

"Please, think about it," she said and turned to leave.

AT HOME THAT EVENING, Abby put down the book she'd been reading and booted up her laptop computer. She'd seen a sheriff's department car slowly cruise by earlier that evening and felt safe and protected, knowing that Henry and his deputies were on the watch.

From her position by the lamp, Mary angled her head to read the book's spine. "*Make Like a Tree . . . and Leave.* That's an unusual title."

Even though she hadn't done anything for which to feel guilty, Abby felt as if she'd been caught with her hand in the cookie jar. Sure, the paperback she'd bought from Beach Bag Books gave scant bits of information on how to disappear without a trace, but she reasoned she wasn't ignoring Henry's request to stay off the case. She was just reading a book for her own enjoyment and illumination.

"This is the book that guy tried to shoplift from Beach Bag Books. There's a lot of humor in it," she said by way of defense. "It's been a long day. I needed something to help me wind down."

"Yes, it has been tiring, but it was good to see Mom and Dad and to talk to Zack, Nancy and the grandchildren on the phone."

Mary's children, both in their thirties, lived off the island. Tampa, Florida, was home to Nancy and her husband and her two children, while Zack traveled the country, playing piano with a jazz band. Although they couldn't come to visit as often as either Mary or they would like, they all stayed in frequent touch with each other. Remembering this morning's lesson about getting right with your brother before offering a gift, Abby knew that the prettily wrapped packages they'd sent Mary paled in comparison to the fact that there was so much love between the siblings, as well as for their mother.

Mary sat with her Bible on her lap, but she hadn't opened it. "At Mom and Dad's today, you sort of grimaced when they commented on your new look." Finnegan sat up beside her chair, and Mary leaned over to rub his neck. "I'm sorry you're not comfortable with it yet, but I think it looks good."

Abby immediately felt contrite. She hadn't intended for her lack of enthusiasm over the new style to make Mary feel bad.

And she certainly hadn't intended to make an expression that could be interpreted as a grimace.

"Mary, I'm sorry I haven't been more excited about the new look. It's just taking me a while to get used to it." She set the laptop on the coffee table to give her sister her undivided attention. "I really do appreciate what you did. For what it's worth, even though I grumbled during the perming process, I really enjoyed the time we spent together."

Mary looked slightly mollified by her reassurance. "Thank you," she said. "But I still wish you liked it."

Abby gave a little laugh. "Getting me all dolled up is like that part of the verse in Matthew: 'Don't cast your pearls before swine,'" she paraphrased (Matthew 7:6, KJV).

Mary pushed up the sleeves of her sweater to her elbows and put on an expression that Abby hadn't seen since she was Bobby's age. Back then, her protective older sister had threatened to clean the clock of an aggressive classmate who'd been trying to goad Abby into a fight. At the time, Abby hadn't been afraid of the girl and had intended to ignore her until she tired of the game. What she most remembered about that day was the realization that no matter how many silly arguments she and Mary might have gotten into, they were always on the same side in the things that really mattered.

"Don't you talk that way about my little sister," Mary said as if she were referring to someone else in the room. She flashed a teasing grin. "She's pretty cool, even if she is stuck in a fashion rut."

The two of them laughed, the tension between them dissolved now. "I *am* in a fashion rut," Abby confirmed. "And that's okay with me."

"It's okay with me too." Mary reached over and squeezed

her hand. "I love you no matter what, and I want to be here for you . . ."

She ended the sentence on an odd note, as if she had started to add "the way you've been here for me" then thought better of it. Abby knew that her sister would never want her in the position of needing anyone the way she herself needed Abby.

"I need you," Abby said. "More than you know. Not necessarily for a makeover though."

She chuckled again, and Mary joined in.

Mary released Abby's hand and leaned back in her chair. "I've been thinking about those verses Patricia taught in our Bible lesson. The ones about getting right with your brother before putting your sacrifice on the altar."

Abby nodded. She'd been thinking about them too. "I suppose I haven't been very gracious about the makeover."

"Not true," Mary interrupted. "Even though it wasn't something you wanted, you went along with it for my sake. And when your hair turned out curlier than expected, I could tell that you really tried to like it. Or at least cope with it politely."

Mary sighed and dangled a hand over her chair to scratch Finnegan's ears. Then she looked up and studied Abby's face intently.

"When I suggested the makeover, I wasn't suggesting you aren't pretty just as you are," Mary admitted. "It's sort of the way I look at the containers we use at the flower shop. If I see a beautiful basket, it inspires me to imagine which plant to put in it, what color of ribbon to tie around it and whether to mix in some ferns. I guess I got carried away and did the same thing with you."

Abby couldn't resist teasing her sister. "So you see me as a basket case?"

Mary grinned in response, but her words were serious. "I see you as someone who's perfectly capable of filling her own basket and tying her own ribbons."

Abby's breath left her in a sigh. That was exactly what she'd been trying to tell her sister all along, and it was heartening to know that Mary *got it*. Relief swept through her as she realized they had just crossed another hurdle in their relationship. Their differences had created obstacles for them as children, then widened into a chasm as they grew older. But now they were finally accepting them. Accepting that the two of them could be quite different, yet still love each other wholeheartedly . . . not *in spite* of those differences, but *because* of them.

"Thank you," Abby said, gazing fondly at the sister who meant so much to her. "I guess this means we're done with makeovers?" she asked hopefully.

"No, I'll still offer suggestions," Mary declared with a glimmer of mischief in her eyes. "I'll just stop expecting you to follow them."

"Fair enough. Although I have to admit, I was really looking forward to putting that hair dye kit you bought into the offering plate for someone who needs it more than I do."

Mary gave her a sly smile that let her know she still had plans for that particular purchase. Abby shrugged.

They shook hands to seal their agreement. Mary picked up her Bible, making it clear that it was now time for her daily devotions. So Abby set the computer on her lap and searched the Internet for Max Rigolo's name.

Mary looked up from her reading. "Why are you working on Sunday?"

"I'm not. I'm just looking up something out of curiosity."

Her sister knew her too well. Mary's eyes narrowed, and her

voice was low as she issued a caution. "You need to leave the investigating to Henry. He's in charge of the matter now."

"This is more about the Damar flycatcher than about the box." Abby filled Mary in on her conversation with Henry yesterday, in which she had passed along the info about the botched drug bust in Seattle. She also mentioned the lure she'd found in the spot marked on the map. "I'm not going to annoy Henry by going around looking for more suspects, but if this information about Max Rigolo will help him find the person responsible for hiding the box on the farm, then I'm certainly going to share it with him."

Finnegan got up and sniffed at the sliding glass doors. Abby felt a shiver go up her spine.

"You couldn't have to go again," Mary told the dog. "You just went out a few minutes ago."

Finnegan sighed and returned to his place beside her chair.

Abby knew that he wouldn't have accepted Mary's command so calmly if someone were outside, but that knowledge did little to quell the uneasiness in her stomach.

Their discussion over, Abby returned her gaze to the information displayed on the screen. In addition to being a highly acclaimed businessman, Max Rigolo was the founder and president of KIND, "Kids In Need of Dialysis." According to the group's Web site, many children with failing kidneys or who were waiting for a donor organ couldn't afford the life-giving dialysis or were refused medical coverage. Thus KIND was established to help desperate families with the sometimes overwhelming costs of keeping their children alive.

The group's slogan, "Be KIND," was blazoned in a banner across the top of the Web page. Underneath the banner, a hyperlink button read, "Support a Child." Abby clicked on the button, and it took her to a page asking for donations to help a child in need. Sponsors were promised a thank-you gift of a bracelet to wear that would also help promote the cause to others. Though it was hard to tell from the grainy photo, the bracelet also appeared to sport the slogan. Givers were urged to donate $250 to receive a gold-plated bracelet, $200 for a silver-plated one, $100 for copper or $10 for fabric. The really big donors could get full gold or even diamond-encrusted bracelets.

Considering that Abby had already written a check today that covered her budgeted amount of giving for the month, she had no desire to go in the hole financially to satisfy her curiosity. But for $10, she could forego her planned dinner out with Ida and invite her over for a home-cooked meal instead.

Her mind made up, Abby clicked the "Donate Now" button and filled in the requested information. But she still had plenty of questions.

How did this philanthropist, Max Rigolo, fit into the mystery? And where was the map they'd found in the tackle box supposed to lead to?

At this point, she couldn't see how the pieces fit together, but next time she saw Sergeant Cobb, she would ask him what he knew about Max Rigolo.

CHAPTER ✤ FOURTEEN

T HE FIRST THING ABBY DID
when she arrived at work on Monday—even before saying
hello to Hugo—was to check on the egg's progress.

The bufflehead duck scrambled around in his cage as she
entered the room. Abby covered his cage with a towel so he
wouldn't continue to be disturbed as she examined the egg and
then refilled the duck's food and water dishes.

As she approached the incubator, no apparent progress had
been made since her quick check-in yesterday. Ida would certainly be disappointed to hear that. Then again, if the chick
were already hatched, she would have been disappointed to
miss the miracle of Newton's entry into the world. Abby only
hoped that he would indeed enter the world. She was reaching
for the stethoscope to see if she could detect a sign of life inside
the tiny speckled shell when she became aware of two male
voices outside the lab door.

The elegant, distinguished voice was undoubtedly Hugo's.
The other—low, deep and authoritative—sounded like Henry
Cobb's.

She stepped into the hall and saw Hugo as dapper as ever and Henry in his smart-fitting green and tan sheriff's department uniform, writing something on a clipboard pad and looking as serious as she'd ever seen him. He hadn't bothered to remove his dark green campaign hat. Judging from his no-nonsense attitude, this was not a casual chat they were having. This was official business.

"Oh, Abby, there you are," Hugo said, waving her toward them. "Sergeant Cobb is here to take a report of some unusual activity we had over at the museum."

"Unusual activity?"

Henry finished his scribbling, then turned to face her. "It started with an automatic alarm to the dispatch center Friday night. I was going to mention it to you at church yesterday, but you were in such a hurry to leave. And on Saturday, I hadn't checked in with the station yet so I didn't know about it when I saw you."

She nodded, remembering being pulled over by Sergeant Cobb in Green Harbor because of her dramatic hair change. She patted her head self-consciously.

"Apparently, someone tried to enter the building through the back door. A deputy responded to the alarm shortly after nineteen hundred hours, but when he arrived, there was no one in the vicinity and no evidence of attempted entry."

"Nineteen hundred hours?" Abby said. "That would be—"

"Seven o'clock." Hugo finished the sentence.

"That would be shortly after Ida and I left. We spent some time together over here in the lab and then we returned to the museum, but we didn't hear anything. I remember resetting the alarm when we left the building." She turned to Hugo. "It's possible that I entered the wrong code, which triggered the alarm. I don't think I did though."

Henry made a note of that on his clipboard. "That's possible, but this morning Hugo found scratch marks in the wood around one of the museum's side windows. We're assuming someone may have tried to force their way in."

Abby rubbed her forehead. Hoping for a benign answer to the questions raised by the unusual activity at the museum, she asked, "What about wildlife? Spring is the time of year when animals are looking for sheltered places to give birth. Maybe a rodent chewed the wood."

"Maybe so," Henry said. "Then again, it could have been caused by pranksters. Hugo, you've been in the news recently, with the story about the Native American tools and things you found. Any time you draw attention to yourself publicly, you run the risk of making yourself a target."

"Why would anyone want to target Hugo?" Abby asked. "He's never done anything to hurt a soul. In fact, he's helped more people than most folks will ever meet in a lifetime."

Hugo smiled, obviously pleased by her adamant testimony.

"True, but not everyone thinks the way we do." Sergeant Cobb rubbed his chin. "Some are jealous when they see others receiving attention for their work and they want to lash out at them. Others are just looking for a target for their mischief. My guess is, it's the latter."

Abby felt her jaw muscles tighten. "Unfortunately, that makes sense. In a sick sort of way."

"And speaking of publicity," Hugo said, turning the conversation back to his favorite subject, the museum, "William Jansen is going to send a photographer to cover the new

Native American exhibit. He's not going to run another in-depth article like he did before, but the pictures and captions in *The Birdcall* will be enough to alert everyone that it's ready for viewing."

"Hugo, that's wonderful!" Abby was always happy to see good things happen to her favorite people. Considering the time and attention he put into the museum, he deserved a lot of good things in his life.

Sergeant Cobb flipped the pages down on his clipboard and tucked it under his arm. "Call the station if you see anything else that looks suspicious," he told them. "Since I'll be in and out, and patrolling the other islands, I may not be able to come personally, but any of the deputies will do a fine job for you. Meanwhile, I'll alert them to make extra runs past the museum during their patrols."

They both thanked him, and as Hugo returned to the museum to work on the Indian exhibit, Abby asked Sergeant Cobb to come back to the lab.

"Sure," he said, following her. "I wanted to talk to you anyway."

She settled into a chair as he took a seat on the other side of the lab table. "You have good news about Sam?" she asked.

"Only if you consider that the good news is that there's no bad news. As far as we can tell, we haven't found any evidence that he's involved in either acquiring or hiding the money. Sam's not currently a suspect, but he's still not totally in the clear."

"So does this mean that Thelma has stopped her accusations against him?"

"No, but we've investigated her claims and have found no evidence of Sam's involvement in her missing money either."

"Of course you didn't find any evidence. Because he didn't

do it." Abby fiddled with a pencil. "Sorry. I get a little heated when people are treated unfairly."

"Perfectly understandable. I have a thing about justice, too," he said, tapping the badge on his chest.

"Well, I'm thankful for any steps in the right direction. Now, once we catch that Jellybean guy, Sam will be vindicated for good."

"We?"

"Er, that was the imperial *we*. As in, everyone who's on the side of the law."

"Quick save," he said.

"The coffee just kicked in. Have you found out anything else about Jellybean?"

"That's what I wanted to tell you. But keep in mind, I can only share what's on public record."

"Of course," Abby said. "Do you think anyone on the island is involved?"

Her thoughts flitted back to the people with whom she'd already spoken. People who had access to large sums of money. William Jansen and his family's diaper business. Rick DeBow and the stockmarket. Even her own Hugo and the museum donations. Her stomach clenched at the thought, but she knew he could have been a suspect at one time. And then, of course, there was Vince Emory. Abby still didn't know what he'd been up to in Bellingham, even after their discussion yesterday. But that was okay with her. He could keep his business to himself, but she hoped he would step out of the shadows and work on setting things right between himself and Cheryl.

"That's still uncertain. It's possible that someone could have been working in tandem with the man involved in the shootout. But apparently Jellybean is only the tip of the iceberg."

"Did you catch him?"

"No, but I spoke with an investigator from the FBI when they came to retrieve the cash. It seems that Jellybean, whose real name is Jason Legowski, was a thug for a man who uses operatives to sell drugs on the street. And the key in the box was to a safe deposit box that holds a list of names of other dealers in the organization. Unfortunately, we still don't know which safe deposit box the key fits."

"What about the map? What's that supposed to lead to?"

"We're still not sure about that."

"And the ring?"

"Druggies fence stolen items all the time. We're checking with some insurance companies to see if one of them paid out a claim for this particular ring. That probably won't get us any closer to making an arrest, but it might return a family heirloom to its rightful owner."

"Now that you know Jellybean's name, the police can track him down and arrest him. And he can tell them which bank box the key fits."

"It's not that simple. Except for a brief contact when Jellybean tried to work a deal with the feds after he disappeared with the money, he dropped out of sight. At this point, it's suspected he may be dead. The last he was heard of, he'd joined a different drug ring and attempted to cheat his new boss. There's reason to believe his criminal cohorts caught up with him before the law did."

"Oh no." Abby felt sick.

"Actually, Jellybean is just a small cog in the wheel. His boss, the kingpin of the whole operation, also goes by a nickname. Mr. Z. He's the one we want. There are a few suspects, but there's never been enough evidence to prove that any of them are Mr. Z."

"What kind of deal was offered to Jellybean?"

"Well, after the bungled sting, Jellybean took off with Mr. Z's money, the hundred and fifteen grand. Naturally, Mr. Z was angry at losing the money, so it's speculated that Z was eager to rub Jellybean out."

Abby touched a hand to her cheek. "What a horrible way for people to live."

"Or die, which Jellybean didn't want to do. So he contacted the feds and offered to turn over the money and testify against Mr. Z on the condition they put him in the witness protection program."

"The little guy goes free so that the ringleader can be taken down."

"Personally, I'd like to see them all go to prison, but it does a greater good to break up these drug rings from the top down." Henry rubbed his fingers over the palm of his left hand, the action akin to washing away dirt. "Anyway, Jellybean agreed to discuss the particulars of the deal, and once he was safely incognito, he would turn over the goods. But before he could do so, Mr. Z was already on his heels. We assume that either Jellybean or an associate of his buried everything in the tackle box and took off."

Abby pondered the situation. "He probably wouldn't trust anyone else with that much money."

Henry nodded his agreement.

"So the items in the box were Jellybean's only bargaining chip with the authorities, and he knew Mr. Z wouldn't kill him until he knew that list of his dealers was destroyed."

"Apparently so." Henry stood and tapped the clipboard against his thigh. "I've given you this information because you were the one to find the box and turn it in, and I thought you'd want to know. I really don't want you to go any further with this, Abby. It's too dangerous."

She considered what he was asking of her.

While she paused, he added, "I can't tell you what to do, of course. I respect you too much for that. But I want you to stay safe."

"I appreciate your concern. And your letting me know the background on this case."

She could tell he was ready to go, but there was one more thing she needed to know.

"You said you and your officers didn't find anything when you went to Dorsal Island. Have you been back to look again?"

"No. The area was clean." He tipped his hat back. "You went there to poke around, didn't you?"

"No poking," she said, "but Bobby and I did have lunch over there this weekend. And while we were there, I found a fishing fly."

"Yeah? So people fish there sometimes."

"Well, because the lure was made of feathers from a rare Damar flycatcher, I checked around and found out it belonged to Max Rigolo."

"Oh yeah, that hotshot do-gooder?"

"You've heard of him?" Abby had been away from Sparrow Island for a number of years, so she wasn't up on who was who in the area.

"All of Washington has heard of him. Rigolo owns a huge logging company and is one of the richest men in the state.

He's also one of the most generous and raises a lot of money for some kids' charity."

Abby rubbed her chin.

"Rigolo's fishing fly on Dorsal Island is merely a coincidence," he said. "Don't waste your time or energy on this. Some of the top law enforcement people are on this case. Let them take care of it."

He stood to go.

"Please, Abby. This is getting serious now, and I don't want you or anyone else getting hurt."

"SEE THE ODD TIP ON THE BEAK?" Abby said later that afternoon, pointing past the large jagged opening in the shell. "That's the egg tooth. Since the baby's beak is rather soft prior to hatching, the hard point is designed to help him break through the shell. Soon after Newton finishes hatching, the egg tooth will fall off and his beak will be like any other house sparrow's."

Ida bounced on her toes. "This is so exciting. I've never watched a bird hatch before." She was still wearing her uniform, having come straight from the café after her lunch shift ended at four o'clock so as not to miss a minute of this time she had waited almost two weeks to see. "He seems tired. Can't we help him a little by taking off that bit of shell that's blocking him from coming out?"

"He *is* tired, but this is something he'll have to do on his own. The struggling actually helps stimulate his circulation and breathing. So the only thing we can do now is watch."

"And pray."

"Yes, of course."

"Poor little Newton. I know just how you feel." Ida exhaled a large sigh. "Life is such a struggle."

The last time Abby and Ida had been together in the lab, her young friend had been down because the bird hadn't shown signs of hatching. And now, although she seemed cheered by the bird's gradual emergence into the world, there was something else on her mind.

"What are you struggling with, Ida?"

The girl turned around and sat on the countertop that lined the lab's wall. "Oh, it seems like everything lately. I know God loves me and wants good things for me," she said, "but sometimes it feels like He's blocking me from everything I want. I try so hard, but all my effort doesn't get me anywhere."

Abby nodded compassionately but didn't say anything, knowing that sometimes it's best to stay silent while a friend vents.

"When I became a believer, I thought things would change for the better. But I'm still in the same boring job, on this same boring island and doing the same boring juggling act to pay my bills. What am I doing wrong, Abby?"

Ida was having a crisis of faith and Abby was aware that whatever she said could either help or hurt her friend's relationship with God. She took a deep breath, closed her eyes briefly and sent a prayer heavenward. A little divine help would be needed to bring this confused lamb back to the flock.

"Could it be that you're wanting God to be like Santa Claus?"

Ida frowned for a moment as she thought. "But the Bible says in Matthew 21:22, 'If you believe, you will receive whatever you ask for in prayer.' I've tried to do the right things. I've been more patient with the waitress who tries to boss the rest of us around, and I've been reading the Bible and getting more active in church. I even stopped watching that reality television show where friends take advantage of each other to win prizes. And that used to be my favorite program."

Abby was aware of the show and was shocked when it had become a big hit. *Chums and Chumps* glorified putting yourself first, and each week it rewarded those who lied to and betrayed their friends to get what they wanted.

"Being a believer isn't about God seeing things our way," Abby said gently. "It's about us trying to do God's will, even when we don't see things His way."

"So I should see that my life is destined to always be a struggle? That doesn't seem right."

At that moment, Newton gave a renewed effort, pushing against what held him back, and finally fell against the padded base of the incubator. His head, shoulders and most of his chest and back were now out of the shell. The fragment that Ida had wanted to remove earlier now lay at the bottom of the incubator beside him. The bird's eyes, still tightly closed, appeared blue beneath the thin pink skin that covered his body. He was panting now from the exertion. Abby knew that, although he was now near exhaustion, the eventual reward would be worth it all.

"Sometimes I wish I could be more like Newton." Abby reached in to take away the shell fragment. Most likely it wouldn't hurt him if she left it there, but she didn't want it to impede his movements. "He doesn't know that his struggle is temporary. He might even think that this is the way life will always be. But he pushes on anyway. That's what faith is all about."

"Yeah, but his struggle is over in a few hours. I want to do

God's will, Abby. But does that mean I have to live like a pauper for the rest of my life? The Bible promises showers of blessings, but I haven't felt any drops yet. So I guess I'll have to water my own garden."

"And how will you do that, Ida?"

"Well, the blessings don't seem to be here on Sparrow Island, so I'll have to go elsewhere to find them. Seattle, maybe. Or perhaps even outside of Washington."

Abby gave her a sympathetic smile. "That's probably the way Sarah felt when God took so long to give her and Abraham a child. They were getting up in years and it didn't look like God was going to bless her with a baby. So she sent Abraham her handmaid, Hagar, to produce an heir."

"So what's wrong with that? During those times it was acceptable to continue the family line through a servant if the wife couldn't conceive."

"What was wrong was that they were looking at the situation through their own foggy perception. God had promised Abraham *and Sarah* a child. Not Abraham and Hagar."

"So what took Him so long to give them the blessing He promised?"

"Perhaps they weren't ready yet to receive it. God was patient, though, and He waited until they had matured in their faith so He could trust them with the blessing."

Sitting on the counter, Ida swung her sneakered feet back and forth. "It's just frustrating to have to wait. Even Ryan is trying my patience. He promised he was going to come to Sparrow Island for a visit, but now he says he's too busy with work. Long-distance relationships are the pits."

"Having kept up a long-distance relationship with my family for many years, I can certainly sympathize."

Ida leaned over from her perch on the counter and stared into the incubator. "How much longer will it take for him to be free?"

"It shouldn't be long now. All he has left to do is kick the shell off his legs and lower body."

While they waited, Abby told Ida her concern that she may have set the security system incorrectly when they left the museum Friday. And that something—possibly an animal—had scratched the ledge outside her office window.

"Speaking of animals," Abby continued, "Mary's dog acted strangely again last night. She's convinced it's a tomcat trying to make time with Blossom, but I have a funny feeling it might be a person."

"Do you think it could have been a reporter looking for something new to write about the money you found? I heard they sometimes go through people's trash cans to get information for their stories."

"There would be no reason for anyone to do that. All they'd have to do is pick up the phone or knock on the door. It would have been easy enough for a reporter to contact me directly."

Ida made a noise that sounded like snort. "I wish Thelma Rogers would contact you directly. It's getting tiresome listening to her grumbling. It has gotten so the waitresses draw straws to see who has to wait on her."

"That bad, eh?" Abby had hoped Thelma would grow tired of her vendetta against Sam and let it drop. Unfortunately, once she got an idea set in her head, it was almost impossible to change her mind.

"More than you realize." Ida paused, apparently weighing her words. "She says she's going to sue."

"Sue whom?"

"I don't know. She just wants her two hundred dollars back." Ida slid down off the counter. "And she's still ranting about that letter she got, saying she never made any donation to a children's charity."

Abby paused in preparing the numbered band that would go around the bird's leg. Generally, the identification anklets were reserved for rarer species than sparrows, but since Ida was already so attached to Newton, this would be a good way to track him in case he turned up again someday.

"Children's charity? Did Thelma say which one?"

"She might have, but I started tuning her out after a while."

Abby paced the floor. Could this be another piece of the tackle box puzzle? Or was it a different puzzle altogether?

The only way to find out would be to see the letter herself.

Ida tapped her arm. "Oh, look! Newton's out in the open."

Sure enough, the chick's fat little body lay like a pink, stubby-winged blob on the bottom of the incubator.

At least one thing was turning out right today.

CHAPTER ❧ FIFTEEN

ABBY ARRIVED AT LITTLE Flock Church early for Wednesday night Bible study and whiled away the extra time chatting with Janet at her desk. Their topics covered everything from Patricia Hale's latest mission project to the hatching of Newton. And, of course, updates on the tackle box.

Janet crossed her legs and jiggled one sandal-clad foot. Abby noticed that she had disregarded the rule from their childhood about waiting until Memorial Day to wear white.

"I heard you and Mary got peeped recently," Janet said.

Abby rubbed her arm. Gooseflesh.

"Mary thinks it's one of Blossom's suitors."

"What do you think?"

"I'm not sure. I *thought* I saw a face the first time we heard the noise outside our window, but it happened so fast I'm not certain what I saw."

"Are you thinking what I'm thinking?"

Considering the wild spins Janet's mind took on occasion,

there was no telling what she was thinking. "It depends. Does it have anything to do with a vacationing actress burying a script on my parents' farm?"

Janet laughed. "That could have happened, I suppose." Then she turned serious. "I'm concerned that the prowling around your house has something to do with your box of money. People get strange ideas in their heads sometimes. Someone could have read that article in the paper and decided to hang around and see if there's more where that came from."

Abby twisted her mouth and gnawed the inside of her cheek. "If that were the case, they'd be prowling around my parents' house since that's where the article mentioned the money was found." She paused a moment and said a silent prayer for God to surround her parents with His loving protection. "It wouldn't make sense for anyone to spy on Mary and me."

"It would if they think you held out on some of the money. For all they know, you could have found twice as much as you claimed was in the box and kept the difference for yourself."

Abby gasped. "Is that what people are saying?"

"Of course not. They just haven't thought of it yet because they don't read as many mystery novels and watch as many thriller movies as I do."

"Let's hope they don't start now."

Abby wasn't sure which was worse, the thought of being peeped in her own home by some sicko, or having someone out there who was bent on stealing money from her that she didn't even have.

"Oh, by the way, Vince Emory wants to talk to you."

It was getting closer to the time for Bible study to begin. Abby stood to go. If she didn't see Vince before the class, she'd try to catch him afterward. "Did he seem upset?"

Before Janet could answer, Thelma Rogers popped in to ask her about the new lesson books for Bible study. They weren't due to be distributed until the end of the month, but Janet gave her one anyway. Thelma had her own ideas of how things should run, and people generally found it easier to just go along with whatever she wanted than try to make her conform.

Thelma threw Abby a suspicious glare and was turning to leave when Abby commented that she hoped she'd found her money by now.

"Of course I haven't found the money yet. Not unless you count the letter I got, thanking me for donating nearly the same amount to some charity I've never heard of."

"Do you happen to have the letter with you?"

"As a matter of fact, I do." The older woman riffled through an overflowing black purse, not an easy task given the number of pockets and zippers it contained. Out came tissues, the most wrinkled of which she tossed into the trash can. Then a breath-mint wrapper with one candy remaining, bent hairpins, ink pen caps, safety pins, a two-inch pencil stub, a nail board with the top layer peeling up, a grocery receipt, a folding hairbrush and assorted papers. Most of those also went into the trash can. The pencil stub, hairbrush and breath mint went back into the purse.

Abby leaned over the trash can and pointed. "Isn't that a bank slip? You might need it."

Still intent on her search, Thelma dismissively waved her hand. "It'll show up on my monthly statement." She was fishing in a different compartment now. "Here it is."

The paper was presented to Abby with a flourish, as if this alone proved Thelma's claims that Sam had taken her money.

Abby looked at the letter. It was from an organization called

Children of America. The body of the letter thanked Thelma for her donation of $225 and invited her to contribute again in the enclosed, self-addressed envelope.

"May I have a copy of this?" Abby asked.

Thelma paused to consider her request. "A copy would be all right. But the original stays with me as evidence for my lawsuit."

Janet pressed the ON button on the photocopier next to her desk.

Abby placed the letter in Janet's outstretched hand and waited while she put the paper on the glass and pressed the COPY button.

"Thelma, I'll look into this for you, but I'd like for you to hold off on your lawsuit a little while longer."

"It looks like I'll have to wait," she declared. "It'll take some time to save up more money to pay the lawyer."

Without so much as a thank-you or a kiss-my-foot, Thelma refolded the letter and stuffed it back in her purse beside the lesson book Janet had given her, then left.

Abby thanked Janet for copying the letter, then followed Thelma out into the chapel. With her focus still on the letter, she wasn't aware of anyone else nearby until Cheryl Emory touched her elbow. Abby jumped, and the paper she was holding went sailing.

In a gentlemanly gesture, Vince picked up the photocopy and returned it to Abby with a bow. His wife smiled at his playfulness.

"I'm glad I found you," Vince said. "I've been wanting to talk to you about what you said the other day."

Abby bit the inside of her upper lip. "Is everything okay?"

"Everything is perfect," Cheryl said. "After you talked to

Vince on Sunday, he came home and confessed everything. Actually, he waited until the next day so it wouldn't color my Mother's Day celebrations, but everything is out in the open now and we owe it all to you."

Cheryl put her arms around Abby and kissed her cheek.

"You saved our marriage."

Abby could only stare in surprise as the happy wife stepped away from her and grasped her husband's arm. "I'm glad that you two have worked out your, er, marital difficulties."

Vince patted his wife's hand. "Just as you suggested, I had been keeping a secret from Cheryl. Unfortunately, that secret made her think I was betraying her with another woman."

"You weren't?" Abby asked.

"Of course not. What happened was that the company I work for suffered some economic setbacks, and they tried to save money by cutting the hours—and the pay—of some of the employees. Since part of my public relations job dealt with the company's charitable endeavors, they decided to cut my pay, cancel the charity work and have me focus exclusively on publicity campaigns that would draw in more business."

Abby nodded. "And I assume the Grace Girls' organization was one of the charities that your company abandoned?"

"I had done so much work to investigate the home and line up a hefty company grant for them. Unfortunately, they weren't the only ones that were disappointed. Due to the drop in my pay, I couldn't fulfill some of my personal charitable commitments either."

Abby knew he was talking about his private donations to the church's yearly Bible camp, but she said nothing about it.

Cheryl affectionately rubbed her husband's back. "Vince was so sweet. He tried to keep the news from me because he didn't want to worry me. The problem was that I had been worrying about something far worse than a financial setback."

Vince gazed down at her, his eyes filled with love. Then, to Abby, he said, "And I have to admit, I didn't want Cheryl to have to work outside the home. My ego kept telling me that I should be the sole provider."

"What he didn't know," Cheryl interjected, "was that with the kids grown and gone, I had too much time on my hands, and I *wanted* a part-time job. So this way we have the best of both worlds. Vince left his job and is going to work from home, organizing fund-raising programs for various charities, and he's going to be a consultant for the Grace Girls' Home. And I'll be working a few days a week as a guest relations clerk at The Dorset. Vince and I will actually get to spend more time together than we ever did before."

"That's right," said Vince. "And that day you saw me at the Monroe Building in Bellingham, I was applying with an executive search agency for a new job. But after praying about it—and your talk with me—I knew I couldn't go back into the cutthroat business world. I had to put my efforts into something that really matters to me."

Abby smiled her relief. "I had no idea all this was going on. All I knew was that you were carrying a heavy burden."

"We're both so excited about our new beginnings," Vince said. "How can I thank you?"

Clutching her Bible under her arm, Abby assured them there was no need for thanks. She was just glad that acting on her Sunday morning Bible lesson had reaped such wonderful results.

Cheryl let go of her husband's arm. "I'm going to go save us a seat," she told him and ambled away.

"There is one thing you could do." Abby thought of the

letter in her purse. "Since you're experienced in working with various charities, perhaps you could take a look at this letter."

She handed him the document Thelma had shared with her. "Can you tell me how someone could get a letter thanking them for a donation they never made?"

He glanced over the letter. "I've never heard of this group before."

"Neither have I, but I tend to focus on just a few charities that either the church recommends or that have special meaning to me."

Vince handed the paper back to her. "It could be that she has donated to this charity before, and the computer database picked up an old list."

Abby frowned and shook her head. "No, Thelma insists she's never given these people any money."

"Maybe she doesn't recognize the name because she donated to a smaller charity that falls under this umbrella group's name. Or maybe they got their lists mixed up. Perhaps they meant to send her a solicitation letter instead."

"Yes, I suppose it could be that." Remembering the one-last-question tactic that she liked to use, Abby decided to ask him a broader-scope question. "Is it possible the charity could have had some corrupt intent when they sent this letter?"

"I suppose it's possible." He grinned. "Do you want me to make like Janet and come up with a scenario that's worthy of a movie of the week?"

Abby returned the smile. "Sure, why not?"

"Well, let's say the organization bought a mailing list of people who've donated to other charities. Then they sent a letter to them, pretending to be one of their charities of choice."

"Why would they do that?"

"It's extremely hard to get that first-time donation from patrons."

Abby knew that to be true from the conversations she'd had with Hugo about the museum's collections.

"But once someone has decided that something is a legitimate and worthy charity, they're more likely to donate again. It's possible this Children of America group was pretending to have received the $225, hoping she would take their word for it and assume she'd just forgotten having done it. Then it would be easier for her to make the choice to supposedly 'continue' donating to that charity."

"How devious."

"True, but it's not very likely to happen. There are government agencies in place to police that sort of thing, and legitimate charities don't want to take a chance on ruining their reputations."

Piano music drifted to them from the front of the church. "That's our cue to take our seats," Abby said.

As she joined her family who just arrived, the things Vince told her continued to weigh on her mind. During the opening prayer, she bowed her head and released her concerns to God so she could focus her heart on worshipping. And she thanked Him for the blessing He had bestowed on the Emorys.

At the back of her mind, though, she wondered if there might be another, more dubious explanation for the letter Thelma had received.

ABBY PARKED HER CAR IN THE GARAGE, next to Mary's van, and grabbed the paper sack of groceries from the passenger seat. After tonight's Bible study, she'd told Mary she'd meet her at home and then made a quick stop at The Green Grocer for oatmeal, then bought some other things while she was there.

She was about to click the garage door closed when she heard something outside. Thinking Finnegan was outside and wanted in, she walked to the backyard. But it wasn't a dog she found by the butterfly bush.

Abby stopped in her tracks and peered into the darkness that was broken only by a flashlight aimed at the ground. Although the moon was partially obscured by clouds, she could make out the shape of someone bending over.

Gripping the grocery bag tightly in front of her chest, Abby quickly debated whether to make a dash back into the garage. But if he'd already seen her, and if she did try to make an escape, he could follow her inside before she could close the automatic door.

Abby's thoughts flashed to Janet's conjecture that someone might want the money that they assumed she'd kept for herself. If that was the case, this could be a matter of survival.

She reached into her bag for anything to use as a weapon of defense, and her fingers closed around a heavy can. The bag made a crinkling sound, and the hulk in front of her straightened and turned toward her. The flashlight shone in her eyes, blinding her as the person made a move toward her.

"Lord, help us both," she cried. Abby flung the can, fully intending to conk the guy senseless. Better him than her. Unfortunately, it slipped as it was leaving her fingers and went slightly off target.

"Ow!"

Immediately, she grabbed another can from the bag. He rushed toward her, and it wasn't until he'd grabbed her arm to prevent a better-aimed throw that she realized he was shouting her name.

"Abby, it's just me."

Her fingers relaxed, and she let out a shaky breath. "Henry?"

He took the can from her grasp, then helped her set the bag on the ground. "Yes, it's Henry."

He turned the flashlight on the can he'd taken from her. Black beans. She had bought them to use in a wild rice and corn dish for her and Mary.

"You were going to 'bean' me with this can?"

"Not you, exactly. I thought you were a prowler." She remembered his cry of pain when she'd thrown the can. "Did I hurt you?"

"Naw, just clipped my elbow. I was more surprised than hurt."

"What were you doing out here, hiding by the bushes? Have *you* been peeping in our windows?"

"No, of course not." He sounded indignant. "Mary mentioned that you two heard something around the house again. After the false alarm and possible attempted entry at the museum, I thought it would be a good idea to come by and check things out for myself."

"Not to mention scaring the life out of me."

"Sorry about that."

The sliding glass door to the back deck opened and Finnegan came rushing out. Mary was right behind him, rolling out onto the porch in her wheelchair.

When Abby bent to pick up the other can of beans—now dented—that she'd thrown, the dog kissed her face. "Where were you when I was out here being scared to death?"

Mary answered for the dog. "He was sitting in the living room by the sliding glass door, wagging his tail. Henry, I didn't know you were coming over tonight."

"While I was driving by, I thought I saw a movement in the yard, so I parked up the road and walked back to the house. By that time, whoever it was had gone, but he left behind a piece of evidence." Henry walked back to the place where he'd been crouching earlier and lifted the heavy flashlight from his belt to shine it on the ground. "Take a look at this."

Abby followed the direction of the flashlight beam. Sure enough, there in the dirt was the imprint of a large sneaker.

"It wouldn't hurt to get a motion detector," Henry suggested. "Then, if someone comes within a certain distance of the house, a spotlight will flood the yard and scare them off."

Abby felt funny about this. Henry was not one to overreact, so his quiet demeanor told her this might be more serious than she'd originally thought. "Maybe Janet was right. Maybe someone is scoping us out to see if we kept some of the money from the tackle box."

"That's ridiculous," Mary said.

"No matter what the reason," Abby said, "I'm not going to sit around while someone trespasses on our property."

Abby was angry now. Until now, the case of the tackle box and money was one of curiosity and a desire to defend the honor of their family friend. But now . . . now it was personal.

"I promised you I'd stop looking into the case," she told Henry. "Well, I don't care about the box or the money anymore. What I do care about is catching the person who's scaring my sister and me."

CHAPTER ✿ SIXTEEN

IT WAS PROMISING TO BE A beautiful May morning. The sun shone its warm rays down on the foursome gathered by Mary's back deck, and a gentle breeze scuttled through the rhododendrons, ruffling the leaves and budding flowers.

The only thing that marred this beautiful Thursday, Mary thought, was the purpose of the visit from her father and Sam. The two men went about their task with grim expressions and few words. Finnegan walked between them in a supervisory manner, first sniffing the ladder George held and then inspecting the stack of tools on the deck before lying down to watch.

Mary tucked the item she'd brought from the house into the corner between her hip and the side of the chair, then fluffed her pink-flowered skirt over it. She pushed her wheelchair to the center of the backyard where she could watch while George and Abby called instructions to Sam, who was up on the ladder installing a floodlight the size of her head. The motion detector attached to the device would turn on the light if anyone should wander through their yard after dark. Mary understood that they were doing what needed to be done, but she wished they wouldn't go so overboard.

"I didn't think you'd be installing circus lights," she told Abby. "That thing is going to light up the whole western side of the island every time a chipmunk runs through the yard."

"We can put in a smaller bulb after the prowler is caught." Abby sighed. "I'm sorry about all this disruption. Perhaps I should have just turned everything over to Henry as soon as I found the box. Before I opened it. Then you wouldn't be dealing with some intruder lurking around your home."

"Don't be silly," Mary said. "First of all, this is our home. And second, you could no more stifle your curiosity than I could stifle my urge to wear bright colors."

Today's designated color was pink. Her skirt featured a riot of pale pink, fuschia and purple blooms splashed upon a background of white. She wished Abby would occasionally let herself go and enjoy the thrill of indulging herself in the gorgeous colors God had given them to enjoy.

"Have you seen the latest *Birdcall*?" she asked Abby. "There are a couple of pictures of the new Native American exhibit that's opening this weekend."

"No, I haven't had a chance to look at it yet. I'm sure Hugo will bring it to my attention when I get to work."

"Speaking of work, aren't you supposed to be there now?" Mary took note of the serviceable slacks and solid beige blouse. What she wouldn't give to be allowed free rein to dress Abby in some snazzy outfits and brilliant colors.

"I told Hugo I'd be in after this is done."

As the proprietor of her own flower shop, Mary had the flexibility to go in and work or turn things over to her manager's capable hands as the need arose. She was glad that Abby had similar leeway to set her own hours occasionally.

Right now, Abby was squinting into the sunlight as she watched Sam install the light on the back of the house. She looked so serious that Mary wanted to lighten the mood.

"So, who do you think this guy was peeping?" Mary asked. "Me or you?"

Her sister seemed jolted from her thoughts, and she turned to face Mary. "What?"

She wasn't getting it, so Mary decided to push the subject to tease Abby out of her solemnity. "It must have been you that he was trying to get an eyeful of. I was fighting a bit of a cold at the time, so he certainly wasn't interested in looking at my red nose. But you..." Mary swept her hand in a graceful arc toward Abby. "You were the one who'd just had that dynamite permanent. I'm sure he was trying to get a peek at the glam creature who dazzled everyone with her simple but elegant beauty."

Sam stopped what he was doing and turned around on the ladder. "You have been looking mighty sharp lately, Abby."

"Of course she looks sharp," George insisted. "What else would you expect from a Stanton?"

Mary agreed. "They're right, Abby. And it's looking even better now that the curls are starting to loosen up."

Even though Sam and George had returned to their work, Abby looked uncomfortable with all the attention focused on her appearance. "Do you want the camera now?" she asked Sam.

It had been the farmhand's idea to install a camera that would snap a picture whenever the automatic light was activated. The bracket to hold the camera was already in place.

"Not yet," he said. "First, I need to secure the sensor."

Mary reached for the item she'd hidden earlier in her skirt folds and handed it to Abby. "While you're at it, why don't you have him install this too?"

Abby gazed down at the can of beans in her hand, and for the first time that morning she smiled. "Why not? It almost worked last night."

"Every woman should carry a can of beans in her purse. When you're not using it to fend off potential attackers, you can lift it ten or fifteen times in each hand to fend off osteoporosis."

Abby giggled, and Mary was pleased to hear the happy sound.

"Mary, I'm really sorry about what almost happened to Henry last night." She picked at the paper around the can. "He was a good sport about it, though."

"Don't worry about it," Mary told her. "I talked to him this morning and he said his elbow isn't even sore. Maybe you should do some pitching practice with Bobby. Improve your aim, you know."

Abby shook her head. "I doubt Sandy McDonald would want me throwing cans of beans at her boy."

Now it was Mary's turn to laugh. It heartened her to know that Abby hadn't lost her sense of humor to the prowler. "Abby, don't you worry about the person who's been snooping around here. It's probably just some kid's idea of a prank."

"If so, that kid has mighty big feet."

"Well, maybe it's a teenager. They shoot up like dandelions. At any rate, they'll tire of us soon and move on to some other entertainment that snags their interest."

"Yes, I suppose you're right," Abby said, but her tone didn't match her words.

"HAVE YOU SEEN *The Birdcall* yet?"

Hugo stepped into the lab where Abby was feeding Newton, the house sparrow.

He didn't sound as excited about the newspaper notice as Mary had when she'd mentioned it earlier this morning.

"Not yet."

Abby had told him about the prowler already. Like the true friend that he was, he had offered to pop in and check on them in the evenings and be on standby in case they needed him. "Any time, day or night," he had told her. "You know my number." And in that gesture she'd been reminded once again that she'd made the right decision to return home and be with her family . . . and the friends who were now becoming like family to her.

He handed her the paper and waited while she read the long captions under the pictures. The descriptions were to the point, identifying the pieces and noting the museum's hours. Abby was a little surprised, though, that a dollar value—a highly inflated value at that—had been assigned to the artifacts they had received from the house on Wayfarer Point Road.

"I don't know why it was necessary to put a price on pieces of history," she told him, "but it could be a good thing. Perhaps it'll stir public curiosity and draw more people to the museum to see what all the hoopla is about."

"In an ideal world, that might happen," Hugo said. "Unfortunately, there's not going to be an exhibit."

Abby set down the feeding dropper and returned Newton to his warm brooder box. "No exhibit?" she said, giving Hugo her full attention. "Of course there's going to be an exhibit."

Hugo rolled up the paper and rapped it against the palm of his hand. "Remember the woman who gave us the items from her grandfather's estate? Well, she read the article yesterday and was intrigued by the dollar signs in the photo captions."

"Oh no." Abby could see where this was heading.

"She wants everything back," Hugo said, confirming what she feared. "Apparently, her son convinced her that she could have sold the stuff on the Internet and made a killing from it. And when she saw in the newspaper what it was worth, she had second thoughts about giving it to us. I wonder where the paper got that ridiculous price tag."

"But she signed a release." Greed was one thing Abby had never understood. With all the blessings the good Lord bestowed on the world every single day, how could anyone think that wasn't enough? "She can't take it back. That paper she signed when she donated the items to the museum is a legal document."

"According to Mrs. Nygaard, we didn't disclose the full value of the materials before she signed them over to the museum." Hugo harrumphed. "She said if she'd known how much everything was worth, she wouldn't have given it to us."

"What are you going to do?" Abby walked over to the cabinet where she kept samples of feathers from every imaginable bird and picked up the Damar flycatcher lure she'd left at the lab after her visit to the Rod 'n' Reel.

Hugo grabbed his jacket's lapels. "I'd rather not have any bad publicity from this. Perhaps we can offer her a token sum to settle the matter once and for all."

Abby looked up from the lure in her hands. "I don't see her taking it."

"Neither do I." He leaned closer to see the feather-covered hook in her hands. "That's the worst job of fly tying I've ever seen."

"That's essentially what Rod, over at the Rod 'n' Reel, said."

"I've never seen anyone stick foil around where the feather quills and hook and spoon are joined. It seems like that would cause inefficient movement through the water."

Her curiosity piqued, Abby gently removed the shiny foil. A few grains of sand fell from the wrapping onto the countertop where she worked. Underneath the foil, a tangled mess of dark string attested to the fly maker's lack of skill.

"Apparently, the aluminum was placed over everything to keep the string from working loose." She set the fly back down on the counter. "Well, we have our work cut out for us, trying to get that woman to change her mind."

"A leopard frog would sooner change its spots," Hugo said.

"If God can change a creature's coloring, then He can certainly change a person's mind."

"May your concern be as a prayer." Hugo rolled the newspaper into a tight tube again.

In a burst of insight, Vince Emory came to Abby's mind, and she thought of the blessing a simple verse had brought to him and his wife. In a similar way, Hugo needed to "go and be reconciled" with Mrs. Nygaard as Jesus had advised in Matthew 5:24.

Without revealing specific details, Abby shared with Hugo the success she had seen when this advice was followed recently. "How could anything but good come of following God's own advice?"

He stared at her for a long moment, almost appearing to peer through her, so deep was he in thought. Then, for the first time since they'd started discussing the dilemma Mrs. Nygaard had presented, she saw a smile return to his handsome face.

Briefly, and so lightly that she was barely aware of it, Hugo touched her shoulder. "You're a wise woman, Abby Stanton."

Lifting his hand, he rubbed his chin as he considered her words. "This isn't about getting what I want for the museum exhibit. It's about getting right with Mrs. Nygaard."

After wishing Abby a productive day, he left with a promise to try to salvage the Indian exhibit . . . and the museum's relationship with its donor.

She was heartsick for Hugo's predicament and did the only thing she could do in a case like this . . . exactly what he had suggested.

Turned her concern into a prayer.

When she opened her eyes, Abby picked up the lure and walked over to the cabinet to store it with feathers of a similar family. She had just placed the piece on the tray when a tiny glint of silver in the tangled string caught her attention.

Pushing her glasses closer to the bridge of her nose, Abby brought the fly closer. Carefully, she picked loose the string so that a single strand dangled from the feathers' quills.

Though it had been dulled by its exposure to the elements, there was no mistaking the black string streaked with tiny silver fibers.

IT TOOK A COUPLE OF NIGHTS for it to happen, but the camera and floodlight finally did their job. Saturday morning Abby sat at the picnic table in the backyard of her parents' farm, the large blowup of the photo in front of her. This would probably be the only picture they'd get of the prowler. Now that he'd been made aware of the floodlight that was triggered by motion in the yard, he would either stop coming around at night, or he'd change tactics to get whatever it was he wanted. So this photo was their one and only shot at identifying him.

In the lower corner of the picture, between the deck rail and the garbage can, was a grainy image of a person walking in a half-crouched posture. Only a small portion of the face could be seen, but not enough to identify him as his head was turned slightly away. He appeared to have short dark hair, but it was hard to tell for certain because of the darkness and shadows that distorted the profile. Abby wasn't a hundred percent certain, but the posture and the general breadth of shoulders led her to believe the person in the photo was a man.

A large sigh escaped her and sent the paper floating a few inches over the rough picnic table planks. Abby slapped a hand down to catch it and gave the photo another closer look.

It was hard to make it out because of the shadows. With the dark background of the night and the dark clothing of the subject, most of the colors in the photo showed up as varying shades of black, brown and gray. Abby studied the figure more intently, going over every single aspect of the clothing.

And then she saw it—so dark it almost looked like just another shade of gray, but once she zeroed in on it, there was definitely a touch of red on the jacket. The subtle red formed a point that hit the apex of the curve of the sleeve where it joined the shoulder. Joining the point, a straight line trailed up the center of the sleeve, forming what appeared to be a stylized upward-pointing arrow.

Abby took off her glasses and hooked them through the buttonhole in her denim outer shirt. Seeking to rest her eyes from the strain of squinting, she let her gaze drift over the landscape of her parents' yard and saw a blur that she could tell was Sam walking toward her from the direction of the barn.

"Were you able to make out the intruder?" he asked as he

approached the table and settled himself on the seat across from her.

She pushed the photo toward him. While he scowled at the image, she resisted pointing out the distinguishing design she'd found on the sleeve. If she stayed quiet about it, he might find something she'd failed to see, so she wanted to let him approach it with a fresh perspective.

"Don't show this to Thelma," he said straightening on the bench and pushing the picture back to her. "She'll swear it's me."

He didn't sound angry about his run-ins with Thelma. Just weary. Abby found herself growing frustrated for him.

She took another look. "There's no way anyone could mistake this person for you. Look, he seems taller and less muscular."

He picked it up this time and held it closer to his eyes. "Abby, forget what I said about Thelma. It's not right to match unkindness with more unkindness."

"Don't you worry about that," Abby assured him. "Sometimes a person needs to let off a little steam to a friend."

He gave her a smile that clearly let her know he appreciated her overlooking his outburst. Once again, Abby was glad that this good-hearted, thoughtful man was such a source of support to her family, both as a farmhand and as a friend.

While he was still staring at the picture, she pointed out the grainy red of the arrow pattern on the person's jacket sleeve. "Do you think there's any significance to that?" she asked.

Slowly he shook his head. "It's been a long time since I hung around with the 'element,' so to speak, so I don't know if that's a gang symbol or just a trendy design."

"Gang?" It sickened Abby to think such influences might have come to Sparrow Island. For the most part they were insulated from many of the things that tempted young people today. That didn't mean there was never any crime on the island, only that there was less opportunity for it to take root and flourish. "Let's hope it's just the latest fashion trend."

"Show it around," Sam urged. "Someone might recognize the jacket."

He was right. Someone might be familiar with the design on the jacket. Fortunately, Abby knew just the person to ask.

AFTER A QUICK TRIP to Holloway's Hardware, Abby found the Springhouse Café packed with an enthusiastic weekend lunch crowd. From her vantage point at the front of the restaurant, Abby could see Ida and the other waitresses busily hustling from table to table. She supposed she should wait to talk to Ida when she wasn't working, then discarded the idea. She decided she could steal a moment of her friend's time by sitting at her table and ordering a cup of clam chowder, always one of the best-selling items on the menu.

When Ida came to take her order, she didn't perch on the edge of the chair as she might have if business had been slower. So Abby got straight to the point.

She handed a copy of the photo to Ida as she rattled off her order and asked if anything about the person in the picture looked familiar.

Ida studied the photo very intently, her expression serious. She reached for her neck, then quickly put her hand back down.

"I took it to Aaron Holloway a little while ago," Abby said, referring to the young man at the hardware store that Mary had wanted to match Ida up with. Since Aaron had lived in Seattle until recently, Abby had thought—correctly, it turned out—that he might be up on the latest trends among the younger crowd. "He said this is a design the 'cool' kids like to wear. Supposedly, it's a very expensive brand."

Ida straightened and handed the picture back to Abby. "On my paycheck, I wouldn't know."

She seemed stiff in her response, and Abby remembered Ida's dream of living a glamorous lifestyle. Perhaps the comment about the expensive jacket had reminded Ida once again of all the pricey things she wished for but didn't have.

Abby held the photo out to her. "Would you mind showing this around to see if anyone else recognizes this person? With all the customers you see during the course of a day, there's a chance one of them might know who it is."

Ida didn't take the the photo from her. Instead, she tucked her hands into the apron that hung from her waist. "I'm sorry, but I won't be able to do that," she said. "My manager might not approve."

Her answer surprised Abby since from the start Ida had been so gung ho about helping her track down leads. But, after giving it a little more thought, Abby realized she'd been wrong to assume her young friend could mix a personal project with her work duties. With tourist season picking up as summer approached, Ida would have her hands full serving so many extra customers. In addition, it was quite possible that Ida was now tired of playing the sleuthing game. After all, not everyone would choose to relentlessly pursue a problem the way Abby did.

"Yes, of course," she told Ida. "Your job must come first."

CHAPTER ❦ SEVENTEEN

Tuesday afternoon, the sun played hide-and-seek with the clouds. For a few minutes, the day would be bright with warmth and promise, and a moment later everything would darken and the air even seemed cooler. Then it started all over again.

No one at church had been able to identify the person in the photo. Abby's family was just as baffled as everyone else. So after a short visit with the family at the Stanton Farm, Abby picked up her binoculars and birding journal and left for a walk down the gravel path behind her parents' house. The path wound between two alfalfa fields to a stand of evergreens and then to her dreaming rock, her special place ever since childhood. It was the perfect place for thinking. Perhaps some time alone with God would help her get her thoughts straight.

She walked quietly along, pausing every so often to wait and listen for the rustle of the tiny feet of squirrels and chipmunks on the forest floor or scan the sky for the dipping, fluttering flight of the yellow-rumped warbler or the direct, fast-beating wings of the curlew sandpiper. As she walked, Abby thought of the bits of information she'd received lately and pondered how they might fit together. The most tantalizing bit was the string on Max Rigolo's fishing fly that matched the string tied around the bundles of cash. Then there was Thelma's missing money and the odd letter she had received. And now the prowler at Mary's house. Something told her these pieces were connected, but at this point she didn't know how.

Not yet, she didn't. But with persistence and determination —along with the good Lord's blessing—she would find the answers.

Behind her, footsteps crunched on the gravel path. Abby turned, knowing before she saw him that her young friend had followed her for an after-school jaunt. Ellen had been expecting the boy to be dropped off at the house. Her mother must have told him where she'd gone.

As Bobby joined her, he slowed to an exaggerated tippy-toe walk and lifted a finger to his lips. "I'm being quiet," he whispered. "Is it okay if I stay?"

So much for meditating. But she knew he would provide some much-needed entertainment. In fact, he already had.

"Sure, let's go find a place to sit and observe."

They bypassed the dreaming rock and walked a quarter mile farther, crossing a narrow ditch before finding a thick tree limb that must have fallen to the ground during the storm a few weeks ago. They checked it first to make sure there were no ants or snakes living on or under the limb.

Once settled side by side on the log, Bobby leaned close and said, "Mrs. Quinn gave me an A on my leaf project."

"She gave it to you, or you earned it?"

He beamed, the broad smile nearly splitting his face in two.

"I earned it. It was fun, so I did extra and even looked up the Latin names of the trees. Mrs. Quinn used it as an example to show the other kids."

"Bobby, that's excellent." She gave him a congratulatory hug.

To her surprise, he sat quietly for a long time, saying nothing while they merely took in the sights, sounds and smells that surrounded them. The scents intermingled—honeysuckle, wild roses and spruce—but the one that Abby enjoyed the most was the rich, heavy blend of earth, moss and moisture. The afternoon throbbed with the distant lapping of the water against the shore and the intermittent hum of bees visiting flower blossoms. A hummingbird zinged past, appearing at first to be an oversized hornet. The crown of iridescent red feathers against a green back, however, gave evidence that this was merely a territorial Anna's hummingbird defending its turf.

It was hard to say what drew Abby's attention to the bigleaf maple that stood at the edge of the clearing. Perhaps a brief, barely perceived glimpse of a wing, or maybe the faint raspy sound of baby birds begging to be fed. Abby lifted the binoculars to her eyes and adjusted the focus as she scanned from the bottom up to the lower branches. There, just to one side of the trunk, a large burl jutted out. From the center of the gnarled growth dangled bits of grass and leaves. The focal angle didn't allow her to see inside the burl, but she watched anyway, certain that patience would grant her a peek at a parent bird either entering or exiting the nest.

Just as she expected, a buff colored female darted out. A moment later, the male came to the edge of the hollow, his beak filled with food to feed his young.

Abby felt a light tap on her knee. Lowering the binoculars,

she saw Bobby watching her, his eyebrows raised with interest and one hand outstretched. He whispered, "May I?"

She handed him the binoculars and quietly described the location so he could find it through the lenses. She could tell when he'd found it because he suddenly broke out in an endearing grin.

He watched for a long time while Abby explained the differences between the male and female birds.

"I can't see the babies," he said.

"Let's move over there."

Since there was no convenient limb to use as a bench, they sat directly on the ground and waited once again for the parent birds to forget they were there.

"I can see the babies," Bobby said. "Man, they're all jammed together in there." He passed the binoculars back to her.

Abby adjusted the focus again and gazed at the crowded nest filled with fluffy carbon copies of the parent birds. One, two, three little beaks.

"They're about the same age as the house sparrow I'm taking care of at the lab," she said.

"How can you tell?"

Once again, she gave the binoculars to the boy. His fascination was evident as he continued to watch the parents' repeated trips to the nest.

"Their level of activity. It'll be a few more days before they leave the nest. In the meantime, every day they become more and more demanding."

"That's what Mom says about me sometimes."

The boy's honesty prompted an amused grin from Abby.

They sat in silence after that, Bobby absorbed by the activity of the birds and Abby surveying the area beneath the nest.

When the birds were ready to fledge, the young saplings would help to break their clumsy first flights. They would scatter beneath the tree, some perching on the lower saplings, perhaps others hiding in the brush. And the parents would scramble to keep up with the youngsters' voracious appetites. Eventually, as the fledglings became more adept at flying and got the hang of following their parents, the older birds would teach them how to forage on the ground and in trees and shrubs for insects, caterpillars, seeds and grains.

If she had found this nest sooner, Abby would have added Newton to the tiny clan. But now the birds had grown so large there was no room for another. Besides, if she disturbed the nest now, the sparrows would most likely panic and fly away before they were ready.

But that didn't mean it was too late for Newton to be adopted into this feathered family. She had plans for him.

ARRIVING EARLIER THAN USUAL for work Wednesday morning, Abby pulled into the parking area outside the museum. She reached back to grab her purse on the back seat, and when she turned around she saw a man running from the building.

Before she could get out of the car to see what was happening, he darted off into the woods. Then, thinking better of leaving the safety of her car, Abby locked the doors and pulled the cell phone from her purse.

Broken glass glinted on the ground outside her office. Abby prayed that Sergeant Cobb would be on duty today.

Fortunately, the deputy at the station was quick to arrive. He made a thorough search of the building before giving Abby the all clear to enter.

The damage to the museum's workroom was not much

financially, but the visual effect of what had happened took an emotional toll on Abby. It seemed that everything that was not nailed down had been overturned or dumped on the floor. As bad as it was, though, her office had fared far worse.

"Let's check the other building and the lab," Abby said.

As soon as she entered the building—after waiting while the deputy checked it out first—Abby walked into the lab, past the scattered files and books, to check the bufflehead.

"Sergeant Cobb is on Lopez Island." The young, uniformed deputy followed her into the room. "He said to tell you he's coming right over."

"Thank you."

The young deputy was quite capable, and Abby had every confidence in him. But right now she preferred the comfort of Henry's kind, familiar face and authoritative manner.

And Hugo. He'd already been informed of the destruction and was on his way over.

The duck was already agitated, so to avoid handling and stressing him even more, Abby gave him a quick visual once over. Fortunately, the splint on his leg was still in place and he appeared not to have been further injured. To help calm him, she threw a towel over his cage, and he quieted almost immediately.

Next was Newton.

Abby nearly freaked at the sight of the empty, overturned brooder box. Newton was nowhere to be seen.

"Stop! Don't move," she told the deputy who was picking his way through the wreckage behind her.

He had searched the lab before letting her in, and she hoped he hadn't inadvertently stepped on the tiny sparrow. Out of habit as much as necessity, Abby closed her eyes and prayed, this time out loud. For some reason, the urgency of the situation seemed to require more than a mentally spoken plea.

"Lord, I know Your eye is on this little sparrow and that he is always in Your care," she said, her voice quavering. "Please, Father, open my eyes so that I might see him too."

She opened her eyes and quickly searched the floor before moving carefully toward the counter where the brooder box lay. Lifting carefully, she righted it, hoping that the bird was safe beneath it. But he was not.

Abby thought of the young sparrows she and Bobby had seen in the nest yesterday. While their parents had been out foraging for food, they had hunkered down quietly in their nest so as not to draw attention to themselves. But as soon as they heard the scratching of their parents' claws gripping the burl, the chicks rose up, beaks open and clamoring to be fed.

The room was quiet, and Abby ran her fingernail over the brooder box to make a light scratching noise in imitation of a parent bird's claws.

Just as she hoped, the sound of Newton's raspy little squeak came to her from somewhere on the countertop, but it was hard to determine exactly where. Books, papers, file folders, charts and maps . . . they were tossed everywhere in haphazard abandon. And it was impossible to tell under which bit of debris he hid.

Abby continued to scrape her fingernail over the wood, and this time she sucked air between her teeth in imitation of the chick's sound to encourage him to compete by calling louder. He did, and in his frenzy for food he jostled the page of an open book under which he was hiding.

Gently, taking great care not to injure the little guy, Abby lifted the book off of him. Seeing that he appeared to be healthy and robust, she lifted her eyes and thanked God for His mercy on this tiny sparrow. Then she prayed that he had no internal injuries.

She scooped him up and returned him to the brooder box while she prepared his breakfast of mealworms and a special cereal formula for handfeeding birds. As she went about her caretaking duties, Abby was aware that the deputy had left the room, but other than that she was operating on automatic pilot. Abby was grateful for the opportunity to let her mind go numb for a few minutes while she fell into the safe, familiar routine of feeding the chick.

When the chick was full and Abby's task complete, she tried to focus on what needed to be done next—anything to take her mind off the senseless disregard for the lives of God's little feathered creatures—but all she could do was stand and survey the destruction of her lab.

For the first time since she'd seen that man fleeing the museum this morning, the full impact of it hit her. The lab that had been built with the purpose of doing God's work— studying and caring for wildlife and using that knowledge to teach others about His divine handiwork—was now in total disarray. They were fortunate that, other than damaged locks on the doors and her desk drawers, no equipment or furniture appeared to have been stolen or destroyed. Even so, it would take some time to restore order to the lab, and to the work-room and her office in the museum.

The whole thing made her so very sad that it felt as if her heart would crack under the pressure of trying to hold back tears. Sadness was the predominant feeling, but she was a little bit afraid, too. Abby knew that God had protected her all along, and that He'd been watching over her every minute of every day just as He had watched over little Newton. She tried to turn her fear over to Him.

Abby's energy—the drive, enthusiasm and excitement that normally accompanied her through her workday—seemed to have vanished along with the intruder who had escaped through the woods. She felt physically and mentally depleted.

It was unusual for her not to know what to do next, and the sensation made her feel even more out of balance. Numbly, she left the lab and the conservatory building to wander back to the museum.

When she entered her office, Abby saw a welcome sight. Dressed in a white gauzy dress and white sandals, not to mention her gleaming silver hair that looked like a halo around her sweet face, Mary appeared like an angel on wheels.

Saying nothing, she held out her arms to Abby.

In the time it took to blink an eye, Abby was across the room and in her sister's arms. Resting her weight against the arm of the wheelchair, she buried her face in Mary's neck and wept.

For a long time she stayed there, Mary's loving arms around her waist while she dripped tears onto the pretty white dress and sobbed like a small girl. She was aware of Mary's cheek against her hair, her gentle hand rubbing a comforting circle on her back and the soft sound of a kiss on her temple. Most of all, she was aware of a love that seemed to reach inside and help heal the hurt that was now pouring out of her soul.

After what seemed like a long time, the gut-wrenching angst began to subside. Something wet touched her elbow, and when she raised up, she saw Finnegan staring at her with concerned brown eyes.

"It's okay, sweetie. I'm going to be all right." She rubbed his neck, and he seemed to understand her words. To Mary, Abby said, "How did you know I needed you?"

Mary reached into the embroidered denim bag that hung from the arm of her chair and retrieved a tissue, which she used to wipe the salty streaks from Abby's face. "I was on the phone with Henry when he got the call."

She handed Abby a fresh tissue.

Rising from her sister's embrace, Abby blew her nose, then pushed the unruly tendrils of hair away from her face.

"Come here." Mary smiled at her as Abby bent to let her rub away the trace of mascara she'd put on this morning. "This is one of those times when it's a good thing you don't wear much makeup."

BY THE TIME Hugo and Henry arrived a short while later, Abby had pulled herself together and was once again the picture of cool, calm composure. She answered all of Henry's questions completely and without emotion, and she helped brainstorm some places the intruder may have gone to hide.

Sergeant Henry Cobb stared down at her, his expression seemingly stern and fierce to anyone who didn't know him. The flat-brimmed, drill sergeant style of hat he wore, with the gold acorn band and hat badge, only intensified the effect. It was a look that probably intimidated wrongdoers, but Abby was aware that this was Henry's way of masking the concern that he felt.

He shook his head. "Abby, you are one of the toughest women I've ever known, save one. To go through something like this," he said, gesturing toward the open lab door, "and still be as together as you are. Well, you amaze me."

Uncomfortable with the undeserved accolades, Abby

turned away and met Mary's gaze. They exchanged knowing smiles, but Mary kept mum about Abby's moment of personal trial.

"There's something you need to know," he said, his tone serious. "You too, Mary."

Abby felt her stomach muscles clench as she anticipated what he was about to say. "This—this vandalism," she said, sweeping a hand toward the wreckage. "It has something to do with the box I found, doesn't it?"

He paused as if considering how best to say what was on his mind. Finally, he just handed her a scrap of paper.

"We found this in your office."

The note, written with the counterfeit detection marker she'd left on her desk, contained only five words: "Return the money or else."

"Is it for real?" Abby remembered Janet's suggestion that someone who'd read the newpaper article might think she'd kept some of the money for herself. "Could it be someone trying to cash in on another person's heist?"

She passed the note to Mary, who read it and returned it to Henry.

Henry placed the paper with his notes. "We don't know for sure, but it stands to reason that it's the real McCoy and not a copycat."

"So Jellybean is alive after all." She walked behind Mary as they went to the back exit. As always, Finnegan padded alongside his mistress's chair. "What does this mean for us?"

"Hopefully nothing. But the guy is scared, so it would be best not to put yourself in a situation where you might run into him alone. Change your routines," he said. "And make sure you have someone with you at all times. At least until we can catch the guy and put him behind bars, where he belongs."

"I can't have someone with me all the time," Abby protested. "I have a job to do, and that means I have to go out into the woods to keep records of bird sightings."

Mary stopped near the exit and turned her chair to face Abby. "You can take Finnegan with you."

The dog's ears pricked up at the mention of his name.

Abby's heart swelled with gratitude for her sister. This was the second time today that Mary had come through with exactly what she needed at exactly the right time.

Henry had his hand on the door, ready to go, but it was clear he wanted to impress upon her the importance of his request. "Don't go outside after dark, not even with the dog." Then, as an afterthought, he said, "And not even with a can of beans."

The unexpected comment broke the seriousness that had gripped Abby's heart since she'd arrived at work this morning. And, once broken, the dam released a second torrent of emotions as the three of them were swept up in a fit of laughter. Slightly hysterical laughter, but laughter nevertheless. For that—and for Mary and Henry—Abby was grateful.

As if sensing that this wasn't their usual good times kind of laughter, Finnegan licked Abby's hand. She knelt and hugged the sweet animal, tears once again moistening her eyes. Yes, she was grateful for Finnegan too. God was, indeed, good.

"Why don't you come home with me?" Mary suggested. "I'm sure Hugo would understand if you take some time off."

"Thanks, but I'm going to stay and work on cleaning up some of the mess. Hugo needs my help." She pushed the curls back away from her face. "Besides, the best thing for me to do right now is stay busy."

Too busy to think about what Jason Legowski had meant when he wrote "or else."

THAT NIGHT, after Wednesday night Bible study, all Abby wanted to do was recover from the day and zone out with some paperwork. Anything to keep her mind occupied with something safe and nonthreatening. She looked up as Mary called from the foyer.

"There goes another cruiser," Mary said. "Seems like they are driving by the house more often now."

"I'm glad they're there," Abby said, as she put the papers on her lap.

"Me too." Mary wheeled into the living room and into her usual television-viewing spot. "Mind if I turn the TV on?"

"Feel free. I'm just going to sort through this mail."

As the TV droned in the background, Abby shifted the papers around on her lap. A small manila envelope worked its way to the top, and the return address prompted her to deal with it first. Kids In Need of Dialysis. She pulled the letter out and read it.

Dear Friend, Thank you for your recent donation of $10. You will be pleased to know that your generous contribution will help. . . The rest was the usual "we got your money, here's how we're going to use it and will you please give us more" type of letter.

Something about the wording of the document rang familiar. On a hunch, she compared it with the copy of the letter Thelma had received. The names of the charities and the overall content of the letters were different, but in three different places the phrasing was identical. It was possible, she supposed, that charities borrowed particularly effective wording from other groups to use in their own correspondence. But to use so many similar phrases in one letter?

Weirder still was that the letter had been signed by a member of the board of directors: Carmella Rigolo Hawkins.

Rigolo. Abby didn't know why she was so surprised to see that name associated with the organization. It wasn't unusual for people with a passion for a cause to recruit relatives to help move a project forward. Still, she wondered how many other Rigolos were involved in KIND.

Abby retrieved her laptop computer and logged on to the Internet. Once signed on, she searched "Kids In Need of Dialysis" and "board of directors." As the screen came into view, she scanned the list of names. Among the twelve names, there were two other Rigolos—Tony and Osgood—as well as three women with *R* as their middle initial. Coincidence? Abby thought not.

Setting the computer aside, Abby returned her attention to the envelope she had dropped earlier. Squeezing the sides of the envelope, she shook the bracelet out onto her lap.

Just as she had expected, the charity's slogan was embroidered into the fabric of the novelty bracelet: *Be KIND.* But there was something else that commanded her attention, prompting Abby to get up and switch on the overhead light for a better look.

And when she did, it suddenly began to make sense.

Tomorrow she would call Vince Emory to help put some of the smaller details together. But in the meantime, the bigger picture was becoming much clearer.

CHAPTER ❧ EIGHTEEN

THE NEXT DAY, ABBY NEEDED time to think, and the best place to be alone without being totally by herself was the church.

With her lab, office and workroom finally put back in order, she had decided to spend her lunchtime here, quietly, where her soul could find rest in God, as Psalm 62:1 advised. From another part of the church building, Janet's radio played familiar hymns. Though the music was barely audible in the chapel where she sat, Abby found herself gently swaying to the peaceful sounds.

She sat on the front pew, her head bent over the Bible in her hands. Flipping the pages, she thought about the wickedness that had been done, first with the drug money, and more recently at the conservatory. In her heart, Abby knew that God's will would prevail, but she wanted to read His promises and be reminded once again that God was in control.

The pages fell open to I Peter, so Abby began reading in the second chapter and continued into the third. Then, just as she was considering flipping to another section of the Bible, she came to verse 12: "For the eyes of the Lord are on the righteous and his ears are attentive to their prayer, but the face of the Lord is against those who do evil."

Abby liked knowing that God's ears were attentive to her prayer. Because praying was something she did so frequently, it was usually easy to pray. But right now, with her heart and mind jumbled from the recent events, she wasn't sure where to start. So she turned to the concordance in the back of the Bible and looked up *prayer*. The first verse, Matthew 5:44, was one she had memorized from her own childhood days in Bible camp. "But I tell you: Love your enemies and pray for those who persecute you."

It was hard to love the person who would put innocent little birds in harm's way. Harder still was knowing how to pray for that person. So Abby turned to the second part of Romans 8:26. "We do not know what we ought to pray for, but the Spirit himself intercedes for us with groans that words cannot express."

And since she didn't have the words to fully express how she felt about what was happening, Abby asked that the Spirit communicate her feelings for her and help her learn the answers to the seemingly unrelated pieces of information that had been revealed to her.

She tried meditating on what she'd discovered about the bracelet and letter the night before, but her thoughts began racing, and the sense of peace started to lift from her. So, instead of meditating on events and information, she decided to meditate on the verse from the book of Matthew. "Love your enemies and pray for those who persecute you."

Abby focused on the words, knowing that as she prayed for the intruder, it would become easier to love him.

And that's exactly what happened. She prayed for the person whose life was so troubled and confused that he had become involved in drugs and thievery. She thought of him as someone's son or sibling who had taken a wrong turn or, sadly, might never have been taught to choose the right path in life. Before long, a feeling of sorrow overcame her for the person who had made money his god, worshipping it to the point that he would hurt others to have it.

As she prayed, an image of the ring from the tackle box blipped into her brain. Abby pushed it aside, determined not to let her own thoughts interfere with the prayer for her troubled brother.

Returning to her prayer, she asked for God's mercy. *Help Jason Legowski find his rightful place*, she beseeched, *and may that place ultimately be among Your flock.*

Again, the swirl design of the ring flashed through her mind's eye, but this time Abby didn't push it away. Instead, she let the vision float through her mind and fill it with the details of the intricately designed jewelry. The gold had been artfully shaped in a delicate pattern of swirls to surround the delicate opal in the center. It was clearly very feminine and elegant in its presentation.

Even while her mind was forming that last thought about the ring's feminine elegance, another impression came to Abby. It wasn't really a mental picture, as the ring had been. Rather, it was a combination of images, feelings and bits of remembered conversation.

And then Abby knew. Knew with a certainty that was beyond understanding, but she knew.

Finally, she saw how the crazy events of the past few weeks fit together. The contents of the tackle box, the prowler who had watched and later threatened her, and even Mr. Charity himself, Max Rigolo. It all seemed so clear now that she wondered how she hadn't seen it before.

Unfortunately, her soul could not rest in the knowledge she'd just been given. Though Abby was grateful for the response to her prayer, she wished the answer had been different.

"THEY'RE BEAUTIFUL," Abby told the proprietor of Siebert's Jewelry during her lunchtime on Friday, "but they're not what I'm looking for. I'm interested in a very specific design."

Abby couldn't help thinking how much Mary would enjoy perusing the various colored stones set in gold and silver. Her sister actually had all the jewelry she wanted, her favorite pieces being those that her late husband Jacob had bought for her, but Mary still liked to study the artistry of a well-crafted bauble.

But today was not for shopping and admiring. Abby was on a mission.

The well-dressed gentleman with the trimmed goatee behind the glass case pulled out a thick binder and opened to a page full of close-up photographs of rings. "If you'd like, we can custom order a piece for you. Or we can design something according to your specifications."

Abby was so intent on the purpose of her visit that she didn't correct his assumption that she was here to buy some jewelry.

"Actually, I'm looking for something like this." Abby pulled out her notebook and made a few swift motions with her pen. It wasn't Renoir, but the sketch clearly showed the design of the ring that had been in the tackle box.

As she turned the paper toward him, she saw the instant glimmer of recognition cover his face.

"The stone is an opal," she said, "and it's set in a delicate yellow gold band."

"I don't have that exact design for sale at this time." Gordon Siebert studied the drawing intently. "In fact, this particular piece belongs to one of our customers, but are you looking for something along these lines? Perhaps we could make something like it for you."

He unlocked a door in the cabinet on his side of the counter and withdrew a tray of small envelopes. The jeweler flipped through them until he found the one he wanted. He put the tray away and then opened the clasp on the paper envelope. With a turn of his wrist, a beautiful gold necklace tumbled out onto the glass display top.

"Oh my!" Abby pushed her glasses up on her nose as she lifted the exquisite pendant to examine it more closely.

The swirls on the design swept upward in a graceful arc around the sparkling aqua and pink stone, giving the impression that they were embracing the gem. It was quite lovely, and it was an identical match to the ring Abby had found.

As she studied the piece, fragments of conversations came back to her, and it all made an unfortunate kind of sense now.

"I haven't taken the time to get it back from the jeweler after the clasp was repaired."

Abby now understood why the owner had taken so long to retrieve the necklace. She hadn't wanted to call attention to herself.

"Thank you, Mr. Siebert," she said. "You've been more helpful than you know."

Still cradling the pendant and chain in her hand, Abby picked up the envelope that was marked with the type of repair that had been done on the piece and slid the necklace back inside. As she handed the envelope back to the jeweler, she turned it so she could glimpse the name of the customer who had brought it here for repair.

Ida Tolliver.

AS FAR AS ABBY WAS CONCERNED, this was one of the hardest decisions she'd ever had to make in her life. Turn Ida over to the law and lose a good friend? Or talk to her, try to enlist her help and hope she didn't make a run for it?

After a restless night in which Abby drifted to sleep and awoke often, she had come to the conclusion that the best option was to offer Ida an opportunity to redeem herself by doing the right thing. Abby just hoped that her own personal wishes were not coloring God's will in the matter. For the umpteenth time this Saturday morning, first while she and Ida had tended to Newton's needs at the lab and now as they set him in his shallow cardboard platform beneath the tree with the nest in the burl at Stanton Farm, she paused to ask for His clear guidance. And she asked that God would open Ida's eyes to the ultimate good that would come of her own difficult role in setting things right again.

When they had set the bird on the ground, he had immediately scampered for cover on a low branch of a nearby bush. It had taken some convincing for Abby to encourage Ida to follow her to the waiting spot where she and Bobby had observed the happenings in the nest earlier that week.

"He's going to get lost," Ida protested, her blond lashes glistening with moisture. "What if the parent birds don't see him? What if they don't want to adopt him?"

Prior to releasing Newton, Abby had turned the binoculars to the burl that had sheltered the birds from the weather. There were only two possible explanations for the vacant bird bed inside. Either a snake had found the nest and dined on the fledglings, or the young birds had given their wings a try and were now scattered below their former home.

Since Abby had seen an adult house sparrow flitting through the underbrush as she and Ida had approached the observation spot, she expected the youngsters were now exploring their environment.

"Just hold tight," she whispered to Ida. "They'll find each other."

As they both sat together on the ground, binoculars pressed to their eyes, it seemed to take forever for anything to happen on the slope of ground in front of them. Newton clung to the bush, obviously confused by his sudden change of environment. Abby became aware of Ida's restlessness.

Finally, her young friend turned to her and said, "I'm working the evening shift today. If they don't come soon, I'm just going to have to go."

"Don't worry, there's plenty of time." Abby patted her arm. "Besides, we need to talk."

A look of dread skittered across Ida's pretty features. Quickly, Ida lifted the binoculars to her face again and gazed toward the burled tree. But she wasn't quick enough. It was obvious to Abby that the reddening of her cheeks had nothing to do with the midday sun.

Reaching into the hip pocket of her jeans, Abby withdrew the folded printout of the picture that she had tried to give Ida a week ago. She wasn't at work now, and Abby would not let her sidestep the issue again.

"Now that you've had some time to think about it, perhaps you'll remember the man in this picture."

Slowly, reluctantly, Ida lowered the binoculars to her lap.

Abby smoothed the picture and pressed it into her hands. "Certainly his image is fresher in your memory now that you've had a chance to visit with him recently."

"I—I don't know what you mean."

Abby's heart went out to Ida as the girl struggled with her response.

"Of course you do, dear." Abby's tone was gentle, but it brooked no resistance. "And you'll most certainly recognize this."

The next scrap of paper she handed to Ida was the sketch she'd made at the jeweler's yesterday.

Ida stared at the hastily drawn design. Then she blinked rapidly, apparently hoping the image might disappear if she would just will it away.

"Ida, I know you're a good person. And I don't believe you'd intentionally become involved in something that you know isn't right."

Finally, Ida's tears overflowed in large splashing drops. She wiped the moisture off the paper and smeared the ink on Abby's drawing.

"I'm so sorry about everything. I never meant to deceive you." Ida drew in a shaky breath. "I loved him, Abby. And I thought he loved me."

"I know. He made a lot of promises, didn't he?"

Ida sobbed harder now.

Remembering the comfort she'd received from her sister after her lab, office and workroom had been trashed, Abby turned to her young friend and took her in her arms.

"He did," Ida said, hiccuping between sobs. "And he lied. He even lied about his name." She pulled back and gazed at

Abby, her expression filled with the shock of her realization. "I kept thinking I could get him to do right. And I even told him some of the Bible verses that you shared with me.

"He wasn't even interested in hearing about the Bible," she continued, her tone conveying that she felt as though her boyfriend had rejected not only God, but her as well.

"I'm so sorry to hear that," Abby said. And she truly was. No one should go through life without God. And only a fool would fail to see what a treasure he had in Ida.

"I'm such a moron." Ida sniffed and rubbed the back of her hand across her face. "I should have seen what he was up to. Asking me to e-mail him and tell him everything that happened on the island." Now she rubbed her ears as if to blot out the memory of his voice. "He said he liked the way I wrote. He even had the nerve to critique my messages and suggest I include more detailed descriptions. Now I know that he just wanted to stay up on what was happening around here . . . see if anybody had disturbed his stupid tackle box."

"You're not a moron, Ida. Anyone could have made the same mistake."

She jerked a shoulder and looked away. "I gave him the tackle box a couple of years ago, hoping he'd take up fishing and spend more time on Sparrow Island. With me. Instead, he covered my gift with dirt, took off and strung me along with lies and empty promises."

"Is that when you realized Ryan—I mean Jason—had buried the box on my parents' property? When you came over to watch us open it?"

Ida shook her head, her blond ponytail brushing her shoulders. "Lots of people have tackle boxes just like the one I gave him. Sure, it crossed my mind, but when I saw all that money, I told myself it couldn't be his."

"What did you tell yourself when you saw the ring?"

Ida flinched as if stung, but Abby knew it was her conscience pricking her.

"That it must have been a popular, mass-produced design. You know, like the tackle box. I really wanted to believe it."

"You clung to those beliefs even though he had told you he was going to give you an engagement ring to match your necklace? A ring exactly like the one in the box?"

"Yes, I believed in him, even when he came to visit me but wouldn't take me out anywhere. I foolishly took that to mean he was losing interest in me or was ashamed of being seen with me," she admitted.

When she met Abby's gaze, she didn't look away. She seemed genuinely confused by her own reactions to her boyfriend's behavior, and Abby was convinced she was telling the truth.

"I just kept hoping all these things were coincidences. Like the part about his favorite candy being jellybeans."

A long silence passed between them.

"Eventually, I sort of knew that the 'sales' job Ryan had was actually drug dealing, and I got scared. If I had told him what I suspected, who knows what might have happened to me? But if I had told you or Sergeant Cobb, who knows what might have happened to Ryan? I just wish I had known how to make him set things right."

"You can't *make* another person do the right thing." Abby lifted the binoculars to her eyes again. "But you can do the right thing yourself."

"What do you mean?"

Without lowering the binoculars, Abby pointed to where Newton had hopped to a lower branch of the bush. On the next branch over, the mother sparrow sat with a moth protruding from her beak as she turned her head first one way and then another. It looked as though she was trying to figure out where this youngster had come from.

Instinctively, Newton lowered his shoulders and opened his beak. His stubby little wings flicked briefly with anticipation. The mother, responding to the need of the little one, whether it was her own or not, came closer and deposited the moth in the open beak.

Abby and Ida both breathed sighs of relief.

In the next instant, the mother was gone again, in search of more insects.

"Newton is returning to his flock," Abby said. "He's being adopted into this family, and he belongs there."

Her anxiety eased now that little Newton had found his way back, Abby set the binoculars down and directed her attention to Ida.

"Birds need to be with their own flocks. Just like people do."

"You're saying that I shouldn't have mingled with Ryan," Ida surmised. "But even after I knew what he was like, I was hoping I could be a good influence on him. You know, bring him to God's flock."

"And that's an honorable plan. People join God's flock by becoming believers. But if they choose not to believe and just want to take advantage of the flock, then they're like cowbirds."

"How's that?"

"Cowbirds take advantage of other birds by laying their eggs in a smaller bird's nest. The mother cowbird abandons the egg to be taken care of by the host parent. As the chick grows, it quickly crowds the other babies out of the nest and greedily takes all the food for itself. The original family's chicks often die from starvation and neglect, and the foster parents become exhausted from trying to fill up the young bird that's even bigger than they are."

"That's terrible."

"That's the way it is," Abby said. "They don't intend harm. They just want a free ride. But they end up hurting others in the process."

"So you're saying that Ryan and I don't belong in the same flock, and if I spend time with him I'll only get hurt."

"You and many others."

Abby waited while Ida took in what she had to say. It was a lot to absorb. It would take some time for her to see that she'd been used, and to understand that it was not due to a failing on her part, but because her boyfriend had chosen the easy path, rather than the straight and narrow.

"Is he aware that you know he's Jason Legowski?"

Ida shook her head. "After I started having suspicions, I stopped e-mailing him with stories about what was happening on the island. I let him think it was because work was keeping me too busy to write." She wrapped and unwrapped the binoculars strap around her finger as she talked. "That's why he thinks you still have the tackle box and money. In fact, he came right out and asked me what you had done with it. I said 'nothing,' so he assumed from what I had already told him about your interest in tracking down answers that you kept it. He assumed you still believed it was someone's life savings and were trying to find the owner without involving the sheriff's department."

Abby considered what she'd just said. "That explains why he broke into my office and wrote the threatening letter, demanding the box back."

With that in mind, she decided on a plan that would deliver Jason Legowski right into Sergeant Cobb's hands. It would be risky, but it would be riskier still to let this criminal continue to harm others.

"Ida, if you're innocent in this—and I believe you are—you need to take action today to clear your name."

She jerked her head, apparently startled by what Abby had suggested. "You mean I would be suspected of collaborating with him?"

"Well, you have been feeding him details about the box. And even after you had reason to suspect that your Ryan was actually Jason, you didn't come forward and share that information with Henry. To those who don't know you, it could look like you were covering for him. A case of guilt by association. You can prove your innocence by helping to turn him in. But I'll need you to give him a message."

Ida looked down at her hands. "I don't know where he is."

"If you don't know where he's staying, then how do you keep in touch?"

"Previously, we had e-mailed each other. But since he came to Sparrow Island a few weeks ago, he either calls or drops by at random times."

"How frequently?"

"About two or three times a day."

"Excellent. Next time he contacts you, here's what I want you to do." Abby briefly outlined her plan for Ida to invite her boyfriend over to the Stanton Farm the next day for lunch. Abby would arrange for Sergeant Cobb and his men to be there ahead of time, lying in wait to capture Jason when he arrived. "And be sure to tell Ryan I'll have the box and money with me."

"But won't he think it's a setup? If he's managed to evade the police all this time, I doubt he'll let down his guard now."

"You won't tell him that you know who he is. Just invite him as 'Ryan Landau,' the boyfriend I've been wanting to meet." Abby tilted her head, considering what would make this invitation a can't-miss event. "During your conversation, let it drop that I've been scared by the note that was left in my office. Tell him I'm in over my head, and I'm going to take the money to the sheriff's station on Monday. That should make him drop everything and come."

Ida looked doubtful about this plan. But Abby wasn't sure whether she was doubtful it would work, or doubtful she wanted to participate in turning in her boyfriend.

"You *will* do it, won't you?" An answer was not immediately forthcoming, and Abby pressed again. "He did wrong, Ida. He needs to be stopped."

"It's hard betraying someone you love."

"He betrayed *you*. And he betrayed the FBI. You read the article about the drug bust. When Jason escaped with the money, two innocent people were seriously injured. Next time, someone could die. I know you don't want that to happen."

"No, I don't." From the panicked look in her eyes, it appeared that she might bolt. "But I also don't want to hurt Ryan. He can be really nice. You don't know him, Abby. You haven't seen how gentle and funny he is when we're together."

Abby put her hand on Ida's shoulder. "I've seen evil. And I know that it often comes disguised as something beautiful."

Ida pulled away from her. "He wouldn't intentionally hurt anyone."

"Maybe not," Abby said. "But people still got hurt because of what he did. And if you don't help, Ida, you'll be just as guilty as he is. It says in the Bible that you're not to put a stumbling block in your brother's way," she said, paraphrasing Romans 14:13. "In this case, not taking proper action to keep him from continuing to sin could be a stumbling block for him."

Ida was crying again, but this time she didn't bother to wipe away the tears that streamed down her pale cheeks.

"You don't even have to be there when it happens," Abby suggested. "You can tell him to meet you at the farm."

She shook her head vigorously.

"Are you saying you won't do it?"

"I'm saying I won't be a chicken. I'll do what you ask," she said, her voice shaking with emotion, "and I'll be there too."

Relieved, Abby gave her a spontaneous hug. She gathered up her things and, after offering up a quick prayer for God to continue watching over Newton, walked with Ida back to the farm. She had accomplished what she had set out to do. She'd received the girl's promise to help. Now she just hoped that Ida wouldn't change her mind between today and tomorrow.

Or, worse, alert Jason to the plan.

CHAPTER ❧ NINETEEN

Henry's reaction the next next morning was pretty much what Abby had expected. He thanked her for the information that Ryan Landau was really Jason Legowski, and he immediately started making plans to assign a watch detail to Ida's apartment.

While Mary finished getting ready to go with Henry to church, Finnegan danced around Henry's feet, and Blossom observed the goings on from her vantage point on the back of the sofa. Henry bent to pick up the dog's rope toy, and they tussled with it for a moment.

"No, a watch detail would only scare him off," Abby said. "He's being very careful, and he won't even tell Ida where he's staying. Besides, I already have a plan in place."

He let the dog win the tug of war. As Finnegan trotted off, prize in his mouth, Henry turned and raised an eyebrow at Abby. "Before you even tell me what it is, the answer is no."

Abby held up her hands. "Just hear me out."

She sat on the couch, and he reluctantly sat down next to her as she outlined the lunch that she and her mother were already preparing for today.

"Ida is going to let him think the tackle box is in the house, with all the money still inside. So while we're outside getting ready for a picnic, I'll do the proper hostess thing and tell him where the bathroom is, which will give him a ready-made excuse to go inside and snoop. You and your deputies will be inside, waiting for him. So when he goes into the house, it'll be a simple matter of taking him into custody."

Henry stood and shook his head as he paced the floor. "No, it's too dangerous. I don't like using civilians in apprehending a criminal."

"I agree." Mary rolled into the room, her hair and makeup perfect, and her pale blue skirt and top combo enhancing her rosy complexion. "You need to let Henry take care of everything. He's a trained professional."

"I know, and I respect that you know a lot more about these things than I do," Abby said. "But how else are you going to catch him? The guy is getting desperate. Desperate enough to stalk us at home, trash my office and lab and threaten me to get the money back."

Henry rubbed his ear and smoothed down the fringe of white hair that he had disturbed.

"We can't wait for this guy to hurt anyone else," she added. "And you don't have to worry about us. We'll all be outside, away from the action, when you do your takedown."

"Takedown?" Mary asked. "You got that from the *Cops and Criminals* show on TV, didn't you?" By now, Blossom had climbed into Mary's lap and was butting her head against Mary's hand, wanting to be petted. "I saw that show once when Henry was zapping channels. The cops tackled the bad guy to the ground and tied him up like a calf at a rodeo."

"Ida has already invited Jason to our picnic," Abby said, determined not to be sidetracked. "And she doesn't have any way to contact him to change the plans."

"I don't like it," Henry said at last. "But I have to admit it does make sense." He moved behind Mary to walk with her out the door, and Finnegan dropped his rope to join them. "You two go on to church, and I'll drive separately so I can leave early. I have to go back to Lopez Island to meet with some other deputies and set things in motion."

Mary reached for Abby's hand. "Are you sure you want to do this?"

Abby was aware that both of them were watching her as she paused by the door. "At this point, we don't have a choice."

ON A NORMAL SUNDAY MORNING, it could easily take the Stantons twenty minutes or more from the last *amen* to the point at which they were leaving the church parking lot. There were so many friends to speak to and details to catch up on. But today they had practically left dust swirls in the driveway as they headed for the farm to prepare for the big event.

Abby tried to talk her family into going to Mary's house to wait, but they wouldn't hear of it.

"And miss all the drama?" George protested. "No way."

"Besides," said Ellen, "it wouldn't look right if you and Ida have a picnic for Jason at our house and we weren't even there." She stood across the picnic table from Abby and helped her smooth a large red-and-white cloth over the wooden table.

"It's Ryan," George corrected. "If you call him by the other name, you'll tip him off that we're on to him."

"Yes, of course," Ellen agreed. She silently mouthed the name. *Ryan. Ryan. Ryan.*

"It also wouldn't look right if you left your sister out of a family gathering," Mary chimed in as she went up the ramp and into the house to gather the picnic dishes and silverware.

Her dog had been taken to a spare bedroom and told to stay. With Finnegan's strong canine instinct, they had worried he might take a disliking to Jason and scare him away before Henry and his men could do their job.

"I'm concerned that Ida wasn't at church this morning," Abby said.

"Maybe she pulled the breakfast shift today," Ellen suggested. "That girl is one of the hardest working people I know."

"Maybe she changed her mind." Abby hoped that Ida wouldn't let any mistaken notions about love prompt her to do something foolish. Like run away with Jason.

George bent to pick up a stick as Mary returned with a stack of dishes on her lap. He said, "I'm more concerned about Henry right now. It's going on twelve-thirty. He should have already been here when we got home from church."

"That's right. Mary gave him the key to your house, so that shouldn't have been the problem." Abby went to take the dishes from Mary, but as her sister was handing them to her, she tightened her grip.

"When I was in the kitchen, I turned on the boat scanner. There's been a serious accident in Randolph Bay. A Jet Ski apparently collided with a recreational fishing boat, and one of the drivers was hurt pretty bad." Mary let go of the plates. "The sheriff's department and rescue people are there. I heard Henry on the radio, and he was in command of the scene, so he must have been the first one to the accident."

A feeling of dread washed over Abby. First, for the people involved in the accident, and then for Ida and the whole let's-catch-Jason scenario she had set up. It was looking like she might have made a terrible mistake.

"We need to pray," Mary said.

They all bowed their heads and held hands as Mary led them in asking for God's help with both the rescued and the rescuers. And she followed with a prayer for all of the Stantons, as well as for Ida and her misguided boyfriend.

Abby felt her breathing grow shallow. Here she was, preparing a picnic while a criminal was on his way to her family's house.

Unless God intervened—and soon—they were sitting ducks.

IN THE MEANTIME, though, Abby wasn't going to just twiddle her thumbs and wait for God to do it all. She busied herself with the preparations, knowing that if she took care of her end, God would take care of His.

Ida and Jason were already late, so it was possible they might not be coming after all. Abby didn't know which she dreaded worse: Jason arriving at the house without Henry and his deputies there to protect them, or having neither of the two of them show up because they were on the run together.

A siren shrilled from the denim bag that hung beside Mary's chair. The unexpected sound created a ripple of startled reaction among the family members gathered in the Stantons' backyard. As an afterthought, Abby remembered that she had jokingly reprogrammed Mary's cell phone to sound off with a distinctive ring for certain callers.

"It's Henry," Abby declared. When Mary paused in a moment of confusion, she added, "On your cell phone."

Mary grabbed the electronic device and flipped it open. "Henry! Where are you?"

They all gathered closer and watched, but Mary soon closed the phone without even so much as a good-bye. "Henry's on his way, but we lost the signal before he could say anything else."

"That's probably why he didn't call sooner," Abby surmised. "He must have been in an area where the signal was weak. In the meantime, we'll need to decide what to do while we wait for Henry and his men to arrive."

After a brief discussion with her family about what to do next, and considering Mary's suggestion to leave, Abby decided that she needed to stay. When Jason discovered he'd been tricked and that there was no tackle box filled with money, it could be dangerous for Ida to be alone with him. And that decided it for the rest of them because her family refused to leave Abby alone as well.

"Let's put some food on the table," Abby said to Mary. "At least we can play the part so it looks real. By doing that, maybe we'll buy some time until Henry arrives. God willing, Ida and her boyfriend will be later than he is."

"I'll get the chicken," Mary said, as she headed back up the ramp to the house.

Concerned that things might not go as smoothly as she had planned, Abby asked her mother to go inside and finish decorating the cake she had made for the gathering. To her father, she asked that he check on Finnegan and make sure the dog stayed inside.

It was clear that George knew she was trying to get them out of the way of potential harm, so to keep him from arguing about the arrangement, she quietly suggested that Ellen needed him more than she did. With obvious reluctance, he went inside, making a comment about searching for a baseball bat.

The back screen door had just slammed shut when Ida's compact car came tearing up the driveway with Jason at the wheel. He circled over the grass and came to a stop with the nose of the car pointing toward Primrose Lane. He got out of the car and didn't bother to assist Ida before heading over to the picnic table. Ida got out and jogged to catch up with him.

He was tall and lean, just like the person in the picture. And he was wearing the same jacket with the red arrow design on the sleeves. From his gray eyes, precisely assembled features and imposing carriage, it was easy to see how Ida could have fallen for him. Abby supposed that when he smiled, the overall effect would be enough to send any red-blooded woman's heart into palpitations. But today he looked serious.

Dead serious.

The sick feeling that had begun in the pit of Abby's stomach just got worse. *It's okay*, she reminded herself. *God is in control.*

"I'm glad you could make it," Abby said, keeping her voice light and steady as she moved the fruit salad from one end of the table to the other. Then, in an idle gesture, she twisted the top of the pepper shaker. "I was beginning to think you two might have gotten so involved gazing into each other's eyes that you forgot our picnic today."

Mary wheeled out onto the porch, the plate of chicken on her lap. When she saw their company, she stopped at the top of the ramp.

Abby pushed back her hair and extended a hand in greeting, a smile carefully plastered on her face. "You must be Ryan. It's so good to finally meet the handsome boyfriend that Ida has told us so much about."

He ignored her outstretched hand. "I'm sure she's had a lot to say."

Ida touched his sleeve, but he shrugged her off in a dismissive gesture. Ida's expression held both shock and apology. Her thoughts were as easy to read as if someone had written them on her forehead. Somehow—probably by her own traitorous face—she had let him know they were all aware of who he really was.

"Where is it?" he demanded. He reached into his jacket pocket. The size of the bulge told Abby it was not a hostess gift he'd brought.

"Where is what?" Still standing near the picnic table, Abby's hand closed around the pepper shaker. All it would take was one quick motion to remove the loosened top and distract him with a faceful of pepper.

"Ryan, let's just go," Ida pleaded. "It's not worth it."

"Shut up!"

Enraged, Abby stared at him through a haze of red. "Young man! We don't use that tone of voice around here."

"Tough," he sneered. When Ida again pulled at his arm, he shoved her, and she stumbled forward.

Abby lifted the pepper shaker higher, knowing it would be of little use if he decided to pull a gun on them, but there was not much out here with which to defend herself.

Apparently realizing that Ida could possibly be of use to him after all, he grabbed her by the ponytail and yanked her against his chest. With one arm around her neck, he shoved his jacketed hand against her side.

Ida's eyes opened wide with fear, but that didn't stop her from wriggling to try to get loose. Jason tightened his grip on her.

"Put it down," he said to Abby, "and tell me where the money is."

Wishing there was something she could do, anything to take control of this precarious predicament, Abby slowly set the shaker on the table. "I'll get it for you."

"No!" He jerked Ida tighter. "Tell me where it is."

She could tell him the truth . . . that the money he wanted had already been turned in, but she doubted he'd believe her. Her thoughts jumping erratically, Abby considered the Bible story of the prostitute who had lied to help the Israelites. God hadn't held that lie against her, and Rahab had even been called a righteous woman because of her quick-thinking actions.

Fortunately, Abby didn't have to tell a lie. Her purse, with a small amount of money, was in the kitchen. She prayed her parents would get out of harm's way when they saw him coming inside.

"It's on the kitchen counter, right inside the door," she said. As she looked up, she caught a glimpse of Mary who had remained on the porch during their exchange. "I'll show you where it is."

"I'll get it myself." Jason pushed Ida toward Abby with a shove that was forceful enough to send them both staggering toward the picnic table, and he turned to start up the ramp.

In the fraction of a second that it took for them to right themselves, Abby saw Mary still sitting at the top of the ramp. Only now, her sister's expression had changed from horror to one of rugged determination.

From that second on, everything seemed to happen in slow motion. Abby grabbed onto Ida to keep her from toppling into the potato salad.

Jason's hand clutched at his pocket and, before Abby could

even think about what she was doing, she let out a wild "*Yee hawww!*" and rushed toward him.

Mary knew exactly what to do. Catching her lower lip between her teeth, she gave the wheels of her chair a mighty push.

Confused by the unexpected noise, Jason swung his body in Abby's direction. In that split second, while he balanced on one foot to pivot himself toward Abby, Mary's wheelchair clipped him behind the knees and sent him careening into the porch, his head hitting the sides of the wooden boards. Fried chicken flew everywhere.

With a loud *whomp*, Jason hit the bottom of the ramp face first and knocked himself out cold.

Ida raced to Jason and knelt beside him. At first, Abby thought she was going to act like a lovesick girlfriend and cry over his prostrate body. Instead, Ida snatched the handgun from his limp hand and set it on the picnic table.

Her heart racing, Abby dropped to her knees and grabbed Jason's hands to tie them behind his back. Fortunately, Mary was one step ahead of her, handing her a length of knitting yarn from the bag on her chair. Like the calf roper that Mary had described earlier, Abby quickly wrapped his wrists and yanked the doubled-up yarn into a tight knot.

The screen door banged open, and Finnegan came tearing down the ramp to stand over Jason's inert body, barking and growling with fury. George was right behind him, baseball bat at the ready.

And it was just in time, too. Jason stirred, and as he tried to right himself he became aware of the binding on his wrists. With a furious kick, he turned himself over onto his back and blasted them all with an angry tirade.

Finnegan lunged toward him, frightening the man sense-less, and then hovered over his neck. Abby knew the dog wouldn't hurt anyone unless that person was actually attacking one of his loved ones. But Finnegan was certainly letting Jason *think* he would tear him apart.

George made a decidedly halfhearted attempt to hold him back. "If you so much as move a pinky finger," he told Jason, "I'm going to tell him to attack."

Only a moment before, the man had been snarling and threatening the women. Now he screwed up his body into the fetal position, protecting his head from what he probably believed was a vicious dog attack.

"Is he all right?" Mary asked, rolling her chair closer for a better look. "I didn't mean to hurt him."

"They're out here," Ellen called. The screen door opened again and slammed shut.

Henry and three uniformed deputies charged toward them. Abby and the others backed away from Jason as the men sur-rounded him. With lightning fast precision, he was secured in handcuffs and yanked to his feet.

For what seemed like the first time in hours, Abby took a deep breath.

After he turned the glowering captive over to his deputies, Henry went to hug Mary and check to make sure that she was all right. When she continued to fret over possibly having hurt Jason, Henry assured her she'd done exactly the right thing. Then he fixed his gaze on Abby.

She wiped her face and was aware that her hand trembled slightly. "You have no idea how glad I am to see you."

"Nice capture," Henry said. "And the hog-tying wasn't bad either."

Abby managed a shaky laugh. "Thanks, but Mary's the hero. She was like a knight in shining wheelchair."

For some reason, that seemed to break the tension. The Stantons gathered together, hugging and congratulating each other for their roles in the capture.

While Henry read Jason his rights, Abby suggested they pray for the young man whose life had gone so wrong. They gathered together, pulling Ida into the tight circle of love. After thanking God for delivering them from harm, Abby asked God for mercy on the troubled young man. Then she asked for His help in forgiving Jason for all the hurt he had inflicted on Ida and others.

When Henry returned to them, Abby reached into her pocket and withdrew the bracelet and letter she had received from the KIND organization. "Here's something you can use as evidence," Abby told him.

Henry took the items and stared at them in his hand. "What's this?"

"Take a close look at the bracelet. It's made from black string with a silver fiber running through it."

Henry's eyebrows rose as he considered what she was saying.

"It's an exact match of the thread that was tied around the money bundles, as well as the thread that was used to tie Max Rigolo's fishing fly."

At the mention of Rigolo's name, Jason's head came up.

"From what I've been able to piece together," she continued, "Kids In Need of Dialysis is one of several bogus charities, along with Children of America. It appears Rigolo's primary purpose in setting up the charities was to launder the money from his drug dealing operations. Most of the charity donations went into so-called 'administrative costs,' which were actually falsified expenses, inflated salaries and perks for his family members who were figureheads on the board of directors."

"Excellent detective work," Henry told her. "Thanks to you, not only will we be able to put this drug dealer and thief behind bars—" He hitched a thumb at Jason. "—but we'll take down his crime boss as well."

Jason broke loose with a string of expletives. "Mr. Z promised me I could quit running dope and have a white-collar job on his charity board instead. But that backstabber gave the position to someone else." He took a step toward them, but the men who were restraining him tightened their grip.

"Is that why you took the money?" Henry asked him.

"Wouldn't you? The way I see it, I just evened the score. And I would have got the money back and been long gone if those stupid biddies and their dog weren't always at home."

"The score's not even yet," Henry said. "But it will be more level when you're locked away in prison where you belong."

"If I'm going down, I'm taking Z with me."

Astounded, Abby considered the turn of events. It was ironic that Jason felt his sense of justice had been violated when, in fact, he had done so many others wrong. Namely, preying on the poor souls who were addicted to the drugs he peddled.

Ida bent her head and wept into her hands. Abby put an arm around her shoulders to comfort her.

Distracted by his girlfriend's distress, Jason directed his anger toward her. "You ought to cry," he taunted. "You're a double-crosser, Ida, just like Rigolo."

Although tears filled her eyes, Ida stood tall and straightened her slim shoulders. "No, *Jason*," she said, putting emphasis on the name. "I only set things right after you lied, cheated and stole." She shook her head. "The sad thing is, the one you cheated the most is yourself."

At that, Ida crumpled to the picnic bench where she broke loose with heartwrenching sobs.

Henry directed the men to take Jason to the car and wait for him there. Then he stuck out his hand to congratulate Abby for smoking out Jellybean and helping them to nail Mr. Z. "This is going to break a major drug supply chain."

"It was a team effort," she said. "I couldn't have done it without Mary's bravery and Ida's willingness to take a stand."

Ida slowly stood and reached into the pocket of her jacket. Slowly, with great deliberation, she pulled out a computer disk and handed it to Henry. "These are e-mails that Ryan—uh, I mean Jason—and I wrote to each other over the past two years." She gazed at Abby, her violet eyes rimmed with red. "That's why I didn't make it to church this morning. I was hurrying to copy the messages before he showed up to drive me to the farm."

"You did the right thing," Abby assured her young friend, and the rest of her family murmured their agreement.

"I feel so stupid for letting him use me. There were so many red flags that warned me he wasn't what he pretended to be. I wanted his love so much that I was willing to overlook the signs." She sniffled. "He only pretended to love me."

Abby patted her hand. "Jason made money his god. There's no way someone like that could appreciate all that you have to offer."

"You're right," she said, cheering slightly. "He didn't just cheat himself of his freedom, he cheated himself of *me*."

"Exactly. God loves you, Ida, and He has someone else in

store for you. Someone who will appreciate you and who loves God as much as you do."

"I just feel so bad that Jason doesn't know God's love."

Mary pulled her wheelchair closer to the pair. "We'll continue to pray for him," she promised.

"Lots of people find God in prison," George said, stepping closer to the group.

"That's right." Abby pulled Ida to her in a one-armed hug. "Sometimes it takes adversity for people to turn from their wicked ways and seek God."

And she prayed in her heart that, like Saul on the road to Damascus, Jason would see the light, leave his sinful ways behind and take the one true path.

CHAPTER ✿ TWENTY

ABBY HAD NO IDEA SO many people could fit on Sparrow Island, much less in the museum for the Memorial Day weekend grand opening of the new Native American exhibit. Some of the visitors wandered throughout the museum, others loitered outside to enjoy the late spring floral display, but most of them congregated in the wing of the museum that boasted the recently added Lummi artifacts and information.

As for Hugo, he was totally in his element. Beaming with satisfaction over the tremendous interest in his newest display, he sauntered past the crowds in the elegant black tuxedo he'd worn to celebrate the event and handed Abby a cup of punch.

"Here's something to wet your whistle," he said. "Take care not to spill any on that pretty red dress."

When Mary had gone shopping with her and insisted this was the dress for her, Abby had her doubts. The slim-fitting waistline and the softly flowing skirt that ended below her knees in an irregular handkerchief hem had seemed too flashy at the time. But now, seeing Hugo's broad grin, she was glad she had relented to her sister's advice.

"Look at all these people," he declared. "Just when you think they've finished migrating in, there comes another gaggle."

Abby smiled, amused that he was obviously trying to entertain her with birding terminology. She lifted her punch cup and tapped the rim against his. "To continued success. And may God bless all that you set your hands to do."

"Hear, hear," he said and returned the blessing.

Ana Dominguez sailed past, barely slowing down to call out to Hugo. "The quilt, it is *muy bonita*. So pretty, like a work of art."

Hugo called out a greeting, then sipped the punch and focused intently on Abby. His deep blue eyes seemed to pierce into her. It was not at all an unpleasant feeling to be the subject of Hugo's undivided scrutiny, but Abby fidgeted under the warmth of his gaze.

"This exhibit wouldn't be here if it weren't for your words of advice," he said.

"I only told you what the Bible said," she protested. It was amazing how one little verse, taught one morning in Sunday Bible study, could affect relationships in such a positive way. "You were the one who was wise enough to apply it to the situation that was creating a problem for you."

"After you told me how you had set things right with your friend before you gave your gift to the church, I knew I had to do the same. The gift I wanted to give was this display of local Native American items. But before I could do it, I needed to get things right with Mrs. Nygaard."

"God works in wonderful ways." Abby recalled the brief panic that had consumed Hugo when the woman had declared she wanted the donations back so she could sell them. But after an evening spent in discussion and prayer over the situation, Hugo had decided the best thing to do was ask her to return everything to the true owner—the Lummi Indian Tribe. To everyone's surprise, she had agreed.

"Indeed, He does. I'm still amazed by the tribe's generous decision to keep them on permanent loan here at the museum." And Hugo had thanked Mrs. Nygaard by installing a plaque near the display which explained that many of the exhibit items had been found in her grandfather's attic. "In fact, the chief and some of the elders of the tribe insisted on staying the entire day to answer our visitors' questions."

Abby's heart filled to overflowing. "I'll look for them to thank them for their generosity."

"Please do," he said. "They've been invaluable in providing information that we could never have found in books." He turned away from Abby, distracted by a family that was looking for the restrooms. "Right this way," he told them, and off he went.

"There you are! We've been looking all over for you." Mary wheeled up to Abby, Henry at her elbow. George and Ellen were right behind them, grinning with a secret they couldn't contain.

Abby stared back at the four of them, wondering what was up. Her parents' expression reminded her of the time Abby had won the school spelling bee, Mary looked as excited as a teenager getting ready for the prom, and Henry . . . well, to say he wasn't wearing his official sheriff's face was an understatement.

"Which one of you ate the canary?" she asked.

They all looked to Henry, who puffed out his chest. Something seemed different about him today.

"You're wearing your dress uniform."

Mary touched the sleeve of his jacket and smiled up at him. "Isn't he handsome?"

Abby nodded her agreement, and Ellen commented on how the dark uniform contrasted nicely with his white hair.

"He's an officer of the law," George said, urging them along. "Let him do his job."

"Job? What job?" Abby glanced around her, remembering the day her office had been ransacked, and wondered what was amiss today.

"Don't worry. It's a good thing," Henry told her. He withdrew an envelope from the inner pocket of his jacket. "First is a letter of commendation from the San Juan County Sheriff's Department, in recognition of your contributions toward capturing a known criminal and identifying a top-level drug lord, which ultimately led to the dismantling of a multimillion-dollar crime ring."

Stunned, Abby accepted the envelope and opened it to scan the contents of the letter.

"Go ahead and tell her the rest," Mary urged.

"Right." Henry reached into his other pocket and took out another envelope. "It turns out there was a reward for information leading to the arrest and conviction of the infamous Mr. Z. It will take a while for the case to go to trial, but Agent Fitch of the FBI wanted you to know that when Max Rigolo is behind bars, you'll be entitled to receive the amount shown here."

He leaned forward to point to the paper, and Abby's eyes nearly popped. "Oh my goodness, there's a comma in that figure. I couldn't take money for just doing my job as a good citizen."

George and Ellen exchanged glances, but it was Mary who

said what was on all their minds. "I told you she wouldn't accept it."

On second thought . . . "But there's no reason some worthy organizations shouldn't benefit from it. After I split the reward with Ida, of course."

Abby didn't need to consider for more than a moment where her own share should go.

"Little Flock Church would, of course, get a portion right off the top. Then the Grace Girls' Home. And the rest could go to the conservatory to buy a computer program and other things we need for the lab." She smiled as she thought of the positive impact this would make.

Mary chuckled. "And I told you that's how she'd give it all away."

Hugs were exchanged all around. George was the one who broke the celebration when he peered across the room to where a man and woman stood carrying on an intense conversation. It appeared as though she was pushing something toward him.

"Looks like Thelma has cornered Sam," he observed. "I wonder if she's giving him another dose of what-for."

"Uh-oh." The last thing Abby wanted right now was for Thelma to create an ugly scene on Hugo's happy day. She thanked Henry again for the good news he had shared, then excused herself to see if she could help mediate the altercation that seemed to be brewing in Sam's corner.

As she approached, she saw that Thelma was giving him a jar of her famous homemade preserves. Not exactly what Abby had been expecting.

"Thelma, Sam, I'm so glad you could make it to Hugo's happy event," she said. And then it dawned on her. Both of them were smiling.

At each other.

Thelma was the one who filled her in. "I was just giving Sam a jar of my strawberry preserves. Because I, um, you know, doubted him." Speaking to Sam, Thelma added, "Next week I'll be baking some fresh bread, so if you'll tell me your preference, I'll make a loaf for you, too."

That was about the closest to an apology Thelma would come, but it was a big step for her.

Although gruff and blustery at times, Sam was also gracious. "You don't have to do that, Thelma. But I'm glad it took a burden off your mind to know that I had nothing to do with the box of cash Abby found."

The older woman looked down at her orthopedic shoes, then back at the strawberry preserves she was holding. "Actually, I found my missing diva dollars."

Abby thought back to what Mary had said about Thelma misplacing things. "Was the money in your loaf pan?"

"No." She paused and gave an embarrassed giggle. "My bank statement came last week, but it wasn't until yesterday that I had time to look at it. Right there on the first page was a two hundred dollar deposit that I had failed to record in my bankbook and totally forgotten about."

Sam cleared his throat. "The missing money."

"Yes." Thelma hung her head. "I'm so ashamed for what I put you through."

Another piece of the puzzle clicked into place for Abby. "That day at church when you were searching through your purse for the letter from the children's charity . . ."

Thelma looked up, her cheeks still pink with embarrassment. "And I threw away all those scraps of paper," she finished for her. "One of those slips was the bank deposit receipt, which would have jogged my memory if only I had taken the time to look at it."

Sam was smiling broadly now. "Everybody makes mistakes sometimes."

"Indeed they do," Abby interjected. "In fact, that's why you received that letter from the children's charity thanking you for a donation of $225."

It was only after discovering that Rigolo's charities were fraudulent organizations that Abby had remembered what Vince Emory had said about charities buying and selling solicitation lists, and she figured out the rest.

"Apparently you had made a $225 donation to another, legitimate charity in the past—"

"Yes, it was in lieu of flowers for a funeral early last year."

"—and when Children of America bought the list from them, the bogus group used it to report that income to governing agencies. By doing so, they laundered the drug money through the charity, pretending that it came from you and others, so their income would look legitimate. And the majority of the money that went to Rigolo's charities was diverted to so-called administrative costs and inflated salaries for his family members."

"That's incredible," Sam said, "but it doesn't make sense that they would send thank-you letters and tip people off to their scam."

"Exactly. Some of the donations are legitimately given by folks who don't know any better, and those people do receive letters." Abby was thinking of the $10 she'd mailed them for the bracelet and wondered how much of it wound up actually helping a needy child. "And some children have benefited from those donations. Unfortunately for Rigolo—but fortunately for everyone else—someone at the charity must have made a mistake and switched lists, which resulted in thank-you letters being sent to the ghost contributors instead of to the real ones."

"It's a good thing you have a PhD," Thelma said. "It would take someone smart to figure all that out."

Sam thanked Abby for clearing things up, and when she left the pair they were discussing the banana nut bread that Thelma was planning to bake for him.

Abby saw Janet and Margaret across the room and after saying a quick hello to Bobby McDonald, who was enthusiastically leading his parents through the museum, she started making her way toward them. Janet was extra dolled up today. The lavender knit shell she wore enhanced the green in her hazel eyes, and her black skirt was a gauzy number that swirled around her knees. Margaret, on the other hand, was wearing something from her school wardrobe—a royal blue dropped-waist dress that tied in back.

"Congratulations on catching that escaped convict," Margaret said. "You and Mary are quite the dynamic duo."

"Well, since Jason hadn't actually been charged with a crime then, he wasn't technically a convict when Mary and I, uh, encountered him. But that should change after his trial."

Margaret either didn't notice or didn't care as she continued with her train of thought. "Given what Janet told me about Lawanna Porter's odd behavior down at Paradise Cove, I was convinced she was the one responsible for the box full of money."

"I honestly think she was just trying to have some solitude while she went clamming."

Janet loudly cleared her throat to get their attention. "Have either of you seen Ida lately? She's been taking a lot of time off from work, and I'm worried about her."

Abby didn't say so, but she was concerned too. Ida had been conspicuously absent from the café lately, and at church she had seemed preoccupied. Abby had expected to see her at the opening of the new museum exhibit, but so far there had been no sign of her. If Ida didn't show up today, she would pay the girl a visit and make sure she was all right.

Janet shifted the tiny purse that hung from her shoulder. "I wonder if she's depressed because of the trauma she experienced that day at your parents' farm. All that life-or-death drama would be enough to send anyone spiraling down into a deep, dark depression. Not to mention losing her first love to a life behind bars."

"What exactly did happen that day?" Margaret probed.

Abby was about to remind them that everything that happened had been covered quite accurately in *The Birdcall* when she happened to see Ida's blond ponytail. "Oh look, there she is, talking to Aaron Holloway."

The two friends exchanged glances and *tut-tutted* to one another. "She must be turning to Aaron for comfort and consolation," Janet said.

Margaret crossed her arms over her waist. "Rebound relationships never last."

Abby shook her head. "There's not much chance of that. Aaron's so shy, I can't imagine him ever making the first move."

She excused herself and headed in Ida's direction, but when the girl saw her, she said something to Aaron and came to meet her.

Abby greeted her with a hug. "I didn't mean to interrupt your conversation."

Ida shrugged. "We were just comparing movies we've seen lately."

Abby mentally recanted what she'd told Janet and Margaret a moment before. It looked like Aaron might do just fine after all, even without Mary's matchmaking help.

"Are you busy helping Hugo with the grand opening of the exhibit?" Ida touched her ponytail, then dropped her hand. "I was hoping for a moment alone with you."

"Hugo and the rest of the crew seem to have everything under control. Why don't we go for a walk on the conservatory grounds?"

As they stepped out into the late May sunshine, a small flock of sparrows scattered from where they had been feeding on the lawn.

Ida turned to watch as the birds immediately fluttered back to the ground to resume their search for grass seeds and insects. "I wonder how Newton is doing."

"I saw him with a flock just yesterday."

"You did?" Ida grabbed her arm. "How did you know it was him?"

"The band on his leg. He's the only house sparrow that I've banded this season, and he was the only young fledgling that was wearing one. I'm sure it was him."

"That's terrific. I'm so glad he has found where he's supposed to be."

They continued their walk. Ida said after a while, "I've found where I'm supposed to be too."

"Really? And where is that?" Abby hoped Ida wasn't still trying to run away to find excitement elsewhere. After all, they'd both seen where that kind of excitement could lead.

"Right here on Sparrow Island . . . with my own flock." She grinned and adjusted the narrow strap of her sundress. "After Jason was taken away, I realized I'd been living in a fairy-tale world, dreaming of a man sweeping in and rescuing me from my humdrum life."

"Humdrum? You always seem so happy talking to the customers at the café, or going canoeing with Ana Dominguez to gather materials for her wall hangings."

"I am happy, and I do love doing those things. But I had convinced myself that I wasn't very smart or interesting because Ryan—I mean Jason—seemed so sophisticated and worldly by comparison."

"'How much better to get wisdom than gold,'" Abby said, referring to Proverbs 16:16.

"You can say that again. He deceived me about a lot of things. But there's one thing he was truthful about."

Abby raised an eyebrow at this unexpected revelation.

"It's true. He told me I was a good writer." She smiled. "Even Sergeant Cobb said he enjoyed reading my stories about the various happenings on Sparrow Island."

"Yes, he mentioned that to Mary as well."

"Last week I took some time off to research online-college-degree programs. There's one in Washington that only requires a few days of in-class instruction each semester. The rest of the time, the instruction and assignments are handled over the Internet." She kicked a small stone a few feet ahead of her. "I haven't decided on a major yet, but I know it'll be something in the liberal arts so I can take lots of creative writing courses."

"That's a wonderful idea," Abby said. And she knew how Ida could pay for it—with the reward money. "I'm so proud of the way you've taken a difficult situation and used it so that something good will come out of it."

"Is there a Bible verse for that too?" Ida teased.

"There's a Bible verse for everything you can imagine. In this case, it's Romans 8:28: 'In all things God works for the good of those who love him, who have been called according to his purpose.'"

"Wow, it's like you have a Bible database in your brain." She caught up to the rock and kicked it again. "I'll wait until September to start my classes. Wouldn't want to miss being the snack lady at Vacation Bible School. Maybe one of these days I'll know as much about the Bible as you do."

"What kind of writing are you interested in pursuing?"

"Fiction."

For a moment Ida remained quiet, and she seemed unusually shy.

"Maybe I'll even write about the mysteries of Sparrow Island. If I keep hanging around you long enough, I'm bound to pick up plenty of story ideas."

EPILOGUE

ABBY SAT AT THE FOOT of the bed, her head bent as she concentrated on the scarlet nail polish she was applying to Mary's toes. After Mary's handiwork with a hair straightener, the relaxed waves of Abby's light auburn hair felt full and soft where they fell against her neck.

"The color should wash out after six or eight shampoos," Mary told her. "In the meantime, I think it looks pretty good."

Abby glanced up from her task. "Me too. Thanks for the glamour lesson, sis."

Even the dog and cat had received their share of pampering. Abby and Mary had brushed them until their coats shone. Then, to make her sister laugh, Abby had gathered the silky white hair that fell into Blossom's eyes and tied a pink bow around the topknot.

Abby added a final touch to finish off the pinky toe and moved to the head of the bed to sit beside Mary. After plumping the pillows for both of them, she laid her hand in Mary's.

"No red," Abby warned. "But that 'Subtle Satin' looks like a pretty shade of pink."

"Then 'Subtle Satin' it is." Mary began dabbing the color to Abby's fingertips.

"It would be a shame to let your 'courting plumage' go to waste," Mary said. "Tomorrow I'll ask Henry if any of his single friends—"

"Don't even think it."

"So maybe his friends aren't your type. Perhaps if Janet put out the word, we could hook you up with a nice widower."

"It's not going to happen, Mary."

Her sister sighed. "Okay, we'll have to take baby steps toward the dating thing. But in the meantime, isn't this fun? Think of all the primping we could have done when we were teenagers."

"It is fun," Abby admitted. "And the best part is being with you. I've always admired your go-get-'em attitude, but I was never more proud than when you took on that gun-carrying felon. It's a wonder you weren't hurt."

Mary smiled. "As he was coming up the ramp, I prayed for God to distract him so I could catch him unaware. And then you hollered, and I knew the Lord was with us."

Abby watched while Mary finished skimming the layer of pink over her nails, then held them up to the light to admire the delicate color.

"Would you remind me to call Dad tomorrow? There's something important I need to tell him," Abby said.

"Certainly I will." Mary set the bottle on the nightstand, concern knitting her brows. "Is something wrong?"

Abby grinned and nudged her sister with her elbow.

"No, I'm just going to tell him not to bother putting speed bumps on the ramp."

A NOTE FROM THE EDITORS

THIS ORIGINAL BOOK WAS created by the Books and Inspirational Media Division of Guideposts, the world's leading inspirational publisher. Founded in 1945 by Dr. Norman Vincent Peale and his wife Ruth Stafford Peale, Guideposts helps people from all walks of life achieve their maximum personal and spiritual potential. Guideposts is committed to communicating positive, faith-filled principles for people everywhere to use in successful daily living.

Our publications include award-winning magazines like *Guideposts, Angels on Earth* and *Positive Thinking*, best-selling books, and outreach services that demonstrate what can happen when faith and positive thinking are applied in day-to-day life.

For more information, visit us online at www.guideposts.org, call (800) 431-2344 or write Guideposts, 39 Seminary Hill Road, Carmel, New York 10512.